IT'S A WIN FOR ME

MAKING THE CATCH
BOOK 1

CLARISSA MAE

Copyright © 2025 by Clarissa Mae Pitre

Cover Illustration By Morimorijulie

Editing By Roxana Coumans

ISBN-13: 979-8-218-69882-9

All rights reserved. No part of this publication may be reproduced, stored or transmitted in any form or by any means, electronic, mechanical, photocopying, recording, scanning, or otherwise without written permission from the publisher. It is illegal to copy this book, post it to a website, or distribute it by any other means without permission.

This novel is entirely a work of fiction. The names, characters and incidents portrayed in it are the work of the author's imagination. Any resemblance to actual persons, living or dead, events or localities is entirely coincidental and not intended by the author.

All brand names and product names used in this book are trademarks, registered trademarks, or trade names of their respective holders. CMP is not associated with any product or brand in this book. All company, product and service names used in this website are for identification purposes only.

Cataloging-in-Publication Data is on file with the Library of Congress.

Printed and bound in the United States of America

PLAYLIST

1. **Heartbreak Girl**- 5 Seconds of Summer (Chapter 5)
2. **Fall In Love Again**- P1HARMONY (Chapter 7)
3. **Crush**- David Archuleta (Chapter 11)
4. **Loose**- ENHYPEN (Chapter 14)
5. **Baby**- Justin Bieber (Chapter 15)
6. **Fakin' It**- April Jai (Chapter 16)
7. **Shivers**- Ed Sheeran (Chapter 17)
8. **Humble**- Kendrick Lamar (Chapter 18)
9. **FRI(END)S**- V (Chapter 23)
10. **Let Me Love You**- Mario (Chapter 27)
11. **S&M**- Rihanna (Chapter 30)
12. **Boom Clap'**- Charli XCX (Chapter 32)
13. **Into It**- Chase Atlantic (Chapter 33)
14. **Just Friends**- Why Don't We (Chapter 39)
15. **Dress**-Taylor Swift (Chapter 40)
16. **I GOTTA BE** -JAGGED EDGE (Chapter 41)

17. **I Wanna Dance With Somebody**- Whitney Houston (Chapter 41)
18. **Versace on the Floor**- Bruno Mars (Chapter 43)
19. **I Want You**- SB19 (Chapter 47)
20. **Warm**- Ariana Grande (Epilogue)

*To those who love rom-coms and men who yearn.
This one's for you.*
magsaya ;)

CONTENT WARNINGS

Dear Reader,

This story contains mature themes, explicit sexual content, profanity, and topics that may be sensitive or triggering for some audiences. Please read with care.

Anxiety
Emotional abuse (involving a parent)
Cheating mentioned (not by a main character)

PROLOGUE
AMELIA

MOVING TO A NEW COUNTRY DURING FRESHMAN YEAR OF high school is not an ideal situation. But change can be good, right?

"You're from the Philippines?"

I glance up from my seat as a girl plops down in the empty chair beside me in our chemistry class, smiling wide. She's really pretty. Deep emerald eyes, yellow ruffle dress, and a cute matching bow in her long brunette hair.

"Yes." I smile back, surprised she knows. "I'm Amelia."

Yes, the Philippines. That's where I was born and raised, at least until my dad got an amazing job at a law firm in West Hollywood. Now here I am in sunny Los Angeles, and it feels like a completely different world from what I'm used to.

No jeepneys rumbling through the streets, no tricycle rides with exhaust curling into your lungs. There are no street vendors selling warm taho or freshly made lumpia in the afternoon, which is absurd if you ask me.

I'll forever miss the Philippines though, the beautiful

islands, community, my friends, it's a lot to process right now.

All I see now is towering palm trees, broad highways, cafe shops, and designer stores on every corner.

I'm holding on to the one thing my mom told me before my first day here. "Anak, don't worry about making friends. You'll find them when you least expect it."

We'll see about that. I'm not sure how easy it'll be to make friends halfway through the school year. Everyone already has their groups, where would I even fit in?

The girl motions toward my bag. "Saw your flag pin." Then she gestures to herself with a laugh. "Tia."

A sharp ring of the bell cuts through the classroom and everyone slips into their seats easily.

I sigh and dig into my backpack for my notebook and pencils, as Mr. Walls walks in. Tie on and a stiff face, which is not exactly screaming friendly.

"We have a new student here today. Amelia Cruz-Taylor," he directs everyone's attention toward me and my cheeks warm up, palms feeling awfully sweaty. "Find a lab partner and flip to page fifty and answer all the questions."

He yanks down the projector before dragging his feet over to his desk, not saying another word as he puts up a PowerPoint.

"Don't worry, he's always like this. Our class can get pretty rowdy." She nudges my elbow, chuckling quietly. "So new girl, want to be my lab partner?"

We hit it off extremely well, laughing at jokes that make no sense, talking about all of our favorite films, then she even invited me to hang out with her during lunch, though she did warn me about her older brother, Caleb.

Apparently he's annoying and if I ever wanted to ditch

her because of him, she'd understand. But rather than annoyance, her voice was filled with amusement.

"And who's this?"

A low warm voice calls out behind me. I peer over my shoulder, my eyes traveling up to a toned guy with tousled deep brown hair, black-framed glasses, wearing a white and blue football jersey. He has to be at least 5'10 already which is insane for someone our age. He holds his lunch tray as he rounds the table, settling into the bench across from Tia and me.

Our eyes meet, and they're a perfect reflection of his sister's.

"Amelia. I'm guessing you're the annoying older brother?"

Feigning innocence, he twists open his soda. "I think my lovely sister meant *charming*."

"Right, of course," I stifle a laugh.

Tia pokes her fork into a piece of potato and pops it into her mouth, eyes narrowing at him playfully. "I meant what I said."

He rolls his eyes, flicking a small pea at her. "Watch it.'

She laughs as it lands in her tray.

I pick up the lumpia my mom packed me for lunch, dip it into soy sauce and take a huge bite. Crispy, savory, perfection. I could cry, it's honestly that good.

I notice Caleb's eyes linger on me for a moment before he juts his chin toward my Troy and Gabriella lunchbox. "Nice bag by the way."

"Oh...um, thanks," I mumble, my voice dipping awkwardly.

I do love it, but all the other students have regular bags. We're not in middle school anymore. Maybe I should just toss it when I get home and—

"Favorite song? Go," he interrupts my thoughts, snapping a piece of carrot into his mouth.

"Hmm." I furrow my brows, trying to think of the many hits. "Bet On It." Classic.

"Mine too," he grins. "Tia wouldn't stop playing that movie all summer, so it's stuck in my head."

Tia snaps her head up, a smile tugging at her lips. "It's a masterpiece and it should be respected and that means watching it at least twice a month."

And from that day on, we were a trio. Best friends. I couldn't be happier about how natural it all came…but the thing is friendships are bound to change.

It was only a matter of time.

But I would've never guessed we'd change this much…

1
AMELIA

Present Day July 10th

"You have everything all packed, anak?" my mom calls out from the living room as I finish packing my suitcase.

After graduating college last year with my marketing degree, I landed a full-time job offer in San Francisco as a social media analyst. I've been staying at my parents' house while I was working but after some time, I realized I miss Los Angeles way too much and needed to move back.

I asked one of my best friends, Maya, who works at a PR agency if they had an opening, and luck was on my side for once because a position opened up last month. She put in a good word for me, and next thing you know I got a phone call a few weeks later for a virtual interview, it went well, and now I'm packing up all my things to start over.

"Yeah!" I grunt, rolling my High School Musical luggage into the hallway with one hand, holding my hoodie in the other. "Remind me why I didn't buy a new suitcase? This is so embarrassing."

My dad meets me at my doorway, laughing as he takes

the suitcase from my hands. "Embarrassing? Come on, you love that old thing."

I stare at him, slipping the hoodie over my head. "Yeah, when I was thirteen."

"Because you said, and I quote 'I'm only taking one flight, I don't need to buy a whole new one'," my mom mimics me in a high pitch tone, poking her head out, using dramatic air quotes.

"Okay well, I regret saying that," I deadpan. "You should've forced me like a normal parent."

An hour later, my parents drop me off at the airport, pulling me to the side of the entrance.

"Call us as soon as you land," my dad instructs.

My mom exhales a deep breath, pulling us all into one big hug. "We'll miss you so much."

"I'll see you soon." I chuckle, hugging them even tighter. "Love you guys."

After that heartwarming goodbye, I do a little wave and roll my suitcase inside, heading toward the check-in as I mentally brace myself for TSA.

"Take your laptops and electronics out of the bag!" the man blares and it echoes all around. There is no reason why we should be getting yelled at this early in the morning.

As I wait in the long line, I can't help but smile thinking about my best friends. Even though it's only been a year, it feels like ten. I haven't gone this long without seeing them, especially Caleb.

He was drafted to his dream team, the LA Vipers, right after college. Football kept him super busy, and that was around the time I moved away, so we haven't kept in touch all that much. We've been texting and calling, but the responses between us slowed...eventually faded.

The one person I don't miss and most definitely am not looking forward to seeing is my ex-boyfriend Jared. He was supposed to visit me last year but I found out he had cheated on me three days prior to me moving.

What an asshole.

After we had dinner one night, I waited for him to get out of the shower. I crawled into bed and his phone lit up on the nightstand.

Now I know what you're thinking…don't check his phone if you trust him, right?

Well, I *wasn't* going to look at first but the screen stayed on long enough for my eyes to move on their own accord. I couldn't help myself after that. When I picked up his phone, my heart started to pound in my ears, throbbing.

He texted her four hours ago that he was at dinner with me. Her reply is still engraved into my brain.

> Hurry up with her and come over later. I know she doesn't make you feel as good as I do.

I scrolled up a few messages, and there was another…

> I miss you, when are you coming over?

I kept scrolling for what felt like hours. All the messages went back and forth for an entire month.

An entire month of pure lies and disrespect.

It felt like someone had dumped a bucket of ice-cold water over my head, washing away the reality I once knew. I physically couldn't move, couldn't cry. I just sat there, tears streaming down my cheeks. Completely numb.

It's funny how I always saw him as my life jacket, the

one who'd keep me afloat. But in the end, he was the one who made me sink instead.

The last thing I remember was yelling "fuck you", grabbing all my things and storming out.

Was our relationship a little rocky that year? Yes. But that's no excuse for what he did to me, when he could've talked to me instead of going behind my back. I thought he would have the decency to respect me even a little, but I was wrong.

That year away from everyone helped me move on faster, even though it still hurts to think about. We were together since freshman year of college, four years of my life, down the drain in a matter of seconds.

After going through TSA easily, I grab my luggage off the ramp, slipping my shoes back on, zigzagging through the crowded airport to find my terminal.

My phone dings, and I fish it out of my pocket, seeing a text from the group chat named:

BADDEST BITCHES
All thanks to Maya.

> **TIA**
> Have a safe flight, noon right?

> Yes, please don't be late.

> **TIA**
> I'm driving, not Maya.

> **MAYA**
> I was late one time and that was in college, relax. I'm a mature woman.

> We only graduated a year ago.

MAYA

Exactly. I've grown a lot since then.

After boarding the plane, I gathered my curls into a loose bun and half an hour later after our flight took off, my stomach was filled with ginger ale and pretzels.

Perfect flight combo.

It lands at exactly twelve fifteen and the chime from the seatbelt sign goes off. I wait for everyone to stand up before even attempting to get off because I'm not exactly in the mood to have my body smashed between people.

Los Angeles airport is packed, as expected and I maneuver my way through, hastily walking over to the pickup area, dragging my suitcase behind me, getting a few stares. I spot their grey Mazda right away.

"Oh Gabriella," Maya singsongs from outside the window, my cheeks instantly flushing.

"Must you be so loud?" I let out a tight laugh, rolling my luggage across the graveled ground.

"I've missed you!" She jogs over, pulling me into a crushing hug.

"Missed you too. It feels so good to be back."

Tia calls out from the driver's seat, popping the trunk. "Ah, hey!"

I place my luggage into the trunk and slide into the backseat. "Hey! So what are our plans later, I know you guys already have them."

"You'd be correct." Maya grins, peering over her seat, looking directly at me. "Wear something hot."

Night out it is.

Later that night, the club is packed with sweaty bodies swaying on the dance floor as I sip my champagne, chatting with a guy I met at the bar. He's pretty cute. Blonde buzz cut, amber eyes, and a scar slashing through his left eyebrow.

"Wanna go back to my place?" he smirks, flashing me a look that screams fuckboy. "We could have a real good time."

You know, I used to be a hopeless romantic until Jared shattered that. Now, it feels like I'm cursed because every guy I could possibly see myself getting to know ruins it the second he opens his mouth.

We've been talking for only ten minutes, if that, and he's already asking me to hookup?

"I'd rather stay here." I force out a chuckle, sipping my drink again to avoid eye contact.

He slides his hand across the bar table, resting it on mine. The sudden contact makes me want to retreat.

"Why, you got a boyfriend?" he asks, cocking a brow.

My gaze lowers down to his hand and my body stiffens.

Tan line. On his ring finger. Oh come on, how unoriginal.

I hate men.

This is exactly why I don't bother trying anymore. It's always the same thing. I don't know if I'll ever find a man who actually knows the concept of love and commitment.

Am I being pessimistic? Yes. Will I change? Probably not.

I don't understand. What's the point of being in a relationship if all you're going to do is cheat anyway? You might as well stay single instead of making others suffer with your poor choices. I've had enough.

I jerk my hand back from underneath his as if it were

burning my flesh and grab my phone off the table. "I'm sure your *wife* won't be too happy about that." Emphasis on the word wife.

I don't normally like confrontation but this guy is testing my patience.

His eyes go round and he quickly shoves his hands into his pockets, like I haven't already seen the tan line. He rises from his seat, stepping closer and I don't move. "I know what it looks like, and—"

"So you're not a cheating asshole who has a wife back at home then?" I cut him off, my arms folding across my chest, a sharp edge to my voice.

He deflates, shoulders sagging. "She... um," he splutters, rubbing the nape of his neck like he's trying to gather some more courage to lie to me again. "I plan on divorcing her soon."

That's the most cliche sentence I've ever heard in my life.

I roll my eyes and turn on my heels, not bothering to listen to his lame excuse as I head back toward the girls.

"Blondie was a no go." I shake my head, slipping back into the booth, resting my head against the plush.

Turning, Maya's eyes turn violent as she scans the bar like she could punch someone, her long jet-black hair flowing over her shoulders. She wore dark kohl liner, accentuating her almond shaped hazel eyes, paired with a burgundy mini dress. "Do I have to kill him?"

"No but I'm sure his wife will one day." I lift my left hand, tapping on my ring finger. "Married."

"He was ugly anyways," Tia scoffs, grabbing her glass of water, because she's our designated driver for tonight.

I snicker, leaning forward and resting my chin in my hand. "I just don't get men."

Tia scoffs, brushing her wispy bangs out of her face. "They're the worst."

"Except Amir," Maya and I say in unison as we snap our gaze to her.

She looks at us over the rim of her glass, hiding her smile.

Amir is her high school sweetheart turned fiancé. Tia and I have known him since sophomore year of high school when he joined our honors English class.

They're officially getting married later in September. Destination wedding in the Bahamas.

He's an amazing man but I'll forever hate him for being related to my ex.

Oh, did I forget to mention that?

Yeah. Jared and Amir are cousins. Lucky me. Now I'm stuck with him.

My mom keeps insisting I bring a date to the wedding, but that's simply not happening. I'm so over the disappointment that comes with men and I don't have the energy in me anymore to entertain it.

I thought I could handle it, but after tonight? It's just too draining. I'll stick to the occasional flirting when I'm in the mood. Anything even remotely close to serious? Off the freaking table.

"Is he meeting us here or back at the house later?" I ask.

She glances at me, hesitant. "I was going to invite him and Caleb, but I didn't want them to intrude."

"No, no, it's totally fine!" I wave her off.

I love hanging around those guys, it always feels like we're all back in school again.

She nods, reaching into her clutch. "I'll text them."

Looks like I'll be seeing Caleb sooner than I thought.

2

CALEB

I'VE BEEN IN LOVE WITH MY BEST FRIEND SINCE HIGH school and she has no idea. The past year felt like a blur, our schedules weren't aligning, and I was an idiot for letting the communication between us die down. I've missed her more than I'm willing to admit. But now that she's moving back, I'm determined not to let it happen again.

"Question. Why the hell are you in a neon pink hoodie?" The deepest laugh erupts from Amir, as he walks into my living room.

I was helping him along with his friends from medical school to pick out a suit for his wedding and we decided to chill at my place while Tia and Maya had…somewhere to go earlier. I forgot where. To be honest, whenever my sister talks to me it goes in one ear and out the other.

"Because it's comfortable," I replied dryly, as I walk over to my couch, digging for the remote that's always somehow stuck between the cushions.

"You look like a tall bottle of Pepto-Bismol." He sneers.

He's around 6'4, deep brown skin with a taper fade. I swear he's been this height since we were fourteen.

"Oh, how funny." I pull the remote out and plop down, turning the TV on.

His phone dings and he's quiet for a moment before rounding the couch, sitting next to me. "You want to go to that nightclub downtown?"

"I'm flattered that you're asking me on a date, but I don't know if I'm in the mood tonight." I chuckle to myself, flipping through the channels.

"First of all, you're definitely not my type." Amir looks at me like I'm a wad of gum underneath a shoe. "And second, Tia texted me because Amelia's back in town and they're over there right now."

My thumb pauses, hovering over the button as my heart beats faster and faster. Why the hell didn't he start off with that?

She's back in town? I heard she was coming back but I didn't know it was going to be this soon.

"I'll tell them you're not coming then—"

"No," I interrupt him mid-sentence, already standing and tossing the remote onto the couch. "Give me a minute."

"Thought you weren't in the mood?" he calls out from the living room all smug.

"What? I can't change my mind?" I shout out from my room, quickly slipping on a black hoodie and jeans. Ruffling my hair enough to make it look presentable for her.

A few spritz of cologne. Gotta make a good impression.

About thirty minutes later, I'm walking toward the front entrance with Amir when a hand suddenly rests on my shoulder. I turn to see a young man smiling at me as he raises his phone. "Can I get a photo with you? When I found out you got signed with the Vipers, I legit threw a party at my dorm, dude."

Fans coming up to me will never get old. It's a reminder of the accomplishments I've made in life this far, even though my father constantly tells me otherwise.

I nod, as we snap a quick photo. "Damn, I appreciate that. Hope you didn't get into trouble with the RA?"

"Uh...the next day I did." He shrugs, with a mischievous glint in his eyes. "But it was totally worth it."

"What's your name?"

"Tyler. I'm actually trying to go pro like you next year hopefully," his voice trembles with excitement.

"Nice to meet you Tyler." Chuckling, I pat him on the shoulder a few times. "You will go pro, just gotta stop throwing parties and pissing your RA's off."

"Will do. Thanks." He snickers, running back over to where his group of friends are.

"Caleb! Do you and Vanessa Noles still talk?"

"Any comment on the rumors?"

"Have you seen Vanessa since?!"

I halt in my tracks, flashes blinding me before I even make it through the damn doors. The questions hit me from all angles, cameras getting shoved in my face, I can't see a thing except white bursts of flash.

"Hey, back up," Amir shouts, grabbing my wrist and dragging me inside. Security shutting the doors before they enter the premises. The bass slams into my chest, vibrating throughout my body, and drowns whatever Amir's saying to me right now. I nod absently, but I'm not truly listening.

It's been an entire month since I made headlines, and it still hasn't died down. Not even close. I've never been caught in a scandal before, sure I've been in the press about women I was *suspected* of dating, but this is worse.

No matter what I do, it keeps haunting me.

It all started when pop diva Vanessa Noles invited half of Hollywood to her album release party. Athletes, actors, reality stars, you name it. Things got a little heated between us for a minute and after…all hell broke loose.

The private rooftop was packed with bodies, clinking glasses, and pop music blasting over the speakers. I had a whiskey in hand, the burn crawling down my throat as I found a quiet spot inside, waiting for my best friend to finish flirting with every goddamn woman here.

"Are you avoiding me?" a soft, familiar voice called out.

When I glanced up, it was her. Vanessa.

Her perfume filled the air. It smelt expensive. A smooth mix of cinnamon and honey. Sweet, like her. We chatted a few times at these events, but nothing more. She was just easy to talk to amid the chaos.

"Nah," I said, taking a small swig of my drink, eyes drifting to the tall window overlooking downtown LA, where brake lights stretched for miles. "Just needed a breather."

Vanessa groaned and stepped beside me, her hip brushing mine as she followed my gaze. "Do you ever get tired of socializing and all the parties we're practically forced to attend?"

"Do I?" I huffed with a small chuckle.

"You're not one to lie, huh?"

"There's no reason to." I looked over at her. Blue silk dress, brunette hair, silver sparkly eyeshadow she's known for. She looked gorgeous, no denying that.

She took my whiskey, brought the glass up to her lips and took a small sip. I couldn't help but watch her, my hands resting casually along the railing behind me.

"That's what I like about you." She handed the glass back, her

perfectly manicured fingers brushing mine, making my mind go fuzzy. I should probably take it easy with the alcohol.

"Probably shouldn't say that." I took a sip and glanced back out the window again. "Your boyfriend might pop up."

"Oh…we aren't exactly together right now," she said, barely above a whisper. Her pinky interlocked with mine and my body tensed. "We're sort of on a break? No one really knows, though."

She's been dating Cam West for the past two years, the producer behind all of her latest hit songs. A beast on the drums, from what I've seen online. I've never met the guy but he seemed pretty solid to me.

"Sort of?" I asked, suddenly invested in her love life.

She sighed. "He wanted to work on his album and I needed to work on my upcoming tour."

"Sounds like an excuse to me."

"An excuse for what?" she asked, her voice dipping into something seductive that made me clear my throat.

"To see other people."

"And what's wrong with that? Space can be a good thing, right?" Her thumb began rubbing slowly across the back of my hand, stirring up some pretty inappropriate thoughts. Damn liquor.

Then she moved in front of me, took my drink, and set it on the floor. When she rose again, her chest brushed against mine, and my gaze dropped…only for a second.

"Have you ever done something that you might regret, but"—she ran her tongue along her bottom lip subtly, keeping those dark amber eyes locked on mine— "you didn't want to stop?"

Her hands pressed against my chest. I forced myself to lean back an inch, my pulse pounding in my neck. "I have."

"I'm sort of in the mood for that right now." A gentle curve lifted her mouth as she closed the gap again, leaning in slowly, cautiously.

This is a bad idea…someone could see us.

"I don't do messy…" I murmured, even as my mind screamed at me to stop and walk away. But my feet were cemented to the ground.

"Me either," she whispered. Then her lips were on mine, warm and soft.

Alcohol was fuzzing my brain and for a second I kissed her back.

Then I heard the faint sound of a shutter or maybe I imagined it, but either way it was enough for me to tense up and pull back. "We shouldn't."

And want to know what happened later that night? Some influencer posted a photo and we were completely visible in the background when someone opened the doors.

I didn't even hear the damn thing open.

Cam saw it. He was pretty pissed off and started shading me on his story, and his loyal fans joined him.

Now I'm labeled as being a homewrecker.

I knew I shouldn't have kissed her back then, but I got too caught up in the moment. They were on a break but the public didn't know that. As far as they were concerned, I was indulging in an affair, just another reckless "stereotypical" athlete who didn't give a shit who he hurt.

And that moment? It cost me.

The truth didn't matter anymore. No one cared. They took the story and ran with it like a goddamn marathon.

Vanessa's team told her to stay quiet. "Let the rumors die down," they said.

She went on tour shortly after and that was all it took to wipe the whole incident from everyone's memory. She was no longer seen as a "cheater" but rather going back to her rightfully claimed beloved pop princess title.

And don't get me wrong, I'm happy for her, she didn't deserve any of the hate we got, especially since they really were on a break. It was mutual and Cam pulled a dick move for doing that to her.

But me? I didn't get off the hook that easily. It didn't

matter if I told the truth at that point, Vanessa couldn't back me up even if she wanted to. So I took the fall.

To this day, every other comment I get is still in connection to Vanessa. People asking if I've *broken any other homes* lately.

Amir and I step further into the dim club, immediately spotting Tia and Maya talking at the booth across from the bar. We excuse ourselves between everyone on the dance floor until we reach them. I need this night out after all.

"Is this seat taken?" I joke, walking up to their table and—

Holy shit, she looks even more beautiful than I remember. Her long curly hair, tawny bronzed skin, and full plump lips.

"Caleb!" Amelia beams, rising to her feet. My eyes rake her up and down before I pull her into the tightest hug I can, snaking my arms around her waist, pressing her body closer to me. I breathe her in, smelling her shampoo, strawberry, her favorite scent. Glad that hasn't changed.

Man, I've missed how perfectly she fits in my arms, like fitting the final puzzle piece.

I reluctantly pull back enough to meet her chocolate brown eyes. "Hey beautiful, how've you been?"

"I'm better now that I'm back." She looks up at me, smiling. "I've missed you."

That catches me off guard for a moment. I was hoping she wouldn't be pissed that we haven't talked much this past year. It's not like I didn't want to. That was never the case. Football's been kicking my ass and I've barely had time to breathe.

"Oh, yeah?"

"Most definitely." She nudges my shoulder and I bite

back a grin. "Congrats on being Rookie of the Year, by the way. Driftwear is huge."

Driftwear's one of the biggest athletic clothing brands in the country. They reached out to our general manager because they wanted to feature me on their cover for *Rookie of the Year* and officially name me as their global ambassador. It's a goal many athletes want to achieve and I still can't believe it's happening.

"Thank you." I hold her gaze before she turns to Amir to give him a swift hug.

Then we all squeeze into the booth like some sardines and Maya says something that makes Amelia laugh until she's clutching her stomach, and I can't help but stare.

God, I've missed that laugh. It's my favorite sound.

3

AMELIA

Hours later, Tia drops Maya off at home because she works early in the morning. I was going to stay at a hotel because my apartment isn't ready until tomorrow, but Tia insisted I stay in their guest house, which doesn't bother me in the slightest. I love her company.

I slide open the frosted glass shower door and flick the water with my fingers to test the temperature. I like it scalding hot, not quite boiling but close. Stepping inside feels like pure bliss. Warm water cascades down my body as I close my eyes, let out a deep breath, and detangle my curls.

I washed it tonight, which practically took a chunk out of my hair.

Okay, it didn't actually take a chunk out, but it sure felt like it as I kept peeling loose strands off my hands.

Stepping onto the white bath mat, I yank the towel off the hook and wrap it around my body, and trot over to the granite countertop. I quickly go through my curly hair routine which only consists of a leave-in conditioner and mousse from my mini travel bottle.

I've decided to let it air dry tonight since I unfortunately don't have the universal diffuser attachments, which, note to self: Buy ASAP. I'd use the regular one but I'm not about to risk it.

Slipping into a pair of sweats and an oversized sweatshirt, I briskly walk across the stone-paved courtyard, feeling like a kid as I leap over the cracks in the concrete. The cool LA breeze ruffles my hair, and I slide open their backdoor, stepping into the warmth of their home, the scent of lavender wafting into my nostrils.

Tia's sitting at her kitchen island, looking deep in thought and my brows furrow as I approach her.

"You okay?" I look down at her wedding scrapbook, open to the seating arrangements page. Jared's name at the table across from mine.

She sighs, exasperated. "Are you sure you're okay with Jared coming?"

"It's fine," I say quietly, biting the inside of my lip.

It wouldn't be fair to ask Amir to uninvite his own cousin from their wedding. It's not his fault that it happened and his whole entire family will be there. I have no right. It's not my day.

She leans in, whispering so Amir doesn't hear her from the other room. "I could tell Jared a lie so he doesn't—"

"No, don't do that." I shake my head, resting my hand on hers. "It's been a year. I'm completely over it already."

A white lie never hurts anyone.

She's silent for a moment, knowing I'm lying but she doesn't push. I'm grateful for that. Am I completely over it? No. But I'm not hurt as I once was. That has to count for something, right?

Four years I was with him. Those feelings didn't disappear like I hoped they would.

I thought that the moment I caught him cheating, it'd be like a fairy waving her magic wand and *poof*, all my feelings would vanish. But life doesn't work that way. I can't turn them off like a switch. We had our moments, and maybe that's what I'm still holding on to by a thread.

A frayed thread.

He doesn't deserve to invade my thoughts and live rent-free in my head, but I know I need to try harder to let him go. Hopefully, I'll get there one day.

"How about we do an old tradition of ours before we call it a night?" I squeeze her hand gently, wanting to move on from this sore topic. I just want to start fresh, not dwell on the past.

We both simultaneously glance at the kitchen clock. 11 p.m. Not too late.

"Movie?" Her eyes light up as she slams the wedding scrapbook shut.

"Movie." I giggle in confirmation and we sprint into the living room like we're teens again, plopping down onto her sectional couch.

Amir emerges from the other room, shaking his head with a smile before tossing a throw blanket. I catch it flawlessly.

He heads over to Tia and kisses her goodnight before heading upstairs. "You two have fun."

Oh we will.

She snatches up the remote buried under the pillow and I shake out the blanket, draping it over us as she puts on a classic.

Mean Girls.

Waking up to the smell of eggs and bacon, my stomach rumbles instantly. Letting out a yawn, I stretch, rubbing my eyes before peeling off the blanket. I unzip my suitcase, throwing on a pair of denim shorts and a blush pink tank top.

After changing, I open the guest room door and pause, confused as to why Caleb is here, cooking with headphones on at 8 a.m.

Black sweats, a plain white tee, and somehow even more toned than the last time I saw him. His Coach really has them working.

He must've felt my presence because, slowly he pulls off his headphones, letting them rest around his neck. He glances over, a familiar grin I know too well spreading across his face, looking like he's up to something. "Hi."

"Morning," I round the mini kitchen island, dropping down onto a barstool. "Don't get me wrong, I'm happy to see you…but why are you here?"

"Tia told me you were getting the keys to your new apartment today," he states, turning back to the stove, not fully answering my question as he scrambles the eggs.

"I am." I eye his back suspiciously. "I should probably go meet them in the house, they're taking me on their way to work."

"They left already," he replies, flipping the bacon in the other pan. "I told them I'd take care of you."

"Wow, how noble of you."

His mouth twitches in amusement as he turns the stove off, sliding the scrambled eggs onto a plate along with the bacon and perfectly stacked pancakes. The smell instantly hits me and my stomach growls again.

"Breakfast is served, milady." He sets the plate in front of me, then gives me the most dramatic bow I've ever seen. "Close your eyes."

I chuckle and do as he says. I'm so used to his antics that I don't bother questioning it. The fridge door opens and closes, followed by a loud hiss of a whipped cream canister.

"Now, open," he murmurs.

I slowly open my eyes to find my pancakes now cutely decorated with a heart drawn in whipped topping with a strawberry on the side.

My favorite fruit.

Warmth spreads through my chest at the little detail. Ever since we were teenagers, he's always done the sweetest things for me.

Freshman Year High School, April 2013

"Hey, remember that early screening movie you wanted to see next weekend?" Caleb asked, taking a bite out of his sandwich as we sit overlooking the rippling ocean.

We always loved coming to Manhattan Beach after his Friday night football practices. It was peaceful and calm. The gentle cool breeze, the salt air, the quietness of it all. Our little escape from reality.

Our bubble.

"Don't remind me. I'm still mad I didn't get the tickets. I was fifth in the queue!" I groaned.

Without a word, Caleb unzipped his backpack, pulling his phone out.

"What?" I frowned, confused.

"Click the movie app."

My thumb pressed down on the app. Bright green text flashed along the top:

Payment Successful. Two tickets purchased.

"No, you didn't!" I squealed, loud enough that the houses behind

us probably heard. "How did you get these? I couldn't even get one and I stayed up all night!"

"I was in the queue too," he chuckled. "Had my phone, iPad, computer, and my mom's phone open. Got lucky on the iPad."

"Why'd you get two?" I stared at him, with the biggest smile on my face. "You didn't even want to go at first."

"Yeah, but you did." He looked at me with that kind, thoughtful look I've seen a million times, and my heart melted. "That's enough of a reason."

"You didn't have to make me breakfast." I say, stabbing the strawberry with my fork, taking a small bite. "But I won't complain."

"Good," he says cooly, pouring me a cup of orange juice. "Now, eat up princess."

4

AMELIA

"THERE'S NO WAY. YOU STILL HAVE THIS?" CALEB TOSSES his head back laughing loudly as he takes my Wildcats suitcase from my hands, sliding it into the trunk of his Mercedes Benz.

He's so dramatic. Granted…I was too, but still. I'm the only one who can be dramatic in this friendship. It's the only way we can function.

I narrow my eyes at him, heading toward the passenger seat. "Don't judge. It's cute and functional."

"Wasn't planning on judging it," he says slyly, slamming the trunk shut with a thump. Then he glances over at me with an unreadable expression. "I agree…it's cute."

I bite the inside of my cheek to keep the smile from slipping out.

As we both climb into the car he passes me his phone. "Here, put your new address in."

I take his phone, feeling the warmth of his touch linger for a second. "Thanks," I murmur, punching in my apartment on Santa Monica Boulevard.

Trees pass by in a blur as I lean against the window taking in the views. Huge billboards lining up with celebrities promoting skincare brands I'm sure they don't use, new movies I need to go see, and oh my...

As we pass the SoFi Stadium, my eyes widen. Caleb's massive billboard spread across the side of the building. He's in his jersey, clutching the football, trying to look all "sexy" for the camera.

"Did they have to photoshop you or something? You're usually not that good-looking."

I'm not blind. Yeah, Caleb's good-looking...*everyone* knows that.

I've witnessed girls falling for him every single day since I met him.

But someone's gotta keep these men humble. He's not exempt just because he's my friend. Sorry, not sorry.

He feigns offense, shooting me a glower before focusing back on the road. "But that means I'm good looking *some* of the time, right?"

"Meh," I say with a smug grin, shrugging as I look out the window. "I guess."

"You guess?" he says, poking my ribs with his finger. I yelp and smack his arm.

"Focus on the road!" I fold my arms, shielding myself from any future pokes as laughter spills out of me.

My thoughts then start swirling in my head as we start approaching my new place.

New job. A fresh start.

I've missed being back in Los Angeles and being with Caleb again. This is where I'm always meant to be. It's comforting, how easily we can slip back into our old routine, like no time has passed at all.

Everything is always better with him.

We pull into the parking lot, the modern apartments look beautiful with massive palm trees surrounding it.

He finds a spot, killing the engine as I head inside.

"Welcome to Sunset View. We are so happy to have you in our community," the woman, maybe in her early 30's with a black bob says. "Our pool closes at 11 p.m. and the gym closes at midnight."

Then I notice she's not even looking at me anymore as she recites all of the information I need. I follow her gaze and of course, Caleb.

Here we go again.

Caleb trails a few feet behind me with my luggage, approaching the desk.

She clears her throat. "If you ever stop by and want to take advantage of our gym here, I'll let you." She lowers her voice, gawking at Caleb like she's ready to eat him whole. "Our little secret."

I'm starting to reconsider my apartment choice. She's completely forgotten about me and all I want are my keys so I can sit on my couch all night, order some leche flan, procrastinate unpacking and binge watch rom-coms until two in the morning.

Is that too much to ask for?

"I'm here for her that's all, but thanks," Caleb says firmly.

"Um…" Shifting uncomfortably, I scratch my temples. "May I have my keys now?"

"Right, so sorry!" She sighs as Caleb doesn't give her any other response before she crouches behind the desk to hand me my new shiny set of keys. "Here you go."

"Thanks." I reach for it, snatching a pamphlet off the table, turning to head toward the elevators. "Have a great day."

"You too," she mutters, disappointment laced in her voice.

"She was flirting big time," I mumble, pressing the up button.

He continues rolling my luggage, then stops beside me. "I know."

"You didn't flirt back?"

"Not interested."

I raise a brow, half-shocked. "She was pretty."

"And?"

"You like pretty girls."

"Okay? I'm not some horn dog that goes after every woman I see." He laughs, glancing down at me.

Interesting choice of words.

"Horn dog?" I press my lips together trying not to laugh.

The elevator dings, the doors sliding open.

"Just get inside," he rolls his eyes, chuckling.

We step inside and I tap my card on the sensor then press the third floor.

After it dings again, we head toward my room. "Do you have any plans later?"

"Not at all," he says quickly, rolling my luggage as I stop in front of my new place. "Why?"

The mahogany wooden door with the numbers 304 written in silver stares back at me. Wow. This is really happening.

I take out my keys, unlock the door, and step inside, taking it all in. The new apartment is quiet and untouched, filled with the crisp scent of wood and linen, with just a trace of fresh paint in the air.

Sunlight streams in, flooding the space with brightness as it glints off the grey wooden floors and marble kitchen island. I take a deep breath, soaking in the warmth pouring through the windows.

"Well, I'm waiting for the movers to drop off my boxes later and was wondering if you wanted to hang out until then?" I half-expect him not to, sure he has other plans on a Friday afternoon than to wait all day for my boxes.

He shuts the door behind me, taking a look around. "Wow, perfect apartment for the perfect girl," he says, rolling my luggage into the corner with a small smile.

"Yeah, I'm not going anywhere anytime soon. You need to give me a tour."

I chuckle and soak in my new space. It feels unreal to be officially back, for good this time. Life in San Francisco was amazing with my parents but this is my home. Where I belong.

I hop onto my new island, sliding my palms across the cool marble, glancing around the kitchen that I definitely won't be using. Cooking's not really my forte but I plan on learning. I can't live off frozen pizza forever.

Unfortunately.

"So, when's your first day at work?" he asks, stepping closer.

I swing my legs, meeting his gaze. "In two weeks. I'm a little nervous though, not going to lie."

"Don't be." He gently squeezes my knee, easing my nerves with one simple touch. "Everything will fall into place. You're a natural at what you do."

Well here goes nothing. To new beginnings.

5
AMELIA

My apartment's getting the finishing touches today, thanks to Caleb swinging by early this morning, like he's been doing for the past few days, 10 a.m. on the dot. He set up my TV, dresser, coffee table, sofa, and computer desk. I didn't expect him to do everything. I was already saving up to hire a moving company but when Caleb found out they were going to charge me an arm and a leg, he offered leaving no room for discussion.

He saved me $2,000 that I can now put toward rent, so I had zero reservations about letting him take over. Also, I'm pretty sure I was getting scammed now that I think about it. It couldn't have been *that* much.

Now he's setting up my new bookshelf that was dropped off fifteen minutes ago. It's a gray oak finish with three tall shelves that stretch floor to ceiling along the free wall in my room.

All the books I impulsively buy after finishing them on my Kindle will finally have a proper wooden home. My 'book trophies'.

"How's it going in here?" R&B music hums faintly as I peek into my bedroom. I step inside and almost trip over a mess of cardboard, bubble wrap, and Styrofoam scattered across the floor.

"Watch your step," Caleb says, his face buried into the instructional manual.

I cautiously step between the mess, popping a squat beside him. He's got a screwdriver in one hand, his glasses are slipping down his nose, flipping through the pages all laser focused.

He looks up at me over the rim of his frames, looking like my grandmother right now. "You know, this bookshelf has a lot of damn screws. Who needs sixty?"

"Because it's fancy." I stifle a laugh. "Want some more water, handy man?"

He's been working nonstop since he got here and the best friend in me is feeling guilty for taking up his whole day.

He shakes his head, a smile creeping onto his face. "I'm fine, but could you please crank up the AC? It's getting hot in here."

"Coming right up." I ruffle his hair, ignoring his groan, then head back into the living room and rapidly tap the buttons down to exactly sixty-nine degrees.

If Maya were here, she'd be proud of that.

When I return, his shirt is discarded to the side, and he's now in only jeans, crouched low in front of the half-built shelf.

"How about we get some lunch when you're done?" I ask, leaning against the doorframe, watching him work.

"Sounds good to me," he says glancing over his shoulder with a grin. "Wanna pick the place?"

"Sure." I chuckle, pushing off the door.

I wander out to my newly setup three-piece modular sofa, sinking onto the plush gray cushions, fishing out my phone and call Maya, hopefully she's on her lunch break.

"Hey hottie," she answers almost instantly. "Is lover boy still working on your apartment?"

I roll my eyes. Please. She's convinced that Caleb and I have hooked up at some point, though she can't prove it.

The closest thing we've ever come to 'kissing' was sophomore year of high school. I was teaching him how to ride my longboard, and we've been out there for hours when he fell on top of me and almost pecked my lips in the process.

"Caleb..." I correct the awful nickname she gave him. "...is still here but we're grabbing lunch after."

"Interesting," she says casually.

"How?"

"Oh I don't know. He's just the sweetest guy, huh?" She snickers, like a wicked witch. "Spending his day helping you unpack rather than sleeping in."

"He's being nice." I raise a brow, suspicious of where she's going with this.

"Nice...right. I'm shocked though, after all these years and you two never—"

"Dated? I interrupt, getting this exact question from my mother every single chance she gets.

"Dating? No." She giggles, then lets out a long exaggerated sigh. "What I'm saying is, he's hot and you're hot. I think it's time you let loose and fuc—"

Ok no. I don't want to think about that.

"I don't see him that way!" I interject. "Don't put those images in my head."

Oof. Too late. I'm picturing it.

"Imagine he's all sweaty on top of you, moaning your

name as he's pounding your—" She lets out a breathy moan.

"Nope. Nope. Nope. I'm hanging up now, bye." I hang up, flinging my phone to the other side of the couch.

Fantastic. Screw her and her dirty mind.

My apartment elevator creaks with a sound that is in desperate need of WD-40. Caleb wanted to go home and freshen up before we went out so it's been a few hours.

As I head toward the lobby, I spot him near the couches. His brown hair is tousled and slightly damp, and a grey t-shirt clings to his broad shoulders and arms. His glasses sit perfectly on his nose, like he just stepped out of a Calvin Klein ad.

He runs his hands through his hair, his shirt lifting enough to flash a sliver of his tanned skin and the waistband of his boxers. Oh, hey I was right...

I chuckle to myself.

His lips curve into a smile, raising a brow. "What're you laughing at?"

I shake my head, a quiet laugh caught in my throat. "Nothing."

"Come on, let's eat before you get all hangry on me," he huffs amused, draping an arm over my shoulder as he steers me through the revolving doors.

By the time we make it to the Grove, the hum of traffic has faded into the distance. We head toward the coffee shop, and I breathe in the fresh air, falling into step beside him.

Caleb has always had this warm, grounding presence.

For most people, silence can feel heavy and awkward but with him, it never does.

The cafe door opens with a light jingle as he steps ahead of me performing the most exaggerated bow, hand pressed to his stomach as he gestures me in. "After you."

"Why, thank you." I laugh, amused by his antics, per usual.

I order a white chocolate latte and avocado toast, while Caleb orders an egg and bacon sandwich with caramel coffee.

We find a nice table outside with a huge yellow umbrella in the middle as Caleb takes a sip from his drink, letting out a quiet hum of satisfaction. "Mmm. Usually caramel coffees are decent but this is good. Want to try?" he asks, tilting his cup in my direction.

"Yeah. Let me grab an extra straw," I tease, pressing my palms against the table. "I don't know where your mouth has been."

He takes another slow sip, then offers the cup back, eyes on mine. "I promise my lips are clean."

"Fine." I shake my head, leaning in as my chest presses against the edge of the table. Then, I wrap my lips around the straw as a low groan creeps up my throat. "This is delicious."

Silence.

When I glance up, Caleb's eyes avert from mine.

"Yeah." He clears his throat. "Delicious."

As we continue eating our lunch, whispers form behind me, followed by the sound of high heels against the gravel. I look over my shoulder and see two women staring right at Caleb before approaching him like prey.

"Caleb?" a blonde with a tight shirt and big boobs squeals. "Caleb Hayes?"

He looks past me, a friendly glint in his eyes. "Hi ladies."

"Oh my god. I told you it was him!" The blonde practically moans from hearing him speak, then shoves her phone into her friend's hands. "Take a picture of us!"

Her friend grumbles, trying to adjust the shopping bags in her hands.

The blonde strides to Caleb's side of the table as he rises, fixing his shirt.

I continue eating my toast, watching him interact with his supporters, which is something I admire about him. Every time I've seen him with one he's never annoyed, never fake, and genuinely treats them like friends.

He wraps his arms chastely around her waist, his touch respectful, but she doesn't hesitate to press her body against his, breaking that touch barrier.

After they snap a photo she leans in, biting her bottom lip. "You're even hotter in person. Could you please sign something for me?"

I wonder what it will be this time, usually fans will bring him hats, shirts, phone cases, I've even seen someone using an unused pad because they panicked at the last minute.

"Of course." He nods. "What is it?"

She points to her cleavage and asks, "Could you sign… here?"

I pause mid-bite, nearly choking on my food as I glance up at Caleb, who's now holding a sharpie she magically pulled from her purse.

Of course she'd have a perfectly working marker.

He looks at me for a second, then back to her, before coughing into his fist. "Uh, sure thing."

She beams, pushing her hair over her shoulder, and he

awkwardly signs a few inches above where she'd asked, careful not to go near the valley of her breasts.

When he finishes, Caleb caps the marker and hands it back. "There you go."

She shrieks, wrapping her arms around him for a hug. "Thank you! I love you so much!"

"Love you too," he shouts back with a polite smile.

I shake my head, returning to my food as he sits across from me. "You have interesting fans. Do they always ask you to sign their body parts?"

"As weird as it may sound, that wasn't my first rodeo." He snorts. "Doesn't make it any less awkward though."

"In that case, maybe I'll get you to sign my forehead? Ever gotten that request?"

"You'd be the first," he grins, taking another bite of his sandwich. "Is that what you want?"

"Yeah. I want Caleb Hayes, written all across."

"Only if I get yours in return." He laughs, tossing his straw playfully at me and I catch it effortlessly.

As we finish lunch, I slide all my trash onto the tray to throw it but Caleb beats me to it. He scoops up both of ours, walking to the garbage can a few stores down.

"Amelia?"

Chills shoot up my spine when I recognize that deep familiar voice...

Jared.

Why do I feel like I've been sucked into a time machine? The memories rush in. The laughs, the petty arguments, the way we'd always watch movies together in my dorm. He'd pull me into his arms, feed me popcorn and I couldn't help the tingles I'd get by being around him.

It's all crashing back.

I shoot upright, stealing a quick glance at Caleb, who's

still busy throwing our trash away. My gaze jumps back to Jared, heart pounding against my ribcage. It's been a whole year since I last saw him, and was counting on the wedding being the only time I'd have to run into him again. Dang it.

"You look great," he says gently, his voice smooth as butter and I'm trying not to get sucked into this familiarity. "Um...how've you been?"

My throat tightens. "Great." I shift my weight from one foot to the other, tapping my fingers impatiently against my thigh. Caleb is taking forever and the longer I stand here, the more awkward I feel.

"I heard about your new job." He smiles, tentative. "Congratulations."

"We can skip the small talk."

There's no need for it.

His expression fades into something more serious. "I know you're mad but please, let me explain."

"Explain?" My fingers twitch at my side as my frustration wells up. "Explain what? That you wasted four years of my life?"

The words tumble out before I can stop them. And just like that, the heartbreak returns.

"Stop." His eyes falter for a split second. "It wasn't a waste, Amelia."

No. Don't cry. Don't cry. Don't let him see you like this.

"You know I loved you but..." he adds, rubbing the back of his neck.

His words fade for a moment as my gaze drifts to the familiar curls that still rest above his thick brows, the same ones I used to twirl between my fingers when everything felt perfect. His tawny skin still glows, just like before.

I hate that I still see him this way. Like I'm wearing rose-colored glasses, only letting myself remember the gentle parts of our relationship. The warmth. The moments that make it hard to stay angry.

Why can't I hate him? I always tell myself I do, but look at me now. Still reminiscing. Pretending to be tough while every part of me aches.

"Loved me?" I let out a shaky, bitter laugh. "Yeah right."

"It's the truth, but I guess in the back of my mind..." He swallows, his eyes flicking away from mine. "I always knew you weren't really mine."

"Bullshit!" I take a step closer, not caring that my voice is trembling. "I was completely in love with you. Fully committed. Unlike you."

"I know, I know but—"

"But nothing. You could've just broken up with me," I snap. "Instead, you chose to sleep with someone else and blindside me for a whole month. Did I mean that little to you?"

I wasn't expecting this. The last time I was this close to him was the night we went out to dinner, before everything went to shit. I can still feel the heat of his hands on my skin, the way he kissed me, only to turn around and do the same with someone else.

"No!" he blurts, panicked. He starts to reach for me, then catches himself, shoving his hands into his pockets. "I just want to apologize. Now that you're back, I can finally tell you something I've been trying—"

His words cut off, eyes shifting past me.

To someone.

"You really think it's a good idea to talk to her after what you did?" Caleb's voice is low and rough as his hand slides around my waist to shift me behind him.

Oh no.

"I'm trying to apologize. Not that it's any of your business, Hayes," Jared snaps.

My brows pull together. It's like someone grabbed the remote to my life and hit pause so I can have the time to process what's going on.

"When it comes to her feelings, it is my fucking business," Caleb hisses through clenched teeth. His eyes never waver.

My head whips up to him. The blue vein in his neck is thick, prominent, as if at any second it's going to burst.

"Hey babe, have you seen my phone?"

The sound cuts through me like a knife. Maroon painted nails loop around Jared's arm and my heart stutters.

She's stunning. Short ginger hair, flowery dress, platform heels. She flashes us a bright, cheerful smile, completely oblivious to the chaos she's walked into.

Is this her? Is this the woman he cheated on me with? Does she know who I am?

My eyes lock onto their hands, now intertwined.

Jared must notice because he clears his throat, gesturing toward her. "This is Kim, my girlfriend."

Girlfriend.

The simple word punches me right in the gut. It shouldn't hurt like this. I should be over it by now and get it together. But the sting is sharp and deep.

"Oh!" She gives us a small shy wave. "Hi."

"Hi." I say with a tight-lipped smile. "Well, we have to go but we'll see you two at the wedding, yeah?" I wrap my hand around Caleb's bicep, tugging him toward the sidewalk, wanting to get out of here but he's solid like a brick.

Caleb stays rooted in place, his gaze solely on Jared. A

muscle in his jaw ticks like he's holding something back. A punch? A yell? I can't tell. But the way his chest rises and falls tells me he's barely keeping it together.

Jared exhales loudly, holding Kim's hand tighter as they turn toward the cafe. Before stepping inside, he glances back and our eyes meet. "See you guys there."

The words hang heavy in the air. This conversation isn't over. I can feel it.

The walk back to Caleb's car feels longer than it should, each step heavier than the last. I find myself walking a little ahead, trying to wrestle my emotions into something more manageable.

Then, a gentle tug at my wrist jolts me to a stop. "You okay?"

I stare at the ground, shaking my head. No. I'm not. I allow myself to tell the truth for once.

He's silent, then ducks his head to meet my eyes. "Talk to me."

I sink my teeth into the inside of my lip, every emotion bubbling up to the surface. "Seeing him felt like reliving that day all over again."

Warmth seeps into my cheeks as Caleb cups my face into his hands as he listens intently.

I sigh. "It just makes me question things about myself. Like the fact that I wasn't good enough…maybe that's why he did it."

Was I doing something to annoy him in our relationship? Was I too much for him?

Caleb's expression hardens, his jaw clenching as he shakes his head.

He leans down, his voice low, meant only for me. "You didn't do a damn thing. You hear me? Don't you dare blame yourself. It's not your fault he couldn't see what an amazing woman he had right in front of him."

"But why do I still feel the same?"

"There's no set timeline on healing." His calloused thumb brushes along my chin. "Four years isn't nothing. That kind of pain doesn't just go away. Give yourself a little more time."

I swallow the lump in my throat. *There's no set timeline on healing.*

He's right, like always. He has this way of making me feel seen, heard, and cared for. Truly my anchor.

After spending this past year apart, I've come to realize I can't imagine going a day without him anymore.

6
AMELIA

I<small>T'S BEEN A WEEK AND</small> T<small>IA AND</small> M<small>AYA MAGICALLY</small> convinced me to go out again. Usually, I need at least two weeks to recover and recharge my social battery, but I don't want to be a party pooper. So, what the hell. I could use a pick me up after the whole running into Jared incident.

"Isn't this a little too short?" I glance down, running my hands down my frame. The smooth black satin skims my palms and stops a few inches shy below my ass. If I so much as bend over, I might as well flash the whole club.

Maya's face fills my screen, in nothing but a black bra and underwear, looking around her closet also debating on what to wear.

"You're kidding right?" She chuckles glancing at me, before pulling a mesh sheer black top from the hanger and slips it over her head. "It's not short enough babe."

I step back from my phone, propped against the mirror, and glance over my outfit once more. The plunging V-neck mini dress clings to my body like a second skin. Not my usual go-to, but damn, do I feel good in it.

It's A Win For Me

I flip my hair in every direction, trying to add more volume, definitely feeling lightheaded now but it's always worth it. Big curls are a must.

"Every guy's gonna be staring at you tonight, wishing they could kiss your feet." Maya says, tugging on a mini black sequin skirt and giving a little twirl to check out her behind.

"I don't want that." I cringe, shivering dramatically.

She laughs. "Do you want me to pick you up? I can swing by. I'm saying no to alcohol tonight."

"Wait, what? You always drink when we go out."

"I work early tomorrow and have a shit ton of brands on my roster to create content for." She groans, snatching her phone up and walking toward her living room. "But, I'm not about to miss a night out."

My phone dings.

CALEB
I'm picking you up.

Thanks but I think Maya's going to take me.

CALEB
Tell her to save gas. I'm on my way.

You don't have to drive all the way here lol!

Caleb?

hello??

k

CALEB
🖤

I tell Maya I don't need a ride after all and we hang up. Not even thirty minutes later, there's a knock at my door.

I swing it open and there he is.

Wearing all black that accentuates how in shape he is. The knitted top clings to him, hugging every inch of muscle. His brown hair slightly ruffled and jawline is still sharp as ever.

"Hey, pretty girl. You ready?"

"Bringing that nickname back, huh?" I tease, giving his arm a playful jab.

"It suits you," he says, scratching his head. "You um… look gorgeous by the way."

"Thanks Hayes, you're not so bad yourself."

"Calling me by my last name now?" he fires back.

"It suits you." I snicker, repeating his words then I snatch my purse off the counter, shutting the door behind us.

I catch the faint curve of his grin as I walk past him and chills ripple through me when his hand brushes against the small of my back, gently guiding me toward the elevator.

It's such a simple gesture, something he always does, but it never fails to make me feel like he's always looking out for me.

Caleb and I walk into the dim club, lights flickering all around us. The DJ, wearing neon glasses at the front, bobs his head while spinning the turntable, and everyone's having a good time. We meet Tia, Maya, and Amir at the reserved VIP area, scooting into the booth away from the chaos and sweaty bodies for a moment.

Tia looks absolutely breathtaking in a yellow mini dress with a halter neckline that pops against her sun-kissed skin, long auburn hair and wispy bangs perfectly blown out. Amir matches her with a yellow button down shirt.

"I'm getting us some shots!" Tia shouts over the music.

"Skip me, I drove." Caleb shakes his head.

Maya raises her finger unenthusiastically. "Me too."

"Water for you two it is." Tia nods, looping her arm through Amir's and head toward the bar. "Be right back."

"And I'm going to dance." Maya singsongs as she rises, smoothing down her skirt before scooting down past Caleb and me, hips swaying as she heads down the steps.

Now, it's only us in the booth. He leans back, resting an arm casually along the back of the seat, and I can feel his eyes burning into me.

I glance over, lifting a finger and circling it around my face. "Is there something on me?"

His eyes avert in an instant, straightening up his posture. "Nah."

As I scan the VIP section, my eyes land on a pretty redhead practically staring into Caleb's soul, clearly trying to get his attention. Which is to be expected.

"You don't have to stay with me, I'm sure you'd have more fun dancing with her." I say, nudging his arm.

"Who?"

I jut my chin toward the woman, who's now twisting her top. "Her."

He tilts his head down, trying to hear me over the loudness of the music. "Say that again."

"The red head over there," I repeat, raising my voice slightly.

He finally follows my gaze, then turns back to me like I sprouted a second head.

"I don't want to talk to her," he says firmly. "Probably not the best move for me right now."

Oh shoot. How did I forget that?

A month ago, I saw online that he was at a release party with our friend Marcus for Vanessa Noles.

Yes, Vanessa Noles, who is in fact in every single one of my playlists. She has a song for every mood.

Lonely? Check. Happy and disgustingly in love? Check. Got cheated on by your boyfriend, the one you thought you were going to marry, but he turned out to be an asshole?

Specific but yes. She does have a song for that too.

Anyway, the next day, my feed was flooded with photos of him kissing her with headlines and comments like:

Hayes isn't who I thought he was.

Homewrecker Hayes should be his new nickname.

I should've reached out and asked him how he was feeling, what he was going through. I should've been there for him the way he's always shown up for me.

But we weren't really talking that much. And I'd only overheard bits from Tia, so I didn't push.

"I'm sorry... I forgot about—"

He gently shakes his head. "No... no. You have better things to worry about than my gossip problems."

Still, guilt twists in my stomach.

"Maybe you can try and have a good time tonight still? Because um, she's coming over here."

"I guess but I'm sitting here with you, she's not gonna just walk over and—"

His voice trails off as she saunters up to our booth, pushing her chest up and eyeing him up and down like a tiger ready to pounce and I take that as my cue.

"Told you...just relax tonight and try not to worry about the media," I whisper before scooting away and giving him space to do whatever he decides.

Tia and Amir trot over with drinks, sliding Caleb his water before handing me a shot.

"Who's the knockout?" Tia slides to the other side of the booth, glancing at the girl who's currently laughing at everything he's saying.

"Some girl gawking at your brother." I reach for my shot.

"Well," she shrugs, grabbing her glass, lifting it in the air. "To Amelia, for starting fresh!"

In more ways than one. New job. New apartment. New life, basically.

I beam, raising my tiny glass of courage and clinking it against theirs before tossing it back. The hot liquid travels down my throat, and I grimace at the abrasive taste. A cough escapes as I wipe my lips with the back of my hand.

As the thumping of the music surrounds me Caleb's words loop in my head. Six words.

There's no set timeline on healing.

Five shots in and the room is tilting with every blink. Heat coils throughout my body, spreading down to my fingertips.

Caleb and the red head are on the dance floor, his hands resting on her waist while hers loop around his neck, pulling him closer. I'm glad he's having a good time, he needs it after the month he's had. One night won't hurt him.

"I'm getting another drink!" I shout over the pounding music as I rise, tugging down my dress and grabbing my purse only to stumble a little on my heels.

"I'm coming with youuu," Tia slurs, pushing up onto her feet, eyes red and glassy.

Amir glances up at me with a full-blown father look. "Sit for a few more minutes."

"No!" I shake my head rapidly. "You two stay. I'll just be right over there. Enjoy yourselves loooovebirds."

"Don't go too far, alright?" Amir calls after me, his voice laced with concern.

"Got it, Dad," I say with dramatic air quotes, already heading down the VIP steps, weaving through the crowd and tossing out "excuse me" more times than I can count.

Finally, there's an opening at the end of the bar and I drop down onto a stool, spinning lazily around.

I raise a finger to the bartender as I lean against the counter. "Vodka tonic, pronto please!"

Maya shimmies her way over to me and twirls my seat around so I'm facing her. "You look like you're having a good time."

I nod as my head lolls forward. "Most definitely."

"It's about time." Maya cups my face in her hands, looking into my eyes like she's examining me. "But, take it easy with the drinks, sailor. You're not a heavy drinker."

I wave her off, laughing. "I'm fine."

The bartender slides my shot across the stone bar top. "Rough night, ladies?" he asks, a thick British accent instantly catching my attention and it warms my insides up.

I still hate men, don't misconstrue. But come on, he's British.

He looks older, only by a few years, with light scruff along his square jawline, dark black hair, and sleeve tattoos stretched all down his buff arms.

Maya says nothing but I'd bet my savings that she's eye-banging him right about now.

I turn my head to check.

Yup. I'm right.

"Not really." I toss the shot back with a laugh, answering for the both of us. "Just having fun tonight."

"Perhaps I could be a bit of a distraction?" His gaze now locks on mine as he pulls the rag off his shoulder, wiping down the table in a deliberate, slow motion. "Only for a minute or two."

Heat rushes to my face.

Maya leans into my ear, whispering, "His accent alone could make me do some questionable things."

My lips twitch in amusement.

He pumps sanitizer into his palms, scrubbing together before offering his hand. "Matteo Hawthorne. Nice to meet you, love."

Maya squeezes my thigh and cocks her head at me, whispering in my ear again, "I'll be watching you from over there, but if he tries anything funny, he'll be missing his dick by morning."

I cough into my elbow at her overly specific threat, dismissing her with a grin.

I turn my attention back to Matteo and take his hand. "Amelia."

"No last name?" he asks, giving my hand a light squeeze.

"You'll have to earn that," I say with a quiet laugh, meeting his dark eyes.

Then the familiar scent of amber and spice wraps around me and I don't have to look to know who it is.

"There you are." Caleb appears beside me, sliding an arm around my shoulders.

"Where's your new girlfriend?" I tease, lifting a brow as I glance up.

"How funny." Caleb huffs, eyes fixed on Matteo.

Matteo's grin falters slightly as he bounces his eyes

between us. "Well, I suppose that's my cue. It was lovely to meet you, Amelia."

He strolls down the bar, greeting the other customers and I let out a quiet sigh.

"Sorry," Caleb says, his jaw tight. "Didn't mean to interrupt."

Did he interrupt? Not at all. It was a harmless exchange and my half-assed attempt at living out the advice Maya's been drilling into my head post-break up: If you can't get over someone, it's time to get under someone new.

I've been getting a lot of advice and I think it's time to start implementing it.

Time to stop sulking around over a man who didn't care, Amelia.

"You didn't," I murmur, fanning my face with one hand.

Saliva pools in my mouth and the alcohol isn't on my side tonight.

"Hey," he says, dipping his head to meet my gaze. "You okay?"

"Mhm," I say, trying to convince myself at this point.

"Doesn't look like it."

I shake my head, swaying. "All good."

"Let's go." His voice firm as his brows knit together. "You look like you're going to barf any second."

"What? No." I try to hold his gaze, but the room keeps spinning. "I'm not leaving."

"You're being stubborn."

"Am not." I attempt a step, only for my legs to betray me.

He catches me instantly, hands at my elbows. His face is right there, inches from mine. "Let's go," he says soft-spoken this time. "Please?"

My stomach flips again. Shit. Okay yeah, I need to get some air.

"We should probably say bye to everyone first," I mumble.

"I'll text them. Come on." He presses his hand against the small of my back, guiding me toward the exit. No room left to argue.

And I had no desire to anymore.

7

CALEB

You want to know the worst part about tonight?

It's that every damn feeling I have for her is still there, lingering like a goddamn pest. It's even stronger now. And I didn't even think that was possible.

Ever since she came back, it's like every feeling I thought I'd buried deep in my gut rose to the surface and now I can't stop it.

Dancing with the redhead earlier was supposed to help. A distraction at best. Something to drown out my feelings for Amelia, even for a few minutes.

Newsflash. It fucking didn't.

And what's with the bartender? Calling her *love* like that? Psh. I hate how much it gets to me. Makes me feel like the same pathetic teenager I used to be.

I lead Amelia out of the club, keeping her close, probably closer than I should as a light wind brushes past us.

Flash

Flash

Flash

No no damn it. Not right now. I quickly shift her to my other side, instinct taking over as I shield her from view.

Flash

Flash

Paparazzi swarm the sidewalk like bees, cameras all pointed directly at us, voices overlapping each other. Hammering me with questions and comments.

"Who's this?"

"Is she taken too?"

I grit my teeth, arm tightening around her as I move us faster. No way in hell I'm letting them snap photos of her like this. This is so fucking stupid. For the millionth time, Vanessa was a single woman and I want to shout it from the rooftops but it's useless.

Ignoring every question hurled our way, her fingers clench tighter at my waist as she clings to me, burying her face in my neck. Her lips graze my skin, and the sudden contact sends a jolt straight to my groin.

"Keys. Now," I bark, slip a hundred into the valet's hand, and follow it with a quick thank you.

A few minutes later, the car rolls forward. I rush to the passenger side, yank the door open, and help her inside. Then I lean over, reaching across her to buckle her seatbelt.

Her breath, warm and laced with alcohol ghosts my skin. I shut the door, circling the car as camera shutters still go off behind me.

Once I'm settled in the driver seat, I shoot off a quick text.

> We're leaving. You guys ok?

TIA

Yeah. Maya's dropping us off. Love you.

Love you too.

"Euugh…" Amelia groans, leaning against the window and clutching her stomach.

I side glance at her, keeping my eyes on the road as I hear her shift. "How much did you drink tonight?"

She lazily turns her head toward me. "Five."

I sigh, grip tightening on the wheel. "Amelia…" No wonder she's about to throw up. "You need to eat."

She pouts, crossing her arms. "Noooo…I want to lay down."

Stubborn as always.

By the time she finishes gagging into an empty bag I left in my backseat, I finally turn onto my street, headlights casting shadows along the apartment gate. I pull into my spot, killing the engine.

I'm out of the car in a second, opening her door as she gags and stumbles forward. I catch her, steadying her with my arm around her waist.

"I'm so tired," she murmurs, her head tipping forward, body slack in my arms. "I don't feel like walking."

I can't help but chuckle.

"Come on, princess."

She loops her arms around my neck as I scoop her up, sliding one hand under her thighs. Snatching her purse from the seat, I nudge the door shut with my elbow.

Walking into my apartment, I lay her down on the bed, smoothing her curls over the pillows.

As I try to pull the covers over her, she shoots upright, clapping a hand over her mouth as a gag tore through her.

She rushes to the bathroom, flipping up the toilet lid as she collapses to her knees.

Following her inside, I dig into my pocket and pull out a pink satin scrunchie. I'm not sure when it started, maybe junior year of high school when she left one behind on my dresser, and I don't know, I kept it.

Since then, I've always kept one handy, just in case. Now that she's back, the habit came back too.

I gather her curls into a loose bun, kneeling beside her and rub slow steady circles along her back. "Let it all out."

She finishes and slumps against the side of the tub, flushing the toilet with a weak hand.

"I'm so sorry. Ugh," she groans. "I can take a car home. This is gross."

"Hey, don't apologize. Just stay here tonight, okay? I'm gonna run to the store real quick."

She sighs, curling her knees to her chest. "Thank you."

I make a quick run to the gas station down the street, snatching up anything I can find at this hour.

Gatorade. Crackers. Bananas. Yogurt. Ginger Ale. Ibuprofen. Toothbrush.

When I get back, I unpack and peek into the bedroom. She's curled under the covers, knocked out already.

Letting out a small breath, I step inside. On the nightstand, I grab a notepad, scribble a simple note and slide it beneath the edge of my ceramic bowl.

Then I shut the door behind me and sink into the couch. I lie there, staring at the ceiling, thinking about last week when we ran into Jared.

Seeing him talk to her, trying to reach out, something snapped inside me. She looked so defeated, and I never want to see her like that again.

God. She has no idea how much power she holds over me.

8

AMELIA/CALEB

Amelia

I genuinely feel like my skull's been smashed with a hammer. Repeatedly.

Sunlight beams through the curtains, and I squint trying to process my surroundings. The thudding in my head echoes in my ears as I struggle to recall what happened last night.

Wait.

Panic creeps in. My heart's pounding in my chest and I freeze. The last thing I remember is Caleb carrying me into his room in his arms…

No.

We didn't, did we? I was pretty drunk last night and I never know what the hell I'm doing half the time. Did I seduce him? Oh God.

I jolt upright, gripping the sheets as I yank them back.

Oh. Still in my dress. Fully clothed. False alarm.

I groan in relief, then glance at the nightstand and spot a small note beside a familiar pottery bowl.

Instantly, I'm back in high school. We used to take pottery classes together whenever we felt stressed and Caleb wanted a breather from his father. It started off as his thing, but after he took me to a class, I was hooked. We've done it together ever since.

I reach for the bowl, tracing the uneven ridges and dips. Flipping it over, I find our initials carved into the bottom, like we'd done all those years ago.

A+C
Best Friends Forever

My eyes soften at the memory. Gently, I set it down and pick up the note.

I'm sorry I couldn't be there when you woke up, I had early practice. Make yourself at home. Feel free to use my car, it's parked in Spot B on the second floor. I ordered a car, so don't worry about it. Text me if you need anything. Oh, and there's a whole bunch of snacks in the kitchen. Take it easy.
—Caleb

I groggily slide out of bed to use the bathroom. After washing up, I glance at my reflection and wince. I look like I visited hell and back…twice.

Mascara smudged, looking like a raccoon. Curls slipping from my bun. And my breath? Reeks.

My gaze drops to an unopened toothbrush on the sink with a sticky note attached with the words *your breath stinks ;)*

I shake my head, a small laugh slipping out as I tear it open and brush my teeth without any hesitation. He's not wrong.

Feeling slightly more human, I shuffle into the kitchen. Bananas, crackers, ginger ale, and Gatorade are all lined up on the counter like it's my own personal hangover survival kit. Caleb literally thinks of everything.

Cracking open the bottle, I take a long slip. The mix of minty toothpaste and citrus is a deadly combo but I need the hydration.

Peeling a banana, I take a few bites, spot my purse on the coffee table, and order a ride home.

Caleb

It's been a few hours since I left this morning. I'm leaning against my locker, waiting for Coach to give us our usual morning prep talk, when a chime goes off inside. I reach in and grab my phone off the top shelf.

> **AMELIA**
> You're my savior. Thanks again for everything, I'm home now.

> You took my car, right?

> **AMELIA**
> No, I just ordered one.
>
> But thanks for letting me know I can drive your car though lol.

> Sent: $100

> **AMELIA**
> Why are you sending me money?

> For your ride.

> **AMELIA**
> It was only $15. I'll send it back.

> Don't want it.

> **AMELIA**
> Fine. I'm paying for something you want then.

> Not possible. It can't be bought.

"Listen up," Coach Banks announces, looping his whistle around his neck. "Our first game's in a few weeks."

His voice snaps me back to the present. I shove my phone into my locker and force myself to focus, even though my brain's still hung up on Amelia.

Coach stands in front of us, dressed in all black, sleeves pushed up as the overhead lights catch the faint stubble along his jaw. His short salt-and-pepper hair is freshly trimmed, his gaze sharp as it sweeps over the team.

The room falls silent. Every eye is on him. No one dares speak when Coach talks. We're not scared of him…well, not exactly. It's more about respect. He looks out for us, but he doesn't tolerate any bullshit.

"We're good, but we need to be better," he barks. "I'll be damned if we start this season off sloppy. Y'all got that?"

The weight of the team's eyes is heavy and the pressure creeps in. I'm the rookie quarterback and I want, no, I need to keep making them proud. I can't afford to disappoint. Not the team, not Coach. And especially not my father.

He'll tear apart every play like it's his day job. Nothing I do is ever enough and I'm really not in the mood to hear him talk my ear off about how shit my plays are.

Marcus, my best friend since college, nudges my arm, offering me a reassuring nod. "You got this, man. Don't stress."

I clap his back. "Appreciate it."

"Because one bad throw and I'll never let you live it down." He grins.

I roll my eyes, but deep down, I'm forever grateful to have him by my side. We met when he asked if I had a spare condom, mind you, we'd known each other for less than an hour in our shared dorm and he's been a pain in my ass ever since.

"With that being said"—Coach claps his hands together—"practice starts now. Let's go, Vipers!"

Practice is brutal. Endless sprints, drills, reps…

Coach stands across the field, eyes narrowing as he watches our every move like a hawk.

We've been running different plays for the past two hours, now wrapping up practice with some simple pass-and-plays.

Sweat trickles down my back as I line up behind my center, Nico. He crouches low, snaps the ball, and drops into the pocket while the defense closes in fast.

Carter, our wide receiver, is a few yards out, signaling that he's open. I nod, dig my cleats into the turf, and launch the ball in a tight spiral.

He takes off.

The defense locks in, ready to level him, but Carter stretches out with perfect timing and snatches it just before it hits the turf. With a sharp pivot, he zig-zags through and bolts for the end zone.

I exhale, watching him spike the ball into the ground. Damn. If we keep playing like this, the Titans won't know what hit them.

Their fans have been up our ass nonstop for months, always pitting us against each other online. The Titans only fuel them, and I'm more than ready to shut them the hell up.

Coach blows his whistle, signaling the end of practice. My shoulders sag with exhaustion. Sweat now clinging to my shirt, I yank off my helmet, running a hand through my damp hair as we head for the locker rooms. The blast of AC hits me like a godsend.

"Hell of a practice," Nico groans as he pulls his helmet off, revealing his black hair and tattoo on the side of his neck.

"Golden boy did good out there," Carter grins, his shirt streaked with grass stains, blonde hair plastered to his forehead.

"Golden boy, my ass," I mutter.

That nickname's been mine ever since I first signed with the Vipers. Coach gave me one compliment on how I handled the clock during the last two minutes of the fourth quarter in my first game. And because compliments from Coach are as rare as Marcus actually committing to one girl…

The name stuck. Unfortunately.

"Please, Coach would build you a throne if he could, or is it already built in his office?" Marcus hollers from his locker, stripping down to his compression shorts. He pulls off his helmet, short curls damp and his light brown skin drenched with sweat.

"Funny. I didn't realize I was in the presence of a comedian." I toss my helmet onto the bench, lazily glaring at him.

"That's why you're Rookie Of The Year, my man," Carter chimes in, leaning against his locker. "Driftwear loves you."

But they avoid scandals like the plague, and I'm already dangerously close to crossing the line. Thankfully, they're still trying to work with me. Their hope is the noise will fizzle out once the season starts. I'll play a good game, and maybe that'll be enough to drown out the bullshit.

I can't afford to screw up now, not with the contract signing in a few months. Driftwear could pull the deal in a second if they wanted.

The locker room door slams open, banging hard against the wall. Coach storms in, looking absolutely pissed off. Damn. I'd hate to be the poor bastard on the receiving end of that glare.

"Hayes. My office. Now," his voice slices through the air before he turns and marches out.

What the fuck?

Silence falls. The entire team all collectively turn around to look at me.

"What the hell did you do now?" Carter pipes up, rubbing a towel across his forehead.

Marcus, who always has something smart to say, stays quiet. Unruly quiet. He gives me a look, one that says you're in deep water. Coach has yelled at us before, but this? This is another level.

I exhale sharply, rubbing the back of my neck.

The walk to Coach's office felt longer than it should. I didn't even get a chance to change, so my cleats echo against the title with every heavy step, loud, making my nerves flare.

When I reach his office, he's already behind his desk. Our manager Daryl right beside him.

Daryl rarely shows up at practices, this must be more than serious.

"Shut the door," Coach says without looking up, gaze fixed on his screen.

I tilt my neck to crack it, then close the door behind me and step toward them. "What's going on?"

Coach doesn't say a word. Instead, he swivels his computer toward me.

I stare at the images, my stomach sinks to my ankles.

"Care to explain?" His voice is eerily cold.

Oh, shit.

9

CALEB

I FREEZE, STARING AT THE SCREEN. PHOTOS. SO MANY OF them. My arms wrapped around Amelia's waist, gripping her like she might disappear. My face all twisted up in concern. Have I always looked that pathetic around her? One shot shows me carrying her into my apartment... How the hell did paparazzi get through the gate? I didn't even see them, or hear a thing. I should've been more careful.

"Caleb, what the hell were you thinking?" Coach scrubs a hand over his beard, shaking his head.

"I was making sure she—"

"I know but everything you do is under a microscope. Don't you realize that by now, kid?" Coach's voice cuts through, sharp. "You're still splattered all over the magazines attached to Vanessa's name. You really think it was smart to be caught with another woman right now?"

Daryl sighs heavily, and then his expression goes stiff like he walked out of Dr. Miami's office.

"It's not looking good," he mutters. "Driftwear called me earlier. They're far from happy."

My stomach drops. This is the last thing I need.

"Yeah, and neither are we. We've talked about this already, don't put yourself in a situation where people can add fuel to it," Coach mumbles under his breath and types quickly, then swivels the laptop back toward me. "Have a look."

I lean in, skimming the comments beneath a sports blog that's infamous for gossip.

Let me guess, this girl's in a relationship too?

Wrecking another home, Caleb? Trying to beat a record?

And that's only a few. The rest are even more merciless. Like people have been sitting there, waiting for something new to pop up to tear me apart.

They rip apart everything about me, my priorities, my character, it's like I'm their own personal punching bag.

I know this is how the industry works. The media lifts you up, only to watch you fall in the end.

But Amelia didn't sign up for this. I was trying to help her and instead I dragged her right into my mess.

"And on top of this..." Daryl scratches his temple, hesitant to spit out whatever else shit there is. "They're considering pulling the deal if this isn't fixed in the next two weeks."

Oh for fuck's sake.

I shut my eyes for a second, dropping into the chair in front of Coach's desk. The leather creaks beneath me like it's had enough too. I squeeze my thumb, trying to shake off the anxiety gnawing at me. Driftwear's probably already thinking of another rookie to replace me by now.

"I don't know how," Coach says, pinching the bridge of his nose, "but you need to fix this before they drop you."

Well, no shit. I bite back the sarcastic comment sitting on the tip of my tongue. Now isn't the time.

I stare down at the floor, jaw clenched so tight that it starts to ache. There's no playbook for this. No perfect pass to fix the damage.

I don't even know where to start.

10

AMELIA

When I get back to my apartment from Caleb's, I kick off my heels, bolting to the bathroom in desperate need of a shower. After scrubbing off last night's chaos, I slip into pajamas and twist my hair into a sleek bun. Orientation at work is tomorrow and I guess it's not too early to call it a day. I'm beat.

I toss a slice of frozen pizza in the oven, unplug my laptop, and settle at the kitchen island scrolling through dresses for Tia's wedding rehearsal. She's not getting married for another three months, so I've got some time.

My phone rings, and speaking of the bride…

"Kamusta ka na," Tia says proudly, propping her phone on the counter as she chops onions. "You know, I really need to learn some new Tagalog words."

"I'll teach you."

"You always say that," she shoots back, waving her knife for emphasis. "And then you forget. It's been, oh I don't know, years!"

"Pasensya na."

Tia freezes mid-chop, squinting like I just insulted her outfit. "What did you say?"

"I'm sorry."

She blinks. "Sorry for what? Did you take my dress that makes your butt look *gooooood*? I told you, you can raid my closet anytime—"

"No, it literally means I'm sorry." I smother a laugh.

"Oh." Her eyes start to water.

"Don't cry."

"Please." She tugs down her sleeve and dabs her eyes. "I don't cry. Especially not over an onion."

"Babe, you cry all the time," Amir calls out, sliding into frame behind her and pressing a kiss to her cheek.

She rolls her eyes, chuckling. "Only sometimes."

After talking for a few minutes, I hang up and check the oven. Mmm, the pizza smells amazing.

I grab a slice, sit back down and resume doom scrolling through a million dresses.

Jared slips into my mind for a brief moment, uninvited. The thought of seeing him at the wedding makes my stomach twist into a million knots.

I'm mid-bite into my hot slice of pepperoni goodness when my phone vibrates against the table again.

This time, it's my mom.

Oh gosh. How many bets, she's going to ask me about bringing a date?

I swallow, wipe my hands, and hit the speaker button as I answer.

"Hi, my favorite daughter."

"I'm your only daughter." I scoff, smiling anyway.

"What are you up to?" Her voice has that devious tone to it. It sounds too sweet and I don't like it one bit.

"Trying to find a dress."

"Oh."

A beat of silence.

"Do you have a date yet?" She spouts.

Ah and there it is. The real reason she called.

I know she means well, she was devastated when I told her about Jared. My dad wanted to punch him, and I was considering it for a while but with him being a lawyer and all, that probably wouldn't have been the best idea.

My mom's always encouraged me to get out there. To trust again. Not all men are bad, she reminds me. I know that. But my heart? It doesn't.

"I'm not looking for one."

Would it be nice not to be alone in the Bahamas? Yes, but I know I'm not ready for anything serious.

"Anak, I heard about Jared's new girlfriend… I know the breakup took a huge toll on you, and that's why I really want you to try and move on—"

We keep talking, or rather, my mom keeps talking about how I need to open up and put myself out there more until we finally hang up an hour later.

As if I wasn't already anxious about the wedding, now her voice is echoing in my head making it worse.

I can picture it now…the pitying looks, the awkward small talk, and don't forget the inevitable *"Are you okay?"* Some of Tia's family are close with me, and the last thing I need is anyone treating me like I'm fragile just because I have history with the groom's cousin.

Okay yeah. I need a date.

All I need to do is:

1. Meet a respectable man.
2. Become his girlfriend.
3. Get him to book a flight to the Bahamas within the span of three months.

Easy enough? No. Ugh, that isn't going to work. All this overthinking is making my stomach hurt. Like IBS hurt.

I huff, shoving my plate in the dishwater, glancing up at the clock.

Only 3 p.m. I have no other plans today so I head into the bathroom, put on a sheet mask, grab my Kindle, and crawl under the cold covers. If I could spend the rest of my life like this, I totally would.

My current read is a billionaire romance with a morally grey MMC and it's spiiiicy.

Exactly my type.

Later that night, my sleep is ruined by my phone buzzing nonstop on the nightstand. Dinging every two seconds.

I groan, roll over, and slap my hand against the table until I find it. The screen blinds me as I squint, only to see Maya and Tia spamming our group chat.

BADDEST BITCHES

> TIA
>
> WAKE UP.
>
> MAYA
>
> Holy shit. Have you seen this?
>
> TIA
>
> ‼️
>
> MAYA
>
> SOS.
>
> WHY THE FUCK ARE YOU ASLEEP? IT'S ONLY 8.

What could be so important right now? I call Tia first, then add Maya onto three way.

"What?" I say groggily, pressing the phone to my ear.

"First of all, why are you sleeping at this hour?" Maya shouts.

"Mm… Why are you yelling?" I slide my palm down my face.

"Have you been on socials today?" Tia asks, panicking. "I was at work all day and we're just now seeing this."

"No." I murmur lazily. "I haven't logged on."

"Check it. Now." Maya instructs.

I groan, putting it on speaker, and open up the app.

My body tenses immediately. My notifications and DM's are flooded. What in the world is going on?

@Calebsgirl28: Are you two dating? Plz say no.

@Mina_2101: Hopefully she's not taken too.

@LAvipersfan15: I kinda ship it.

Panic settles and my heart pounds as I swipe over to the homepage. It's everywhere. Oh no. My fingers move at lightning speed, swiping and it's never ending.

I sit up straight, yanking the blanket and knocking my bonnet off in the process and zoom in.

This looks insane. Paparazzi photos of me and Caleb look way too intimate from the angles they captured. It's completely wrong. One photo shows my face pressed into his neck like I'm kissing him. Another has him carrying me bridal style into his apartment! What the—

This is bad. Really bad.

I was clearly NOT kissing him.

"Everyone thinks you two are a thing." Maya shouts through the speaker. "It's viral."

I tune out as Tia and Maya begin to talk over each other, but it sounds like gibberish.

"I gotta go!" I hang up.

I can't scroll more than three times without seeing a new angle of these images. This couldn't have happened at a worse time.

We aren't reckless college kids anymore. I can't afford to have this follow me around and have my reputation on blast. I start work in the morning and now my face is all over tabloids labeled as Caleb's new hookup?

Unlike Caleb, I don't have a career to fall back on yet if this ruins me.

I get up, pacing my apartment like a wild animal, pressing my lips together, trying to think and wrap my brain around what the media is saying. There has to be something…

So much for a fresh start.

11

CALEB

"You didn't tell me you were hooking up with Amelia." Carter pants, sprinting on the treadmill, cranking up the speed.

I needed to blow off some steam after what happened today so the guys and I hit up our private gym. Working out is the second best thing to pottery to handle stress. I throw my body into something that'll hurt. The gym, the burn, the weights, it's the only thing that'll quiet my mind.

"I'm not." I mutter, annoyed walking over to the rack and grabbing the 70-pound dumbbell with my right hand.

"Ya'll looked pretty cozy to me." Nico doesn't speak much, but when he does, infuriating sarcasm is always wrapped up in a damn bow. He smirks as he pulls his chin over the bar and starts a set. "Thought you grew some balls for a second, Hayes."

Ha ha ha.

"Caleb wishes." Marcus snickers from the bench press, adjusting the pin for his weight before lying back. "I don't know why you don't just tell her already."

"Tell her what?" I ask, gripping the cold metal harder, pushing the weight over my head and my muscles tighten with every pump.

"That you want her," Marcus says. "The comments clearly love you two."

Up. Down.

"Doesn't matter. I'm just her friend." My voice tightens with each rep. "Always have been."

Up. Down. "And besides, I'm sure she's not looking for another relationship. It's called being respectful."

"It's not about being respectful, you're just being a little bitch." Marcus grins, pushing his weight up.

Okay, it's time for me to find a new best friend.

"How do you know what she wants, if you never even asked?" Nico drops from the pull-up bar and walks to spot Marcus. "You can't assume."

"It's not that easy." I rebut. "Besides, I need to apologize to her for all the fucking tabloids about us. I've got bigger things to worry about."

Nico scoffs, bending his knee more and sticking out his hands underneath Marcus's barbell. "Excuses. This is actually the perfect time."

I switch arms. My shoulders burn but I don't stop. These guys always have shit to say but if they were in my shoes they'd be feeling the exact same way.

"You gotta make something happen, golden boy." Carter hops off the treadmill, sweat dripping down his temples. "Amelia's hot."

"Watch it," I scoff, gripping the weights even tighter.

Carter raises an eyebrow. "I'm just telling the truth, don't get all pissy at us because you've never made a move. Do it before I do."

My nostrils flare, knuckles turning white as I grip the metal bar. Like hell I'd let that happen.

"It's called a joke." He flashes that stupid grin. "Lighten up…don't ruin your throwing hand."

"Whatever. I appreciate the advice, fairy godmothers, but I don't need it."

The three of them stare at me. I clench my jaw, forcing myself to walk to the weight shelves, trying to shake off the heat crawling up my neck.

I drop the dumbbell with a hard clank. "So let's drop it."

They're quiet for a beat, and just when I think they've finally shut up—

"You should take my advice. I give great ones." Marcus smirks, sliding off the bench press and walking over to the punching bag, slipping on his gloves.

I walk to the mini fridge, snatch a water bottle, and twist the cap off roughly.

Marcus throws a few jabs at the bag. "Hey, since we're your fairy godmothers, mind buying us a little wand too?"

I scoff. "Next time, I'm working out alone."

It's already 9 p.m. by the time I drag myself to my gym bag in the locker room. My arms and legs feel like jello. I dig out a towel and dab the sweat from my neck, trying to cool down.

My body's spent, but my mind just switched back on… and it's spiraling. I need to apologize to her in the morning since we haven't had the chance to talk today.

My phone rings and I toss the towel on the bench, digging it out of my bag. The screen lights up with a name that makes my heart skip like I'm fifteen again.

I click accept.

"Hey, um...I hope I'm not interrupting," Amelia says quietly.

She could never. "Not at all, do you—"

"Can you come over?" she cuts in. "I really need to talk to you."

She's definitely seen the photos. I was hoping I'd have the chance to tell her myself first.

I'm already packing my bag in record time as she speaks, the guys looking at me confused. "Give me thirty minutes. That okay?"

"Perfect."

Marcus jogs over, trying to listen in. "Who's that?"

I mouth Amelia's name, covering the phone.

"You need me to come over too?" he says, way too flirtatious for my liking.

She chuckles softly and my jaw locks. I've seen them joke around like this for years. I know they get along but he does this shit on purpose, always pushing and knowing exactly how to get under my skin. Normally I don't care as much but now it's irritating the hell out of me.

"Tell him I said hi." She laughs again, but her voice fades back into seriousness. "I'll see you soon." Then she hangs up.

I don't tell him she said hi.

After freshening up, I head over to Amelia's place. I knock once, and the door practically swings open. She's in an oversized T-shirt and sweatpants with her curls pulled back in a low bun. She's the most distracting thing.

Jesus.

"Hey," she says, stepping aside.

I slip off my shoes, leaving them by the entry before locking the door. "Hey."

Her living room is dim, lit only by the glow of her stovetop light. She's pacing with her arms folded, the only sound is the soft scrape of her slippers against the hardwood floor.

I sink onto the couch while she remains standing, her thoughts clearly racing. I decide it's time to address the elephant in the room.

"I'm gonna assume you saw the photos."

She nods, chewing the inside of her cheek. "They're everywhere. Every single gossip account is talking about us. Even a freaking sewing company's!"

I fight a smile, because this is serious. "I've noticed. Driftwear's already ticked off about it."

After the talk with Coach, my notifications have been blowing up nonstop, apps crashing from the number of tags I got. I had to put my phone on Do Not Disturb just to breathe. But before I did, I noticed a lot of comments supporting Amelia and me. Usually, I can't scroll through five comments without seeing Vanessa's name.

"Hmmm." She hums, pacing even faster around her living room and I watch her every move. I wonder what's going on in that pretty head of hers.

"Why don't you sit down for a second?" I say, patting beside me.

"Can't. I'm thinking." She waves a hand, still pacing.

"I'm sorry your name got dragged into this." I heave a sigh. "I'll think of something to get you out of it and keep Driftwear happy. I just haven't...gotten that far yet."

She halts, turns toward the couch, arms folded. "Your online image hasn't been great. At all."

"Thanks for the reminder."

"When was the last time anyone mentioned you and Vanessa?"

"Haven't gotten a single comment last time I checked."

It's eerily quiet.

"See?" Her eyes go round. "They're all talking about *us*."

I blink. "Okay? Yeah?"

Not sure where she is going with this but I listen.

"Listen, this is going to sound…insane." She takes a breath, voice picking up speed as she drops down beside me. "But what if we used this to our advantage?"

Used it?

"We should pretend to go out," she blurts out. "It'll solve your problem."

My brows lift, she's not suggesting what I think she is, right? My brain short circuits. I must've misheard her… I'm tired from the gym and I barely slept last night.

"Are you suggesting we—"

She sighs, covering her face. "I knew it sounded ridiculous, just hear me out!"

I shake my head. "No, no, I'm just trying to process what you're saying. You want us to pretend to date?"

"Yeah."

"Pretend date…each other?" I blink. "How would that solve anything?"

"Yes, Caleb. Keep up," she groans, fidgeting with her fingers as her words rush out. "This could work. The damage is already done. The more people talk about *us*, the less your name is tied to the Vanessa drama. *AKA* Driftwear won't have any complaints. Plus I've got something you could help me with too…"

Okay, wait. I've seen this look before, back in college

when she'd practice marketing pitches and campaign strategies with me.

She's fucking brilliant.

But wait, what does she need my help for?

As I'm about to say ask, she immediately continues. "My mom called earlier."

Ah. Her mom. Sweetest woman alive. Tia and I went over to her parents' house all the time for movie nights. She made us the meanest bowl of Pancit.

It was this stir-fried dish that had different vegetables and meat. I'm drooling just thinking about it. She also made us Halo-Halo with shaved ice, milk, leche flan, and ube. That has been my favorite dessert since. Filipino food is top tier. Yeah, I said it.

"She asked if I had a date for the wedding."

I tilt my head, teasing. "Any luck?"

"Nope. Men suck," she says wryly. "No offense."

"None taken."

I don't blame her for feeling that way.

"She keeps telling me to move on, and I'm so tired of being asked about it every five business days," she sighs. "Plus, running into Jared with his new girlfriend, sucked so…maybe we can help each other? I'll be your girlfriend to get the Vanessa gossip off your back, and you'll be my date."

I stare at her. My heart shouldn't be pounding this hard. But it is. This would solve everything but it can't be that simple, right?

"What do you think?" she asks, nibbling her bottom lip as she waits for me to say something, anything. Her eyes locked on mine as her knee bounces a few times.

"You sure about this?" I ask, squeezing my thumb anxiously. "What if it goes south?"

"It won't," she says confidently. "I know the algorithm like the back of my hand." She lifts her hand, flipping it back and forth to emphasize her point and I can't help but laugh a little. I can see the shift in real time, her marketing brain kicking into overdrive. It's the hottest thing I've ever seen.

Focus.

Is this really happening? I've imagined this moment a million times before, but never like this. God. Pretending to be hers when I've wanted the real thing for years will ruin me. None of this will affect her in the slightest.

But for me? It's going to tear me apart. Limb by fucking limb. I'll be the one tortured in the end.

I clear my throat. "You think our families would believe us?"

"I think so," she says, playfully nudging me with her elbow. "But you have to stay near me when your Aunt Barbara shows up."

Love my aunt, but she's always asking hard-hitting questions and has been pestering me about marriage ever since Tia got engaged.

"Promise. I'll be attached to you by the hip." I tease, patting her thigh.

"So…what do you say?" she asks, tilting her head.

I have a hunch that this is going to be an absolute train wreck for my sanity, at least. The need I have for her is already at an all-time high and adding this into the mix won't do me any good.

But, fuck it.

"Okay."

"Yeah?" She sits up straight, surprise filling her eyes.

"Yeah," I confirm, rubbing the nape of my neck.

"Now we need some ground rules," she says, morphing into work mode Amelia. "Ready?"

I pull an invisible notepad and pen from my pocket, flipping to a blank page. "Yes, ma'am."

She holds up a finger. "Rule number one: Tia, Amir, Marcus, and Maya are the only people who'll know. That way, if we need backup, we've got it."

"Agreed. Rule two?"

Second finger goes up. "Rule number two: We only touch in public. When we're out, we can hold hands, act cute, be flirty, whatever sells it."

Touching her. That didn't even occur in my mind. Of course, we'd have to. It's part of the act. Why are my palms sweating? The pressure coils in my chest and no amount of deep breaths will help me. Nothing even happened yet... relax.

She nods toward my invisible notebook, laughing. "Write that down."

I shake my head, continuing my fake scribbling.

"And lastly, rule number three: Let me handle what we post. I know what the fans want."

"Simple enough." I lie through my teeth. Nothing about this is simple. Not with her.

She gets up and walks over to the kitchen and when she returns, she plops down beside me with her laptop. Her strawberry scent drifts up, her arm brushing mine, sending goosebumps across my skin. God, I'm pathetic.

"I'll find some poses we can do," she murmurs, already typing away. "We'll hard launch soon on your profile."

"A what?" The hell is that?

"Hard launch," she says without looking up. "It's when no one knows you're dating someone and then BAM, you post a photo with them. It blows up because no one's expecting it. Let the people do all the talking."

I stare.

The more she talks, the more it sounds like a rocket launch experiment, if you ask me.

She catches my expression and chuckles, dragging out the words. "Old man."

"Old man?"

"Mhm." She hums.

"I'm only six months older than you."

"And aging quite fast," she adds, lips twitching as she sinks deeper into the cushions, grinning behind her laptop. "I'm noticing a few wrinkles."

I lean in and tilt the screen down with one finger until our eyes lock. "Say that again."

Her eyes gleam with mischief as she feigns innocence. "Say *what* again exactly?"

"My apparent new nickname."

"Old man?" she teases, cocking a brow.

That's it.

I bite back a grin, without warning I slip my hands under her thighs as I lift her off the couch. She shrieks, giggling uncontrollably as I carry her into the bedroom.

Again. My favorite sound.

I gently lay her down in bed, a soft warmth lingering on her face.

"Definitely not an old man," I say, pinching her chin before letting go and head toward the door. "Sleep tight. Thanks for helping me."

"That's what friends are for," she says quietly, setting her laptop aside and pulling up the covers.

The way we fall into rhythm so easily, it's one of my favorite things. It's effortless, like breathing. When I'm near her, the noise fades, my worries disappear, and I'm just... me.

I watch her shut her eyes and a pang hits my chest. I used to think it was hard watching Amelia date Jared. But "hard" doesn't even come close to how I feel now. It's been this quiet hurt simmering under the surface, and now this fake relationship? It's like the icing on a damn ugly-ass cake.

Freshman Year College

The six of us were chilling at Amir's parents' house, after stuffing our faces during Friendsgiving dinner. Now we're all sprawled out across the floor and couch, controllers in hand, trash-talking each other as we played a zombie game. Per the girls' request.

Amelia was on a mission to beat my high score in zombie kills. She didn't.

"NO!" Maya yelled, arms flailing as Amelia missed a zombie by inches. "You almost had that one babe."

Tia laughed, grabbing her soda off the coffee table, before cuddling back up with Amir.

"No freaking way. Marcus come on, you totally saw that," Amelia said, sitting beside me on the floor, legs crossed, poking out that adorable bottom lip. "I totally hit it."

"I plead the fifth." Marcus chuckled from the couch.

"You were close to hitting that zombie... by hitting the door next to its head." I laughed, nudging her shoulder.

Then came a few heavy knocks.

Amir slowly untangled himself from my sister and went to answer it. The second it opened, my stomach dropped.

Jared.

Amelia's whole face lit up, brighter than I'd ever seen. She dropped the controller next to me like it was nothing and sprinted into his arms like she'd done a thousand times before.

He gave her that stupid grin, lifted her up, and peppered her lips with kisses.

The sight made me want to claw my eyes out.

I felt Amir and Marcus's gaze burning into me. They didn't say anything, and they didn't have to. It was a quiet understanding.

Sympathy.

I set my controller down and stood, trying to play it cool as I walked into the kitchen. Even a few feet away it made it easier to breathe, but it was torture all the same.

Every second of it.

I step into the hallway and shut her door gently behind me as her words replay in my head.

That's what friends are for.

Whoever invented the word friends is on my permanent "fuck you" list. I didn't know a seven-letter word could make me feel this damn irritated.

She's my person. I know it.

But it hurts like hell knowing she'll never feel the same. It'll never be me.

Still, as long as I get that smile from her, I'll take what I can get.

Even if it kills me.

12

CALEB

THE NEXT DAY, WE'RE IN THE MIDDLE OF DRILLS. Thankfully, the weather feels good today, not as scorching as usual.

I've been doing this for about an hour now, my body on autopilot as I dig my cleats into the turf. My muscles tense, every nerve in my body coiling tight. I squat low, feeling the burn in my legs as I settle into position.

The piercing whistle blows, and I charge forward, driving with my legs, pushing with all my strength as I crash into the dummy with force feeling the vibrations throughout my chest and arms.

It topples over with a heavy thud, adrenaline surging through me. I exhale hard, ripping off my helmet to meet the cool air.

"You busy for lunch?" I pant, using my helmet as a visor to block the sun.

"You paying?" Marcus asks, coming up beside me, gearing up for his red light-green light drill, one of his favorites.

Orange cones line the field as he readies himself, feet flat on the ground, body low and locked in on each bright marker. Coach blows the whistle and instantly Marcus sprints forward in three quick steps to the first cone. His moves are sharp and calculated.

His footwork is one of the most impressive I've seen in the league, he knows how to keep it light and controlled. If you blink even once he'll already be halfway down the field by that time.

"I'm paying."

"Then of course I'm not busy." He jogs backward toward me, chest rising with every breath, winking.

This guy.

After a long few hours of practice, we head to In-N-Out, posted up in one of the red and white booths, chowing into our burgers and fries like it's our last meal. And I tell him everything.

Not our cheat day, but screw it. I need this.

"YOU AND AMELIA ARE WHAT?" Marcus practically shouts, nearly choking on his half-eaten burger. A few heads turn our way, some curious, some amused, but no one approached.

"Don't blab," I say in a hushed tone. "Only you, Amir, and the girls know."

He zips his lips and tosses the invisible key over his shoulder.

"How did that even happen? I specifically told you to tell her how you feel. Not…get into a situation where you can't." He suppresses a laugh. "Was I not clear?"

I roll my eyes and bite into my burger.

"And you're cool with that?" He leans back against the booth, crossing his arms.

"Yeah, why wouldn't I be?" I shrug. "We both get what we want. Problem solved."

My image gets cleaned up. She has an easy time at the wedding. I get another reason to fall harder. Fan-fucking-tastic.

"Partially."

I glance up. "Partially."

He's right. At the end of the day, what I really want is her.

I picture it all the time. Her hand in mine, waking up to her in bed in my T-shirt. But then I blink and it's gone. It's only a dream.

Marcus watches me like I'm a wounded puppy.

"Don't look at me like that." I scoff.

"Just don't start reading into anything," he says, his tone filled with concern.

I press my lips into a thin line. "I know."

After lunch Marcus and I return to the training center, and I head straight to Coach Banks' office.

"It's open," Coach calls out.

I slowly push the door open, stepping inside. "Hey, Coach. Got some good news for you."

"Yeah?" He cocks a brow, and closes his laptop, gesturing me in.

I sink into the old leather chair across from him, squeezing my thumb. "Our problem is handled. Give me a week."

"Alright, we'll see about that," he says curiously, already reaching for his phone. "I'll let Daryl know, maybe he can get Driftwear to cool down in the meantime."

I force a smile, even though my stomach's tying itself into knots.

No good is going to come from this. Not a damn thing. I

spent years, years coming to terms with the fact that I'd only ever be her friend. And now? Pretending she's mine? This might be the hardest thing I've ever done. Harder than football.

Maybe us "dating" will change something. At least, that's what I'll keep telling myself.

It's the only way I'll survive it.

13

AMELIA

"This post alone boosted the brand's engagement by 20%." I reiterate to my manager Jess, who leans in with her coffee, eyes narrowing at the campaign graph on my double monitor.

It's my official first week at the new PR firm, and so far, I'm signed to a major cosmetics brand for the next few months before signing on to more, just to get a feel for how things operate around here.

Soft Muse. They sell all sorts of makeup and skincare products and they do work but it costs more than a month's worth of groceries for two products alone. Moisturizer is $130, serum is $100, and their most viral face mask is covered in gold flecks that's worth a whopping $220 for five sheets. I'd purchase it myself if I wouldn't enter bankruptcy status after.

Is it wrong that I agree with the comments calling them overpriced? Oops. Don't tell my manager I said that.

Oh and did I mention I have my own office? I'm right by the break room, which means daily espresso with Maya, who's already got me hooked. There's also a massive window that overlooks the city from the twentieth floor. Perfect view of traffic I'll be facing at the end of the day.

"Oh damn," Jess blurts, clapping a hand over her mouth with a laugh. "Excuse my language. I forget I'm someone's manager sometimes."

I chuckle.

"And what about the like to follower ratio?" She leans in closer, her citrus perfume seeps into my nose.

I switch to the sentiment tracker tab and angle the screen toward her. "1.5%. Highest it's been in sixty days." I beam, proud of the progress I've made in such a short time.

"Perfect." She grins, rounding my desk. "Let's pretend I'm not your manager for a second."

I click out of the tab, brows pulling together. "Is everything alright?"

"Totally. So, are you and Caleb really dating?" Jess sips her coffee, nonchalantly. "I keep up with the blogs."

I freeze for a second. Time to fake it.

Jess has been a solid manager so far but she's also wildly invested in my love life. Borderline unprofessional, but I'll let it slide.

"Oh. Yeah we are." I clear my throat, hoping it doesn't sound fake. I know data and algorithms, never said I was an actress.

She flashes me a wicked grin, eerily familiar to Maya's. "You know, they're an older brand in desperate need of a refresh. And you've already delivered their highest performing post only on your third day. Your stats are impressive."

She's not wrong. Soft Muse has been around for over fifty years, but their visuals and techniques are painfully outdated. Stock images with zero depth or style.

Plain and predictable.

That's what I'm here for. Maya helped me rework the whole grid by creating content in a soft beige aesthetic to bring into today's standards.

"Thank you." I chuckle. "Maybe we can have him hold up a product or something."

"That's not a bad idea." Jess smirks, a devious one that makes my skin crawl.

"Oh, I was only kidding."

"No you're right. You should take over their campaign for the new lip product next month…with a little help from your boyfriend. Do a cute video together, a little kiss even."

"Huh?" I cough into my elbow, stalling. Kissing? No way. "Jess, I…I don't know about that."

I belong behind the scenes of brands. Not starring in a couples' skincare ad with my fake boyfriend.

"Imagine." Jess lingers in the doorway, swirling what's left of her coffee. "A campaign with the NFL's best rookie and his new beloved girlfriend. It'll do numbers."

Of course it will. It's "authentic" and his fans would absolutely love it. Soft Muse's brand would easily gain followers overnight with one single post if we did that.

"You might even get a raise if all goes well," she hints, wriggling her brows.

A raise? Damn it. I need all the money I could get, my apartment is beautiful but the rent…not so much.

"I'll…think about it." I flash her the best smile I could offer. It's a 'please leave my office' smile.

"You do that." Jess grins, slipping out the door.

This brand could make or break my future at this company. No pressure.

When noon hits, I make a beeline for the break room, fix Maya and me coffees, and dart straight to her office, hearing it slosh dangerously inside the cup before I slam the door shut behind me.

"SOS." I pant.

She swivels around, raising a brow. "You look awful."

"Thanks," I deadpan, handing her the coffee.

She chuckles, taking a sip. "Thanks. So what happened? Did Jess say something weird again? That woman is entirely too comfortable with us."

"Kinda but first…" I plop down in one of her rolling chairs, gliding across the carpet toward her. "Caleb and I did something insane."

"Yes!" Her eyes gleam. "You two fucked already?"

I scrunch my nose, setting my scalding hot coffee on her desk. "No."

Definitely not. Why is that always on her mind?

"Oh like having sex with him would be the craziest thing you've ever done."

Ignoring her statement, I continue. "We're dating."

Maya freezes mid-sip. Her cup hovering in the air before she places it down, slamming her desk with a bang, sending her stapler flying off the edge with a thud. "This is the best goddamn thing I've heard all day."

"It's only one in the afternoon." I say dryly.

"Exactly."

"Wait, so you didn't have sex yet? Are you guys taking it slow or—"

"Fake dating," I correct, blurting it out before she gets too excited.

"Boring." She frowns. "But, what the hell? Why?"

"Basically, I need help and so does he. I'd rather not listen to people at the wedding comforting me like I'm some wounded deer on the highway. So, I came up with an idea."

"Makes sense, but damn, until the wedding? That's a long time."

"I know, but there's more…"

She slides back into her chair. "Spill it."

"Jess wants me to use my 'new relationship' for Soft Muse."

"No shit." She sips her coffee. "This is gonna be a golden fucking ticket for that brand. Are you gonna do it?"

"I don't think I have much of a choice." I groan, resting my head on her desk. "We haven't even posted official photos and she's already trying to make us a face for the campaign."

Maya lets out a wheezy laugh. "Tia's gonna laugh so hard."

"This isn't funny."

Later in the evening, Maya and I head straight to Tia and Amir's house after work, telling them everything.

"No way." Tia leans back against the couch, already laughing. Of course.

"Come on, this isn't a joke." I whine, grabbing a pillow and smashing it over my face. "Between his campaign and now mine. I'm overwhelmed already."

I'm used to the stress that comes with analytics and brand management. But now that Caleb's tangled up with my job, it's turning into a whole other level of chaos I'm not ready for.

Amir walks in, handing us all water bottles. "What exactly would you and Caleb have to do?"

"She wants me to kiss him, guess the scent, and smile wide for the camera. Please kill me now."

When I got back to my office earlier, Jess had sauntered in again with a campaign brief in hand, already talking deadlines. It's called *Soft Muse's Summer of Romance*. The brief mentioned that we'd kiss each other and try to guess what the flavor is, but I am not doing that. I'm tweaking it. Kissing him would be the most awkward thing ever.

"She's going to full on make out with your brother," Maya says, winking at Tia.

Tia's face contorts, horrified. "Okay, gross. What's the brand called again, so I can block every account associated with it."

"I'm not kissing him." I hurl the pillow at Maya.

I'm not even bringing it up to him until Jess circles back. The campaign's a month away, by then, it'll blow over, and I'll come up with something better (less lip-locked).

Amir chuckles. "What's the first step of this plan?"

I heave a sigh. "I'm thinking Venice Beach. Post some photos from his main account and officially start this."

"Oooh!" Maya grins. "There's an ice cream place with a photo booth there. You two can lick off each other's cones."

She's actually insane.

"Please don't word it that way." Tia winces. "My ears are bleeding."

I pull out my phone and shoot Caleb a quick text.

> You free this weekend?

Operation: Fake Date Caleb.
Starts now.

14

AMELIA

JULY 28TH

As we make our way to the pier, we stop to take in the rippling blue water. The sun is shining, and a warm breeze carries the scent of salt from the ocean and fried food from the boardwalk vendors. The funnel cake is calling my name.

It's our first official date as a fake couple. Time to work my magic.

"Take a photo and post it to your story," I say, shielding my eyes from the sun as I glance up at Caleb.

He lifts his phone, aiming it toward me. "Smile, pretty girl."

"Not of me," I laugh, nudging his arm. "Of the view."

"You're part of my view."

I roll my eyes and guide his phone toward the ocean with a finger. "Just take it."

He grins, snaps the photo, and uploads it.

The paparazzi should see that in no time. Now it's time for important business while we wait.

"Let's get funnel cake," I announce, striding toward a vendor.

"Is that all you want?" Caleb asks, catching up.

I nod, my mouth watering already. I can almost taste the powdered sugar on the tip of my tongue.

"Two funnel cakes, please," he says, sliding his card into the reader.

A few minutes later, we're handed perfectly golden cakes dusted with sugar. We thank the older man and take a seat on a nearby bench.

As always, Caleb eats like a caveman. Three bites in, and his cake is nearly gone. He's basically a vacuum.

"Why do you always eat like it's your last meal?"

"I don't know what you mean." He leans down, taking another monstrous bite.

"You eat like you're afraid I'll steal it."

"Well, are you?" He tilts his head.

"I wouldn't even get the chance."

"My point exactly."

I chuckle, taking another bite with a satisfied hum. "Mmm."

Caleb's gaze lingers on me, then flickers down to my mouth. He reaches over and brushes a crumb from the corner of my lips.

I blink at him for a moment, then glance around the pier, and over my shoulder. Paparazzi.

"Good call."

His brows pull together. "Huh?"

I jerk my chin toward the photographers, tearing another piece of funnel cake. "Bet it looked great from their angle."

He clears his throat, nodding. "Right. Yeah."

"Smart." I pop another piece into my mouth.

After we finish eating, we stroll along the pier. I cast a quick look back and see the paparazzi still trailing, keeping a respectful distance. I step a little closer to Caleb.

"Hold my hand."

He doesn't hesitate. His fingers slide between mine, and I burst out laughing. We've never held hands like *this* before. It's weird.

Caleb groans, though there's a hint of amusement in his voice. "Why are you laughing?"

"Sorry. This feels odd." I try to smother a giggle and fail. "Don't look at me."

He rolls his eyes but tugs me closer, our hands swinging between us.

That's when I see it. The ice cream shop Maya told me about, with the photo booth.

My eyes widen. "Come on," I say, dragging him along.

When we get there, I yank the curtains back and pull him inside. A few murmurs float from outside, probably fans.

The booth is cramped. Our shoulders and knees knock together as we sit, his warmth bleeding into mine.

The machine swallows my five-dollar bill and I scroll through the film options until I land on one with tiny red hearts framing it. "This one?"

Caleb leans in, close enough I can feel the brush of his breath. "I like it."

I tap the screen and the countdown begins.

Five

"Cheeks together," I say.

He leans in, squishing his cheek to mine and I laugh.

Four

"Laughing again, huh?"

Three

I cup his jaw, stroking his chin. "It's hard not to."

Two

"Say cheese," he murmurs, smiling against my skin.

One

"Cheese." We laugh in unison.

SNAP.

"Next one." I say hesitantly. "Maybe you kiss my cheek?"

Caleb straightens, nodding. "I…yeah, I can do that."

The countdown starts again. I keep my eyes on the camera, my smile frozen in place. Caleb leans in, closing his eyes, then gently presses his lips against my cheek.

My skin tingles.

SNAP.

One more to go. I need the last one to be perfect and savable for socials. I unzip my purse and pull out a tube of red lipstick I brought just for this.

Caleb watches as I swipe the color on. I cup his jaw again, my fingers pressing into the sharp lines of his face.

"My turn," I whisper.

The countdown ticks.

I kiss his cheek, leaving a perfect red stain.

SNAP.

Then the machine spits out the strip, and he pulls it free, staring at the four frames quietly.

"Which one's your favorite?" I ask.

He holds the corner of the strip, tapping the last photo.

I watch as he pulls out his phone, takes a photo of the strip in his hands, and posts it to his feed just like we planned.

No warning, no caption, a simple hard launch.

After Caleb drops me off, I freshen up and toss a pizza in the oven…again. I really gotta learn how to cook some adobo or something.

My phone lights up and starts ringing. Mom.

Oh shoot. I forgot to tell her about Caleb.

I answer, and her voice blares straight into my ear, making me squint an eye.

"You two are dating? Why the hell didn't you tell me anak?" She squeals. "Finally!"

My mom's always adored him. When we were teens, she was always dropping hints about how we'd end up together someday. I shut that idea down real fast. He's my best friend and that's all he'll ever be. I don't know why she was so convinced otherwise.

"Mom, I promise you it's not that big of a deal." I scratch the side of my temple, leaning against the counter. "Trust me."

"Not a big deal? I beg to differ, young lady." Her voice sharpens. "Guess you two are next? I should start planning your wedding now!"

Oh dear lord.

"Listen to me, Mom! Do *not* do that. This is so new for us. Marriage isn't even in the cards."

At all.

"I'm just glad those two finally got it through their thick skulls," my dad's deep voice filters in from the background. "She keeps saying she doesn't want another guy in her life but look at her now…all happy and shit."

"Hi, Dad. And I can hear you perfectly clear, by the way!" I groan.

"Good," he says flatly.

"Where do you want to get married?!" my mom jumps

back in. Let's just say, I figured out what I want my future wedding dress to look like by the time we hang up.

For a definitely nonexistent wedding.

August 8th

We make it to Pacific Park for our second fake date, the air fills with screams, laughter, and the chiming bells of people winning those prizes I could never win growing up.

"You know the drill, Hayes."

"That I do." He grins, already pulling out his phone to snap a photo of the huge sign looming over us.

Then I reach for his free hand, threading my fingers through his. He gives a gentle squeeze and leads us through the crowd.

The looks come slowly at first, people trying to be discreet by pointing and whispering.

Caleb lifts our joined hands and presses little kisses to the back of mine. My heart jumpstarts at the unexpected contact before I stifle a laugh.

He glances down at me, rolling his eyes. "Amelia, not again."

"What!"

He gives me a stern look. "How are we supposed to sell being a couple, if you keep laughing every time I do something remotely romantic?"

I take a deep breath, pressing my lips together. "You're totally right. Sorry."

"I can't be that bad of a fake boyfriend, right?" Caleb raises a brow, half-amused, half-challenging.

I shake my head, fighting another smile. "No, definitely not. I promise, I'll be serious."

I bury my face into his arm, laughing into the fabric of his sleeve so he can't see me cracking up.

"You're annoying, have I ever told you that?" he mutters, but the grin on his face gives him away. He keeps walking, steering us toward the balloon burst game.

"I'm only annoying to people who can't handle me."

He stops, squeezes my hand, and suddenly leans in… way too close.

My pulse jitters as he tilts his head, dipping toward me like he's about to kiss me right here, in front of everyone.

What the hell is he about to do? We agreed to PDA but we never talked about doing *this*.

His lips hover over mine before he shifts whispering into my ear instead. "I can handle you just fine."

Then he pulls me closer, his hand settling on my waist. I gasp, heart pounding so hard I swear I can feel it in my throat.

Whispers from behind me draw my attention, snapping me back in the moment.

"Oh my god that's Caleb Hayes."

"Wait, they're so cute."

"That's his new girlfriend!"

"We look good together," he says with a faint grin as we approach the stand.

"Caleb Hayes! Big fan," the man lights up, sporting a huge red-and-gold top hat as he hands him three weighted bags. "Game's all yours. Three pops and you win the big bear."

"Thanks. I appreciate it." Caleb hands over a ten-dollar bill.

I spot the gigantic blue bear and suddenly have the need to bring it home with me. "That's so cute."

I pull my phone out, snapping a few photos.

"This one's for my beautiful girl over there," Caleb says, throwing me a wink before tossing the first bag.

POP.

The balloon bursts perfectly.

POP. POP.

The bell rings, and the man cheers. "And we have a winner!"

He pulls the bear off the wall and hands it to Caleb, who turns and gently settles it in my arms. "For you."

"This is gigantic." I laugh, cuddling the bear close. "I love it, thanks."

"Of course." He pinches my chin, intertwining our hands again and thanks the man with a nod.

We stroll through the park, playing more games, snapping more photos, and stopping every ten minutes as fans swarm.

Word got around that we're here because the crowd keeps on growing.

And once again, the way Caleb interacts with his fans is so admirable. His energy never fades. He thanks each person, gives handshakes, and signs autographs, giving each person his undivided attention.

His latest post is full of positive comments, not one Vanessa mention in sight.

Even Driftwear commented with heart eyes and called us a perfect couple.

Everything is going according to plan.

15

CALEB

It's been a few weeks now since Amelia and I started this fake dating thing, and I can honestly say it's been the best and worst few weeks of my life.

Every time I hold her hand, I feel the need to pull her closer. Every time I kiss her cheek, my eyes flick down to her lips…aching to kiss them. And every time she goddamn laughs when I do something romantic, I feel myself sinking further into the friend zone than I've ever been.

And that says a fucking lot.

Coach changed our schedules this week to 6 a.m., which is the epitome of evil. Whoever decided that we as human beings should be up and functional at this hour deserves jail time.

My phone rings on the way to practice, and I glance at the dash, wondering who's calling at this hour.

Then I see the name. Thomas Hayes.

I reluctantly press the accept button on my steering wheel. His voice is the last thing I want to hear.

"Heard you and Amelia are together?"

Hello to you too.

I lower the window as cold air smacks me in the face, I already know this conversation is going to piss me off.

"Yeah, and?"

"You're doing it again," he snaps. "Keep bullshiting around."

Right on cue. Like clockwork. Because in his world, football has always been the only thing that matters. Not love. Not rest. Not even happiness.

"You think Driftwear will stick around if you start spiraling again? What if you two break up and then what? More rumors? They could replace you in a snap of a finger."

"You really called me at six in the morning to tell me that?" I grit my teeth, flexing my fingers around the wheel. "You keep talking like I'm seconds away from ruining everything."

"You weren't exactly focused after Vanessa, were you?" His voice is cold. "You skipped interviews, practices, and workouts during those first few weeks acting like a coward. You couldn't handle it, and now you're letting some girl from your childhood ruin your focus yet again."

The old guilt flares in my chest. It's true. Those first few weeks were hell, trying to deal with the comments and media was something I never experienced before but I pushed through at the end. And yet, no matter how many games I win, he still sees the worst version of me. I'm never enough.

The wind rushes louder through the cracked window,

howling through the car. "She's not some girl. Don't reduce her to that."

Because she's not. She's my only fucking breath of fresh air.

Before I even realize it, I'm pulling into my designated parking spot outside the facility.

He doesn't say goodbye. Just lets the silence stretch between us until the line goes dead. I groan, letting my phone drop into the cup holder with a dull thud.

The engine ticks and I rest my head against the back of the seat, exhaling a slow breath.

What a great way to start my fucking morning.

My jaw's tight as I storm down the hallway. The fluorescent lights are way too damn bright, the air smells like sweat and ass, and I'm squeezing my thumb so tight it might break.

Everything about today is irking my nerves. I shove open the double doors, and of course, the first voice I hear is Marcus.

Him being an early bird never sat right with me, especially not when he's blasting "Baby" by Justin Bieber, which happens to be one of his pre-workout anthems. He even moans the last part of the chorus to be obnoxious.

I toss a jersey at him. "Shut the hell up."

He catches it and grins.

Carter joins in, hyping him up, doing this weird ass dance to Ludacris's part.

"Leave that to the talented people. I'm begging." Nico groans, shuffling over like a zombie, reaching into his locker for his helmet.

I agree.

The door slams open.

Coach Banks storms in, heated. "If I hear another note

from Marcus and Carter Bieber over there, I'm making everyone do an extra twenty pull-ups."

We ended up doing an extra twenty pull-ups.

By 9 a.m., we've already been at it for hours. Drill after drill. Play after play. Our first game's creeping up fast, and we *cannot* lose against the Titans next month.

Coach calls me into the office after practice, and when I walk in, he looks happy. It's kinda weird.

"Hayes, have a seat."

I plop down into his old chair, and I feel like I've been in this office more in the last month than I care to be.

A few knocks at the door, and our GM, Daryl, strolls in holding a folder and a half-drunk cup of coffee.

"Sup," I say, trying to sound casual, but my shoulders are already tensing up.

"Relax," Darryl chuckles, dropping the folder on Coach's desk as he leans against it. "You're not in more trouble. Actually it's the opposite."

I sit up straighter.

"Driftwear's thrilled about how things are going," he continues. "I'm glad you and your girlfriend are having fun because this is helping the fans love you again."

Coach nods, folding his arms with a half-amused grin. "I don't know how you managed to get a girl to fall for you, but perfect timing."

My shoulders sag in relief.

"Mhm." Daryl glances at Coach, then back at me. "They want more of you two. It's the best scenario that could've happened. Contracts are approaching, so as long as your relationship's going well, we've got nothing to worry about. You're off the hook."

After our talk, I walk out of Coach's office, my thoughts are spinning with positivity for once. Driftwear's happy. The rumors about me are fading and everything is going according to plan. We just have to keep it up.

Marcus jogs up behind me.

"Hey lover boy," he says, voice dipped in sarcasm with a side of jackass. "Who knew you could be such a romantic."

He waves his phone in my face, showing me tabloid shots of me and Amelia as she holds the massive blue bear that's still circulating online.

I roll my eyes.

She looks so cute though.

We step into the locker room and whistles erupt out of every player's mouth.

"Golden boy is in love!" one of the linebackers shouts, grinning like an idiot.

Little do they know it's all fake. But I still find myself smiling, as I swing open my locker door.

"I am."

Because at least that part isn't a lie.

16

AMELIA

August 28th

It's been a full month of pretending with Caleb, posing for photos, curating captions, and letting the internet do what it does best:

Run their mouths.

Tia and Maya won't stop texting about our "dates." They're all over their feed. I've made a few graphs of my own to analyze the responses so far.

Driftwear's account has gained over 20,000 followers since we dropped the Venice photos. Their comment ratio? Skyrocketed. Practically every post is flooded with fans begging them to sponsor Caleb.

This is huge.

Plus, they've got over five thousand comments on one post alone and for an account with 300 million followers… is impressive to say the least. The engagement percentage is through the roof. Even the search bar autocompletes with "Caleb and Amelia" now, which is odd to see, but it's working. I borrowed Caleb's phone a few days ago and the analytics on his page from the last thirty days hit *fifteen million*.

Yeah.

Fifteen million.

But when I was scrolling through my phone earlier, there were a few comments that stuck out like a sore thumb:

@Mandy21: Is this real?

@Vipersaremylife_: She hasn't even shown him any affection. Let me be his girlfriend, I'll rock his world.

@KING_23: I'll bet money on this. FAKE.

Sauntering into Maya's office during lunch break, I nudge the door shut behind me only for it to jam halfway. I glance down to find bright neon green toes peeking out under the frame.

"Hi, ladies." Jess gently pushes the door open with a wide grin and my face falls.

The Soft Muse campaign is this week, and I still haven't pitched or submitted a new idea. I'm drawing a blank for the first time in my life. Not to sound cocky or anything, but analytics are my bread and butter.

Having to kiss Caleb to promote a lip product? Is not. And it's definitely NOT happening.

"Oh hey, Jess." I force a smile, lowering into the rolling chair.

"Jess, what are you doing barging in my office?" Maya says bold as ever with a smirk on her face. "Miss me already?"

I swear Maya has no filter. It doesn't matter who she's addressing.

Jess waves her off with a laugh, then turns to me. "May I steal you away for a minute?"

No.

"Of course!" I chirp, standing up fast. My chair rolls

backwards and hits Maya's desk. I mouth *help* to her as I shut the door behind us.

Jess leads me down the hallway, passing by my other coworkers' offices until we're tucked away into the conference room.

"I wanted to talk about the campaign," she starts, her eyes faltering. "I'm thinking of pulling you from it."

My heart stops.

"Wait...I'm sorry," I stammer. "Why?"

She gives me a tight-lipped smile. The kind that says sorry that I'm being *that* kind of manager. "Soft Muse needs more engagement. And right now, the buzz isn't quite what I expected. I thought you'd have the video by now, it's almost Friday—"

Okay what? I didn't think she'd actually remove me entirely. Crap, crap, crap. I know I didn't want to do it, but this is my career. It's what I've worked so hard for and moved cities to pursue.

Maya would probably say it's a no-brainer. That it's only Caleb, not some random stranger. Everyone already thinks he's my boyfriend, so I just need to fully embrace the role.

I'm at one of the top agency firms and I'm getting pulled from my first major project? I've put in real work helping Caleb with Driftwear and I haven't even leveraged my connection to him to boost Soft Muse's numbers, even though I could have.

"Actually we filmed it already!" I blurt out. "I meant to tell you that...uh...Caleb's been super busy with practices so it look a little longer than expected. I'll have Maya send the file over tomorrow night."

"Oh?" Her eyes beam like she won the lottery. "In that

case, disregard what I said! Knew I hired you for a reason. Can't wait to see."

She flashes me a final grin before strutting out and I stare at the glass door.

I'm either getting fired or a huge raise. I'm hoping for the latter.

My feet bolt faster than I could process what happened. I burst into Maya's office, slam the door behind me and run up to her desk. "I need help."

Maya chokes on her bagel, dabs her mouth with a napkin, and narrows her eyes. "Okay, what the hell happened over there?"

"I told Jess we filmed the video. I blacked out and panicked!" I say, breathless, my neck sweating as I pull my curls up only to realize I don't have a freaking scrunchie.

Note to self: pack panic scrunchies.

"You what?!" Maya shoots upright, rounds her desk with bagel crumbs on her sweater and dusts them off.

"She was going to remove me from the campaign! I couldn't let that happen. Is there an opening at the studio? Jess is going to kill me—"

She grabs my shoulders and turns me toward her. "Breathe. When did you tell her she'd get the video?"

"Tomorrow night." I mumble under my breath.

She laughs out of panic. "So we have less than twenty-four hours to book the studio, get Caleb, film, and edit this?"

"Yes," I say, my nerves spiking at an all-time high.

"Fuck, okay. Talk to Caleb and go to the Luxe studio around nine. I'll book it for you and edit everything once you're finished. Darius owes me a huuuuge favor."

Darius is the owner by the way.

I nearly collapse in semi-relief. "Now I owe you, big time."

She winks, already pulling her phone. "Knowing you're kissing him is more than enough, babe."

I pull mine out too as she gets on the line and my thumbs go flying across the screen.

> Can you come over tonight? I get off at six. Need to talk asap.

CALEB
Of course. Everything ok?

> Okay…ish?

God. My heart is beating so fast I can feel it in my neck, face, and throat.

Thud.
Thud.
Thud.

Right on time. I slowly open the door. Caleb stands there in a black T-shirt, glasses, and gray sweatpants. He slips his shoes off and I close the door behind him, trailing him into the kitchen where he leans against the counter, folding his arms.

His eyes find mine. "Okay…ish?"

Kissing Caleb has never crossed my mind before. He's always been my best friend. I know he respects my boundaries and wouldn't do anything I didn't want to but how the heck am I supposed to ask him this?

"I lied." I take a deep breath. "It's worse."

"Worse how?"

I move past him, fidgeting with random things on the counter to keep my hands busy. "My manager was going to remove me from this campaign I'm supposed to do."

"She didn't though, right?" He glances over his shoulder, following my every move.

I shake my head and step back in front of him. "No. But, the campaign isn't exactly easy."

"Is there anything I can do?"

"Um…unless you want to kiss me on camera to sell lip products, then yeah." I spew, out of breath. "That's what she wants. Maya already booked a studio for nine tonight, but I'm freaking out."

I gather the courage to meet his eyes.

He's just blinking. No emotion. Great. I broke him.

"You're stressed about kissing me?"

"Of course I'm stressed!" I utter. "I'd be stressed kissing anyone on camera, matter of fact! And with you it'll be so awkward plus you didn't even ask for this and now—"

He pushes off the counter, stepping nearer. "Then let's practice."

I blink up at him, backing away. "What?"

"If you're worried it'll look awkward," he clarifies, getting closer. "It'll be like research."

Why is he so calm about this, like kissing your best friend is the most normal thing in the world. But honestly, I don't have much of a choice.

My fingers shake as I swallow hard. "I guess so."

"I'm only trying to help."

"Uh, do you kiss top, bottom—" I trail off, stepping away until my back hits the wall with a muted thud.

Caleb completely closes the gap, towering me. I can feel the warmth radiating off his body, even though he isn't touching me yet.

"Let's not overthink it."

I am.

"Right. It's only a kiss." I gulp. "No big deal."

"Yeah." Slowly, he raises his hand, tucking my hair behind my ear before gently cupping one side of my face. His thumb grazes my cheek, leaving a trail of fire in its wake. "Just a kiss."

My heart is pounding against my ribs, anxiety is through the roof as I bite the inside of my lip. If I shift even an inch, I would probably feel *a lot* more than I should.

"Can I?" His voice drops lower, rougher.

My breathing picks up. It's only a kiss. We're adults, we can handle this.

"Mhm."

Caleb's gaze lingers on my lips, his chest rises and falls in a slow, deliberate rhythm, as if he's savoring every second.

His thumb brushes my cheek once more, silently assuring me that I can pull back at any time.

I don't.

My breathing grows heavier, and the silence between us is deafening. I've never seen this look from him before.

His grin slowly curves upward, and my stomach flips as if it's training for the Olympics.

He tilts his head, removing his glasses with such smooth ease that I nearly forget to breathe. My lips tingle as his brushes mine, slow and teasing as his tongue barely grazes my bottom lip, then he captures it.

The kiss is slow at first, like he's gauging my reaction.

When I don't pull back and lean into him instead, it's like a flip is switched. His hand, which was cupping my face, moves higher, now tangling in my hair.

The pressure is firm but careful as he gently fists a

handful of my curls, tugging just enough to tilt my head back. A breathy gasp escapes me, and then he smiles against my lips.

This kiss is unlike any other. Sure, I've had good kisses before, but this? It feels like every inch of my body lights up, awakening every nerve.

My fingers move on their own, curling around the strings of his sweatpants, drawing him closer until there's no space left between us.

This feels good.

He nips my lower lip as a soft groan escapes him. But just as quickly as the warmth consumed me, it slips away.

A chill settles over me, like something is missing. I lean forward, chasing the heat of his body like a moth to a flame, but all I meet is air.

He lets me go, and my hands fall uselessly to my sides. My body now aches from the sudden loss of contact.

"How was that?"

There's a slight unevenness in his breathing.

"Good." I say, struggling to catch my breath. I part my lips to say more, but he interrupts.

"Cool." He avoids my gaze. "I'll um…pick you up in a few hours, yeah? I gotta go do something."

He pulls his keys from his pocket and rushes out without another word.

The door closes behind him with a quiet click. My heart is racing as I tilt my head back against the wall to steady my breathing. But the fluttering in my chest won't stop. I run my fingers gently over my swollen lips, tracing the lingering sensation.

Caleb and I kissed.

And now I won't be able to stop thinking about it.

17

CALEB/AMELIA

CALEB

I kissed my best friend.

For a split second, I thought maybe she felt something real, but reality came crashing in reminding me it was all for practice. Am I an idiot for leaving like that?

Yes. But I didn't have a choice.

Pretty sure she would not have appreciated her friend having a full hard-on in her goddamn kitchen.

So yes, I had to leave. In dire need of a cold shower.

The moment I get home, I head straight to the bathroom. The freezing water pours over my shoulders doing next to nothing to wash her out of my head. I close my eyes, tilt my head back and yep. There she is. Clear as day. Those gorgeous brown eyes, the way she kissed me back.

It's too much for one man to take.

I flip the water off, the cold air hits me as I step out, wrapping a towel low around my waist as I curse under my breath.

I'm screwed and now I have to go kiss her again for a damn campaign that I agreed too in an instant without even looping in my manager first.

Fuck me.

AMELIA

I'm setting up the ring light in front of the white backdrop in Luxe's studio. Maya gave me the pin code so I could set up everything for the shoot.

I twist the maple wood tray at an angle on the table, lining up the five new lip balms from Soft Muse's flavored collection. There's cherry, mango, vanilla, cinnamon, and my personal favorite scent...strawberry.

My lips still tingle from the way he kissed me earlier, the way he claimed my mouth like it belonged to him. It was the polar opposite of the Caleb I knew growing up, he was the one who never pushed boundaries, and never crossed lines. It makes my heart race all over again just thinking about it.

"All set up," I announce, placing my phone on the mount and flipping the camera around.

He walks over and before he can scan the flavors I block his view and step in front of him as I reach for the blindfold on the table.

"You need to put this on first."

"Now I'm being blindfolded?" He grins, takes it from me, and slips it over his eyes.

"Yes, you have to guess the flavors. It'll be easy." I adjust the mask, my fingers brushing against his smooth skin.

After hitting the record button and guiding him to the stool beside me, I grab the first balm and pop off the gold cap. I slap on the fakest PR smile I can offer as I talk into the camera. It's a very strange, but new feeling.

"Kiss test time! Caleb's going to guess every flavor of Soft Muse's lip balm collection. Should be pretty easy if he kisses me right." I cringe speaking into the camera as I hear a snicker from him and I nudge his arm.

I glide it across my lips, rub them together, and lean in just enough to hear him suck in a breath. His finger lifts my chin, then he kisses me. It's not rushed, just slow and delicate.

I pull back, my breathing uneven and shakier than I intended. I can't help but stare at his mouth. "Well?"

He licks his lips slowly. "Can I try again?"

"Only one guess."

"Vanilla." He smiles downward.

"Correct." I nervously laugh, reaching for the second balm. This one's my favorite, its sugary scent hits my nostrils, sending a warm rush through my body. I rub it on and lean in again. "Next."

This time, he inclines forward, parting his lips and I press mine against his. His hands grip the stool beneath me, right between my legs, not touching me as he pulls me closer.

A breathy sound slips out of me before I pull back quickly, the sudden awareness of the camera snapping me out of the moment.

"Easy." He clears his throat, voice gone quiet. "Strawberry."

By the time we finish the video, I can barely look at him. Not because it's awkward but because every time our eyes meet, something in my lower belly stirs in a way I don't appreciate.

We clean up in silence as I drop the lip balms into my purse while he coils the cord.

"Was that good?" He asks, flipping the light off and plunging the studio into a softer dimness.

"It was perfect, thanks."

"The kiss or the video?" he adds, sneaking a quick glance my way.

Both, I want to say. I want to admit that he's the best kisser I've ever had, but unraveling that thread would be the worst idea.

"The video." I force a laugh, keeping my cool as I shove the maple tray back into my bag a little too roughly. "The kiss was…okay."

Translation: best kiss of my life.

"Mhm. I'll grab the car," he says amused before disappearing toward the entrance.

Once he's gone, I pull out my phone and send the video to Maya.

Heaving a sigh, I sling my purse over my shoulder and double check the studio to make sure we didn't leave anything behind.

Caleb's already waiting at the curb and I take a deep breath before walking over.

This is too much already…I'm not supposed to feel like this. This is fake.

Fake.

"That video was hot." Maya whispers into my ear making me jump and squeal.

I'm halfway down the hall early this morning with my

overpriced iced coffee in hand and I whip around so fast I nearly spill it. "Jesus, you scared me. And seriously?"

When I was watching the video back… it was hot, I won't lie. Something about him being blindfolded was a sight for sore eyes to say the least.

She laughs, following me into my office. "Oh 100%, it's probably my best edit yet. Soft Muse is going to love it."

My cheeks burn as I set my coffee down and place my keys on the desk trying to ignore the pit in my stomach.

"Jess saw it too, she's just as obsessed with it," Maya adds just as Jess waltzes in like a tornado, clutching her tablet.

"Congratulations," she announces. "Amelia, you have earned yourself a raise."

"What?" My eyes widen.

This is what I've wanted. To do well at work and build something for myself.

"You have a bright future in this company. That video was exactly the vision they wanted and you captured it perfectly." Jess flashes me a smile. "They're posting it after the Viper's game."

"Wow, thank you! That means a lot coming from you."

"Keep up the good work." She beams as she spins on her heels out of my office.

"Told you. You and Caleb are hot together." Maya grins and traces a heart in the air with her fingers. "Lovers."

I roll my eyes. "Not even."

I doubt he's thinking of our kisses the way I have. I'm the one who brought this whole thing up and he's probably waiting for the day we can put an end to this.

18

AMELIA

It's been a few days and you may be wondering if I've stopped thinking about the kiss.

The answer to your question is no. Not even close.

I quickly change into a pair of jeans and slip on a white tank top. Caleb's on his way up, and I take a deep breath. Caleb and I need to kiss during his first game because the engagement will be at its highest so when Soft Muse uploads our video, it'll cause a ripple effect.

Thud

Thud

Thud

The knocks snap me out of my thoughts and I open the door for him as his cologne fills my apartment instantly, a mix of amber and spice. He's also wearing his glasses again, backwards hat, carrying a small backpack, and grey sweatpants.

Don't look down. Don't look down. Don't look down.

My eyes betray me anyway. What the hell is going on

with me right now? A few kisses and I'm already acting like a teenager.

"Hi, Caleb."

"Hey, pretty girl," he murmurs, taking off his shoes.

We sit down and I shift uncomfortably on the couch, my eyes drawn to him. I quickly look away, focusing on anything else to distract myself. His face? No. His chest? No. The little birthmark on his tanned neck? Absolutely not helping me.

"Amelia, you're drooling."

I blink and wipe my chin frantically. "Uhh, what?"

"I'm joking." That infuriating smirk tugs at the corner of his lips. "What's on your mind?"

Warmth seeps up my neck. What's on my mind? Oh, nothing…just thinking about how I can't wait to kiss my best friend again. "I was thinking of some ways we can pull off Sunday."

"I'm all ears." He reaches up, biceps flexing as he adjusts his hat, my eyes can't help but follow the movement.

"This Sunday," I say, trying to reel myself back in and not get off track, "you'll need to call me your girlfriend during the press interview. You've never said it publicly, so when you finally do, it'll stir things up again."

He leans back, spreading his arms along the top of the couch. "Girlfriend," he echoes, his eyes flicking to mine. "I like the sound of that."

I cough lightly, and straighten up. "Right…and shout out Driftwear too, wear one of their shirts after the game."

"Anything else?"

"And you need to kiss me when the game ends."

"Yes, ma'am." His Adam's apple bobs. "I do have one request, though."

"Request?" I tilt my head.

"Wear my jersey."

Next Sunday comes fast. Caleb's already at the stadium getting ready, so it's just Tia, Maya, and Amir piling into the shuttle he arranged for us. I sleek down my hair in a low ponytail, edges are swooped. Half of his #1 jersey is tucked up, flashing a little midriff paired with denim baggy jeans.

Back in high school, I used to show up to his games with a foam finger, screaming my lungs out from the bleachers. Now I'm wearing his name across my back and it feels nice.

"You look amazing," Tia gushes, nudging me with her elbow as we step into the shuttle. Her wispy bangs styled as the rest of her hair falls over her shoulder in a loose French braid, and a Vipers bomber jacket.

"Like super gorgeous, if you need a fake girlfriend I will gladly apply," Maya adds chuckling. She's in baggy ripped jeans sporting a Vipers cap with gold jewelry.

"You two look beautiful too. I might have to ditch Caleb," I tease, settling into my seat.

As the bus veers through rush-hour traffic, it takes about thirty minutes for the SoFi stadium to come into view. My nerves twist into small knots when the sound of cheering fans grow louder with every mile. I clench my fists in my lap, leaving half crescent shaped indents in my palms.

This is the first time we're doing something like this in front of everyone. The *entire* stadium. Sure, we've walked around holding hands but this? This is intimate. And there will be many eyes on us.

Including the most important ones, Driftwear and Soft Muse.

Amir leans over, patting my shoulder. "Hey, it will be fine. You got this."

"Thanks."

As we pull into the stadium lot, a sea of yellow and blue jerseys floods my vision. Fans are yelling, waving oversized signs, foam fingers, and chugging beers as they funnel inside.

When the bus rolls into our designated spot, Tia and Maya both reach for my hands.

Tia whispers. "It'll be over before you know it."

"Fake it till you make it," Maya adds with a wink, giving my hand a squeeze. "We'll be at our seats, I'll order you a beer, you're gonna need it."

I step out of the shuttle and feel two large hands land on my shoulders. I whip my head around, startled, and find an older man with an earpiece, a Vipers lanyard, and a crooked smile looking down at me.

"Hi ya, I'm Randy. Caleb told me to come get ya as soon as your shuttle pulled in."

"Oh hi, I'm Amelia," I manage to say as he hurriedly ushers me into an *Authorized Personnel Only* entrance. He leads me through a maze of endless hallways, twisting and turning until we reach a sleek lounge tucked away from the noise.

"I know exactly who you are," he says with a teasing grin. "I couldn't scroll two posts without seeing ya two on my feed."

"Sorry about that." I chuckle.

Randy lets out a deep, throaty laugh as he leads me inside the private VIP players' lounge waiting area. Plush ruby leather chairs, a mini fridge stocked with every sports drink known to man, and a foosball table in the middle. A couple of players I recognize are lounging around and some doing high-knee stretching.

He gently squeezes my arms. "Be right back," as he speed walks to wherever he needs to go.

Caleb's sitting on the singular plush couch, lacing up his cleats. His head snaps up when the door slams behind us and all his attention is on me. "You're here," he says finishing up, stepping closer.

Was he always *this*…attractive? Everything he does now, even something as simple as tying a freaking lace is making me go crazy.

"It looks good on you." His eyes rake over me, lingering on the way the jersey hugged my frame. "Really good,' he adds, grazing his fingers against the spot where I tucked it under my bra.

I press my lips together trying desperately to ignore the way my pulse flutters as he splays his hand across my waist. His gaze is so intense, I'm torn between holding it or looking away.

Seriously, what the hell is going on with me.

"Thanks," I mumble, biting the inside of my cheek. God, he's making me nervous. In all nine years of knowing him, I've never struggled to speak. "Oh, um, don't forget to kiss me…after the game."

"I won't," he says, his eyes darkening just a little.

"Alright boys. Let's go!" a man with salt and pepper gray hair shouts from the other side of the wall, disrupting our moment.

"I'll let you finish." I turn to walk away but Caleb's hand grasps my wrist gently.

"Stay where I can see you, alright?" His voice is gentle, but the intensity in his eyes makes my heart race.

I nod.

He reluctantly pulls his hand away and I take a step back, feeling his gaze burn into me. "Good luck out there."

"You're my good luck charm. We've got this."

Randy appears out of nowhere, gripping my shoulders as if I might somehow drift away. "Cmon, let's get you to your seat," his voice chipper, steering me forward.

He maneuvers me toward the bleachers and I start to see some of the players slowly gathering near the tunnel. The stadium roars around us. The screams, the chatter, the stomps of their feet against the metal bleachers. I spot Tia, Amir, and Maya waving me over, foam fingers held high and their beers in the other hand.

This is the perfect seat. The row is low enough to be visible to Caleb over the railing. Jesus, this moment feels so real now.

"Enjoy the game!" Randy tips his hat, sprinting around the grey railing surrounding us to run along the sidelines.

Shortly after, the stadium lights flicker and fade, the metal beneath my feet begins shaking. The chorus of "Humble" by Kendrick Lamar blares through the speakers, sending vibrations through me.

Then, Caleb emerges from the tunnel, the first to step onto the field. His broad shoulders filling out the jersey, his confidence at an all-time high. I'm not looking at my best friend right now. This is Caleb Hayes, Top Rookie Quarterback.

The entire stadium instantly screams "Caleb, Caleb, Caleb!" I scream his name along with the other fans. The players sprint out further into the field and the screams only get louder. They break into a dance and I can't help but laugh and dance with them from my seat along with Tia and Maya.

The game kicks off, and Caleb moves with ease. He

snaps into formation, scanning the field as his biceps flex with the first pass. It's spiraling through the air and right now he's full on commanding this game. I'm so beyond proud of how far he's come, knowing how tough his father has been on him throughout the years. I know this is Caleb's home. His happy place.

During the second quarter, Caleb shuffles his feet left to right, observing the field for an opening. Damn it, there is none. Without a second thought, he bolts and my heart races. I spring to my feet, inching closer to the railing, my eyes locked on him.

He speeds through the defense, racing past the yard lines, and my palms are getting sweatier but I can't look away. The opposing team closes in, pushing him toward the sidelines. He's barely clinging to the edge of the white line, passing the 40-yard mark…then the 30…then the 20. He's almost there.

One last defender dives, but Caleb sidesteps as one of the Vipers defense pushes him out of the way and Caleb tumbles into the end zone.

The announcer's voice erupts over the speakers, "Caleb's made a full run down the field, down the sidelines, into the end zone. TOUCHDOWN VIPERS."

I gasp and sink back into my seat as if I was the one running the field. I forget how stressful being at a game is.

"Ow!" I yelp, reaching for my right arm.

Tia quickly pulls her arm back, realizing she's been squeezing mine in a death grip. "Sorry!" She winces. "I might need to go to the bathroom until this is over. I'm overstimulated."

Maya laughs. "Tell me about it."

"Oh, come here." Amir says, tugging Tia into his side. He wraps an arm around her, and she nestles against him.

Two quarters to go.

The game is coming to an end, the crowd begins to roar as Caleb looks around the field. This is the final play. If they don't get this…it's over.

24-24.

Caleb steps back scanning the defense. With one fluid motion he rears his arm back, throwing the ball, sending it spinning through the air like a missile. It had to be over 90 yards.

"YES!" Tia shouts.

The ball continues to soar and my heart is pounding. It's aiming toward Marcus, and in a blink, he's already in motion stretching his arms out. His feet move swiftly like clockwork. Defenders close in from every direction, but he fakes left, spins past one, then jukes right, dodging another.

"Go, go, go, go!" Amir begins chanting.

"He's going for it!" Tia hops up, jumping up and down, nearly spilling her beer.

"Go Marcus!" We all scream in unison as he charges down the field. He passes the 30-yard line and just as we think he's about to get tackled, he jumps over the defense, diving his body into the end zone.

"WOOOOOOOH!" the crowd erupts, the stadium trembling with energy.

The announcer's voice booms over the speakers, "What a play! 79 YARDS. Unbelievable! Marcus Reed made a clean dive in. Touch down Vipers!"

Marcus leaps up with a grin plastering his face, clutching onto the ball. He starts doing the Dougie, and soon the rest of the team joins in, celebrating their insane win. Caleb jumps on Marcus's back, laughing along with everyone.

We're all on our feet, clapping and screaming along with the crowd, the sound deafening. "Vipers!"

Caleb pulls his helmet off, brushing his hair back with a wide grin. He scans the crowd, and then his eyes lock directly with mine, as if I'm the only person here.

My breath catches in my throat as he jogs toward me, a camera now following his every step. Maya smirks nudging me closer to the railing. And there he is.

His gaze is steady, gripping his helmet by the guard with one hand. "Ready?" he asks breathlessly, tilting his head up.

My heart is pounding out of my chest as fans around us stare, pulling out their phones. I'm suddenly hyper-aware of how many eyes are *actually* on us.

"Yes." I lean down over the railing.

Caleb reaches up, his fingers grazing the collar of my jersey, curling around the fabric giving it a tug. The noise fades as he closes the gap, our lips meeting.

The crowd roars loud, but it feels distant as Caleb's lips move against mine. He grins against my mouth, the small movement sending shivers down my spine. Then he kisses me again, deeper this time.

This kiss is nothing like the last. Our tongues brush softly against each other's and a quiet involuntary moan escapes me. I forget where we are for a second until he pulls back enough to look at me, his green eyes several shades darker.

He throws me a wink, then jogs back toward the team and my legs have turned into complete mush.

Maya spins me around, slapping her hands down on my shoulders, pulling me in and whispers, "You sure you two have only ever been friends?"

I swallow hard.

Tia has a hand covering her eyes, groaning. "Is it over yet?" Amir leans in, whispering something in her ear, and she hesitantly cracks open an eye before chuckling. "Seeing my brother kiss my best friend is not a sight I want to see. No offense, but all offense."

Maya laughs, reaching into her pocket, swiping through her phone, and hands it to me. "There's a livestream on the Vipers page."

I glance at her screen, and the comments are flooding in so fast, my eyes couldn't keep up with the pace.

Footballfanatic: Omg that was hot.

Calebsgirlfriend69: Nooooo!!!

Marcuswife_footballlover: AS LONG AS SHE DOESN'T TOUCH MARCUS I'M FINE.

Heat rushes to my cheeks.

Tia opens her own phone, scrolling through the comments. "You two have broken the internet."

Everyone saw. Everyone knows.

I am officially Caleb Hayes' girlfriend.

19

CALEB

Kissing Amelia sent adrenaline through my veins more than the game itself. Her lips will be the death of me. And seeing her in my jersey? Fuck.

I blink rapidly, trying to clear my thoughts as I head for the locker rooms. The buzz of our winning game surrounds me, but I'm barely paying attention. My mind's locked on one thing…her. As always.

I pull my helmet off, shoving it in my locker.

"Hayes, you've got a minute?" Coach Banks sticks his head inside the room, gesturing toward the reporters outside.

I nod and take my jersey off, digging into my bag for a white Driftwear shirt and slip it over for the press.

As soon as my foot steps out into the hallway, bright lights of cameras hit my eyes. A swarm of reporters surrounds me, firing off a bunch of questions.

"Caleb! Caleb! That throw was insane!" a reporter says, her voice unable to hide her excitement.

"Marcus played a hell of a game, that fake and run to

the end zone was one of the best plays I've seen," another man calls out.

Pride swells in my chest.

"Thank you guys. We showed out tonight. I'm beyond honored to be a part of this team and—"

A microphone is damn near shoved in my mouth as an older man cuts me off with a condescending tone. "We haven't seen you with Vanessa Noles in a while. This woman's single right? Try not to break up another home."

It's the first time Vanessa's name has been brought up since Amelia and I started this and the fact that he brought it up now pisses me off more than ever.

"Next question?" I bite out, clenching my jaw as I scan the crowd.

A blonde reporter now chimes in, fiddling with the wind dust cover on the microphone. "Is she a hookup or a fan that got lucky?"

My eye twitches.

"Never been a hookup," I say firmly. "And a fan? Nah. If anything, I'm my girlfriend's biggest fan."

The simple word feels natural.

Gasps ripple through the crowd, chatter rising.

"Girlfriend?" the blonde repeats, shoving the mic even closer.

I glance around at the other reporters before meeting her gaze, leaning into the mic so everyone can hear me loud and clear. "Girlfriend."

The crowd of reporters erupts into more questions, but I don't stick around to answer. I simply flash a smile and offer a quick nod to the group, and head back toward the locker room to freshen up.

I finish and make my way over to the private lounge.

"Caleb! Have you seen this yet?" Marcus sprints out of

the locker room, dressed in a gray sweatsuit, dropping his phone into my hand.

"Seen what?" I murmur, glancing down at the screen.

Our kiss. *1 million views*. It's only been an hour.

"You and Amelia are already crowned couple of the year." Marcus lets out a laugh. "Look at the comments, even though that dumbass reporter talked about Vanessa, there's *none* from fans."

"Oh, shit." I scroll, comments filled with our names, hearts flooding the screen. Some people are even saying they want to buy the shirt I was sporting from Driftwear.

Amelia, Maya, Tia, and Amir walk into the lounge, their faces lit with huge smiles.

"WOO VIPERS," Tia giggles, waving her foam finger.

"Congrats on the win." Maya says.

"That spin was insane." Amir nods, giving Marcus and I a quick dap. "And Caleb that throw? Perfect aim."

"Preciate it." I nod back.

Marcus wastes no time, his gaze locking on Maya. "Oh, look who actually showed up. Couldn't stay away?"

Maya arches a brow, her smile sweet as ever but her voice is the opposite. "I'm here for them—she motions toward Amelia and me— "Don't flatter yourself."

I can't help but shake my head letting out a small laugh.

"Ow, my poor heart," Marcus clutches his chest. "You don't have to lie to me, angel."

Maya rolls her eyes.

Amelia laughs, stepping beside me, and all I want to do is wrap my arms around her and kiss those lips but we're not in public. I straighten, trying to keep my composure in check.

"You were amazing out there," she says, glancing up.

"Thanks, beautiful."

We make our way to the shuttle, exiting the stadium from the back entrance. The cool air greets us, which is much needed after tonight's game. A small group of reporters somehow managed to get in the back past security, cameras raised high pointing it directly at us.

"*Caleb! Over here, we have a couple more questions!*"

Flash

Flash

Flash

I instinctively wrap my arms around Amelia's waist pulling her close, as they start to swarm around.

"Amelia, right?" one of the reporters calls out, the camera flashes becoming more abrasive.

"Hi, yes that's me," Amelia says, her voice warm as she wears that gorgeous smile of hers.

The reporters' cameras begin clicking furiously again. "How does it feel to be the lucky girl dating Caleb Hayes?"

"I'd say it feels pretty good," she says, a bit shy. "I'm proud of him."

She's proud of me.

I lift our hands, pressing a soft kiss to the back of hers, as we turn to head down the alley toward our shuttle. "I'm the lucky one here, not the other way around. Thanks guys, goodnight."

Amelia's gaze drops for a second before she glances over her shoulder and gives the reporters a small, hesitant wave.

We make it to the bus and as she walks past me to go up the steps, I can't resist the urge to reach out, wrapping my fingers gently around the base of her ponytail. "We're good at pretending, huh?" I murmur, my lips brushing the shell of her ear.

I hate that word. Pretending.

But I don't want her thinking I'm trying to cross a line. It would only make everything more complex. I need to be smart. Maybe once the wedding's over, once this passes, I'll tell her everything I've been holding in.

"Yeah." Her lips part slightly, voice barely above a whisper. "We are."

She climbs the steps first, and I let the strands slip from my gasp, a grin tugging at the corner of my mouth.

I watch her, my fingers flexing at my sides, itching to reach out to her again but I can't.

She makes her way to an empty seat next to Maya, and plops down.

"I'm actually going to sit next to... him," Maya grumbles, jerking her head toward Marcus as she gets up, but not before tossing me a wink. "Seat's all yours."

Why is she looking at me like that?

But I'm not wasting time, so I make a beeline straight for the seat next to Amelia.

Their voices begin to fade as the weight of tonight hits me. We pull out of the stadium and I rest my head back against the seat, weightless as it slides across the headrest and my eyelids grow heavy.

Amelia chuckles beside me and she shifts closer, her warmth surrounding me which is exactly what I needed.

I don't remember much after that as exhaustion takes over and I doze off instantly.

For the first time in a while, I feel genuinely at ease.

I feel...at peace.

20

AMELIA

I'M NOT MUCH OF A COOK, AND I DEFINITELY DON'T FEEL like trying at seven in the morning. I head over to my freezer, pulling out my handy dandy box of waffles that never lets me down, and toss them in the toaster.

I lean against the cool marble countertop, reaching for my phone from where it's plugged in and unlock it.

A week has passed since I became officially known as Caleb Hayes' girlfriend and it's been an interesting one to say the least. I open the newsfeed app and click on the team's profile. Caleb's interview from last week's game is now pinned at the top.

Setting my phone back down on the counter, I listen to it while I walk over to grab my waffle that popped up.

Fan? Nah. If anything, I'm my girlfriend's biggest fan.
Girlfriend?
Girlfriend.

Heat spreads across my face. I know it's all fake but is it bad that I like the sound of him calling me his girlfriend, even if it's for one second? It's a fleeting thought, but it lingers longer than I want it to. I'm sure this is only a phase, maybe it's because I haven't been physical with a man other than Jared in years so my mind is spiraling.

I've spent all morning in a webinar with Jess and Soft Muse's creative director and brand manager going through their analytics from the past week. I'm more than impressed, their lip product launch has succeeded with over 250,000 units sold which surpasses the initial projections. There's also a ton of videos being posted from influencers going in stores to buy all the shades and gave it raving reviews.

It's more than a success and the numbers keep skyrocketing with every refresh.

Now, I'm taking a much-needed lunch break before the numbers start merging together from my soon to be eye strain. I'm working from home which means I have more time to read my romance book.

Laying down on the couch, I've been losing myself in the story for the past thirty minutes, then my phone buzzes on the coffee table. I sit up, flinging my Kindle beside me.

> **TIA**
> Cake testing at 3. Don't forget. Caleb's coming too, he practically begged me.

Tia asked me to join her cake testing because Maya's taste buds are non-existent. She'll literally eat anything and that's not helpful for making important decisions so she opted out.

I've been waiting for this day for months. Free cake is not something I would ever pass up. Also, it's impossible for me to forget appointments. If I have something as simple as a doctor's appointment, I can't focus on anything else other than that. I'll stay home and pace back and forth, convinced I'll miss it somehow. Going to the store prior? Nope. Grabbing a quick bite? Not a chance.

> Do you know me at all?

Hours later, Jess texts me that I can clock out early because I finished all my spreadsheets, giving me just enough time to freshen up before I leave.

It's warm outside, so I go for a flowy white-floor length skirt paired with a navy blue crop top and my white crossbody purse. It's two-fifteen and as I'm hooking my hoop earring, I glance out my window, only to see the sun shining down on Caleb's Mercedes Benz that's pulling up into the parking lot. I'm so confused because he didn't tell me he was picking me up.

I snatch my kindle off the couch, stuffing it into my purse and take my phone out to call Caleb and peek out my window again.

"Yes?" I can tell he's grinning.

"Why do I see your car parked outside?" I faintly laugh.

A few minutes of silence, and then theirs knock at my door. I walk over to answer it, my eyebrows furrowing as I meet his eyes, quickly hanging up.

"Your chariot awaits." He chuckles.

Then his eyes rake over me and I can't help but feel my skin ignite.

Caleb's hair is more tousled than usual, and he's wearing a brown knitted short-sleeve top that clings to his tanned, muscular arms, paired with black dress pants.

Wow, he looks handsome.

"I could've ordered a ride."

"I can't have my fake girlfriend driving herself, now can I?" he teases, a sly smile on his lips. "Besides, how else would I be able to give you these?"

Before I can even internally complain about him using the word *fake*, my eyes nearly pop out of my head when he pulls out a bouquet of books from behind his back.

A *book* bouquet. Oh. My. God.

Five of the latest romance novels on a stick, with flowers surrounding them.

"What the—" I yank him into a hug, feeling his hands slip around my waist as the bouquet squishes together and I gasp pulling back to fix it. "Did you make this?"

He rubs the back of his neck. "Yeah."

Caleb actually looks nervous, just like he did when I turned sixteen. He's always like this when he gives gifts to people, and it's the most adorable thing.

Okay, adorable isn't exactly the first word you'd think of when looking at a 6'2 man, but somehow it fits him.

"Happy birthday!" They all clapped, jumping up and down.

"Make a wish, pretty girl," Caleb whispered in my ear as he leaned down.

I closed my eyes, pursed my lips, and blew out the candles.

"I'm going to grab some plates, you guys head into the living room and open some gifts," my dad smiled, walking into the kitchen. Tia followed him, asking my mom for more Chippy chips.

"You're old," he teased.

I swiped some of the icing off the cake with my finger and tapped his nose. "And you're older."

He laughed, wiping it off. "I got you something."

"Oo show me!"

He took my hand and led me into the living room. A small box sat near the fireplace. He plopped down and gently pulled me beside him.

He handed it over, the tip of his ears a little pink. "Here."

I tore it open and my eyes widened.

He rubbed the back of his neck and squeezed his thumb. "I...hope you like it."

It was a scrapbook with our photo on the front. I traced my fingers over it and flipped it open. There were a bunch of pictures of us, some he must've taken while we were studying at the library. I laughed when I saw another one of us gathered around a Kamayan feast, food spread out on banana leaves. Another was a selfie we took from our favorite spot...Manhattan Beach, at sunset, the orange hue pouring in behind us.

"God, I love this." I hold the bouquet in my hands. "What's this for?"

"For everything." he says softly. "You've helped me in more ways than I can count."

My eyes flicker down to his hand and my expression falters, he's fidgeting with his thumb. Gently, I reach for his hand, stopping him, and weave our fingers together.

"You've helped me too." I say quietly. "Thank you."

He exhales a deep breath, as his thumb brushes mine.

"So does this mean you're now my personal chauffeur?" He opens the passenger door and I look into his eyes.

"I'll be whatever you want me to be."

Oh.

Caleb sticks the key into the ignition just as his phone rings from the cup holder. He grabs it, answering with a quick tap and puts it on Bluetooth.

"Driftwear loved that you wore their shirt," a deep voice fills the car, filled with excitement. "They want to bump up the contract signing to two weeks from now, right when they get back from Paris. But don't think I forgot about that little stunt you pulled. Promoting a brand without my approval? Don't pull that shit again, Hayes."

Oops.

My head snaps to Caleb but he waves me off mouthing "Don't worry about it."

He clears his throat, voice dropping to that fancy business tone as he starts talking more about the contract. I take that as my cue to mentally clock out. Reaching into my purse and pull out my kindle, flipping it open to the chapter I started earlier.

Tia's cake testing spot is in Beverly Hills, a thirty-minute drive, giving me plenty of time.

A few minutes into the car ride and of course the spiciest scene would pop up now. The story is getting too good and screw it, there's no turning back. I lower the brightness and pinch the screen to minimize the font.

My fingers tap the screen, flipping the page and the characters are about to get it on in the shower and my pulse flutters fast.

He throws me over his shoulder, giving my ass a hard slap before setting me back on my feet. "You like this, don't you?" He murmurs as his fingers find the wetness between my thighs.

I clamp my legs shut, fighting the heat rising up my neck.

I steal a glance at Caleb who's still talking and shift in my seat, leaning against the cool window to hide my device while I continue.

"Fuck." A breathless moan escapes my lips as he slips a finger inside me.

He bends me over and pulls his co—

"What are you reading?" he asks casually, after hanging up the call.

I jolt and my fingers fumble as I try to lock the device.

"Wha..huh?" my voice stammers, coming out a little higher-pitched than I'd like.

He glances at me, cocking a brow. "You look pretty invested."

"Oh, um…it's just a silly romance book."

Please let this conversation end already.

His eyes lazily drift down to my lap. "Can I read?"

Absolutely NOT.

"You're driving, so maybe next time," I lie straight through my teeth.

The universe is somehow playing some sick twisted game with me today because as soon as the words leave my mouth, the light turns red.

"Come on," he says, turning his right signal light on. "I've always wanted to get into romance books. We can start our own little book club."

"And we can. Just not with this one."

He then turns into the gas station and my brows furrow, confused. I peek at his dashboard and it's a full tank. "You don't need gas?"

Pulling into a spot, he switches the gear shift in park. Then his hand shoots out, grabbing my Kindle in one swift motion.

"Caleb!" I gasp, flustered as I notice my book is still on the screen and didn't properly lock.

Oh crap.

My body warms, watching his eyes skim the page. His tongue darts out, wetting his lips, and the sight of it has goosebumps dancing across my arms.

I could crawl into a hole and die of embarrassment.

All I'd need is a shovel.

"This turns you on?"

Our eyes lock and for a second, I forget how to breathe. Then I blink, forcing myself to look away, rolling my eyes to cover the heat blooming beneath my cheeks. "No…maybe…umm—"

He mumbles, "Jesus," then runs a hand over his mouth, placing the Kindle back on my lap, and reverses the car.

And he doesn't press further after that. Doesn't tease me. Just silently reaches for the volume knob and cranks up some music.

Out of the corner of my eye, I catch the sharp line of his clenched jaw as he pulls back onto the main road, his fingers tapping against the wheel.

I sigh, leaning my head against the cool window, trying to calm my mind and body racing like a maniac.

Just my luck.

21

CALEB

Fuuuck.

If I grip the wheel any tighter, it might crack. I shift in my seat, praying she didn't notice the apparent bugle pressing against my jeans from what I read. Never thought I'd say that about a book, but here we are.

I sneak a glance at her out of the corner of my eye and she's biting the inside of her cheek, still reading that goddamn book.

That's not helping.

I suck in a breath, forcing my hands to relax on the wheel and shortly after we pull into the parking lot of Sweet Cakes, an all-white building with a massive, swirling splash of purple icing coming out of a piping bag right above the door.

How fitting.

I head over to the passenger door, pulling it open for Amelia, who's busy digging for something in her purse. What the hell is in there? I'm afraid she'll pull out a rabbit at this rate.

"AHH you guys are here! Perfect timing. The baker is ready for us," Tia squeals.

"Hope you guys are hungry," Amir says.

We step inside, and I'm hit with the sight of a long table filled with cakes in every flavor you could think of. Chocolate, mint, red velvet, coffee, raspberry, marble and if I keep naming them, I'll start drooling on the spot.

"Hi everyone, my name's Henry and I'll be guiding you gorgeous people through today's cake test." He gives us a warm smile, sliding his gaze over to the soon to be married couple. Tia leans over, pressing a small kiss to Amir's cheek.

"And of course, you two will be tasting first," Henry adds, gesturing towards the fun sized sample cakes in front of them. "This first one is the Bourbon Butter cake, it consists of bourbon whiskey, and brown sugar, my personal favorite… it feels like having an orgasm in your mouth!"

Amelia bursts out laughing beside me, a loud startled sound that makes Henry smirk in satisfaction and says, "You'll get to experience it, don't worry!"

She tries covering it up with a awkward cough, but fails miserably. "Can't wait."

"Nice one," I murmur low.

"What? He can't just say things like that and not expect a reaction," she whispers back, pressing her lips together in the cutest attempt to stifle more laughs.

Henry hands my sister and Amir a small sample cake.

"Mmmm." Tia hums as she takes a bite.

Amir follows suit, taking a forkful of the cake, pausing to chew it thoughtfully. He nods at Tia, raising an eyebrow. "This one is actually good, not too sweet."

"Told you." Henry grins wide. "An orgasm."

Tia and Amir laugh with Henry as they bond over the bourbon sample.

Amelia walks past me, a little cough escaping her as she heads straight to the chocolate near the end of the table, no surprise there. She's always loved chocolate, but there's one flavor she's been fixated on since we were teenagers. Nougat Cocoa.

Amelia had an exam tomorrow, and she'd been stressing out over it all month, so I wanted to surprise her with something special. The chocolate she loved was sold out at all the local markets here, but after a quick search, I found it in a city over. I begged my mom to come with me because I needed an adult in the car, having only a learner's permit. The drive was a little far, but my mom didn't mind. She knew I really wanted to surprise Amelia. My father on the other hand had way more to say but I didn't care. If it were up to him, I'd never have friends during football season.

When we got there, I found a whole row filled with her favorite Nougat Cocoa. Jackpot. As I walked toward the checkout counter, books and accessories on a few shelves caught my attention. I remembered Amelia just finished a book on her Kindle that she'd been gushing about a few weeks ago, so I grabbed a copy because I know she liked to have the physical copies of all her favorite books. I also got some…sticky tab things? A pink bookmark. Oh, and I couldn't forget the highlighters.

The next day, I spotted Amelia by her locker. Her long curls flowed down to her waist. She looked so beautiful. I probably looked like a fool with how wide I was smiling as I walked over to her, holding the basket.

"Hey."

She shuts her locker and turned to face me. "Hey!"

Her gaze shifted down, and then she tilted her head, curious.

"I know you've been stressed with your exam…" I said, my cheeks warming up, which only ever happened with her. "I got you a little Good Luck basket."

"Is that Nougat Cocoa?" She squealed jogging in place all cute.

"I've been trying to find these bars all week! I can't believe you found them." She picked up a bar, slowly peeling back the wrapper and taking a small bite, humming. "I'll never get sick of these. Ever."

"Keep digging," I chuckled as she wrapped the candy back up. I reached out to take it from her so she can use both of her hands.

She dug further into the basket, gasping when she picked up the book. "*The Love Between Us*, oh my god."

"I know how much you love adding those different colored tab things in your book, and I know you just finished it on your—"

My words were cut off as she quickly put the basket near our feet, slammed into my chest, hugging me tight. My arms wasted no time wrapping around her, pulling her closer, our breaths moving in sync.

She squeezed me again, and all I heard was a sniffle. My eyes widened, and reluctantly, I pulled back and cupped her face. Her eyes shimmered with tears.

"What's wrong?" I stammered. "Is that the right book?"

"Yes."

"Then why are you crying?" I smiled, relieved, and swiped my thumb near the corners of her eyes.

"I'm the luckiest girl in the world, to have a best friend like you."

Best friend. If that's all I'll ever be…I'll have to accept that title because there's no way I can go through life without her.

"Oh my, this is so good," she mumbles, her words half-muffled as she stuffs her face with the chocolate cake, one hand under her fork. "I think this is the best chocolate I've ever tasted in my life. You're so going to agree."

I can't resist. I step in beside her as our shoulders brush and I feel a jolt of electricity. "Better than Nougat Cocoa?"

She gasps, peeking over her shoulder to double check that Henry is still busy with my sister and Amir. "Oops I take that back. Nothing is better than Nougat Cocoa," she leans closer, whispering with a hushed giggle. Chocolate smears on her chin, but she doesn't notice. "I stand on that."

That giggle always hits me harder than it should.

"You're trying not to make a mess, but you're doing the complete opposite." My eyes flicker down. "Come here." I gently lift her chin as she steps in and the gentle brush of my skin against hers sends a rush of heat through me.

Our gazes meet and there's a beat of silence before I hover my thumb near her mouth, then gently wipe the chocolate away, slow and deliberate.

I bring my thumb to my lips, tasting the sweetness as my eyes never leave hers. "You're right." I slowly lick my lips, savoring the sweetness. "It is good."

22

AMELIA/CALEB

AMELIA

Tia and Amir decided on the marble cake, so everyone can get the best of both worlds at the wedding. Perfect choice, in my opinion, because that was definitely an "orgasm in my mouth" as Henry would say.

FYI, according to him, every single cake was an orgasm.

It's still early, and I have no plans after, so I ask Caleb if we could stop by the makeup store before he drops me back off. I need a restock and to have a little splurging moment. It's been a while.

"Is this a lip liner?" Caleb lifts a brow pencil, swiping a few strokes on the back of his hand.

"No, it's a brow pencil." I walk over the lipstick section, choosing a brown shade, and swipe a few strokes to the back of his hand next to it. "This is a lip liner."

He furrows his brows, squinting at his hand. "They look exactly the same."

Oh, such a clueless man.

He wanders around the store like a little kid, grabbing every lipstick he can find, swatching them on the back of his hand, and asking me if I like the shade.

He finally swipes a color with a nice mauve undertone. "What about this one?"

I give him an impressed look. "I'd wear it."

He tosses it into a little basket he's suddenly carrying.

"What are you doing?" I take a peek inside and all the products I mentioned getting next time are in there.

Leave-in conditioner, lipstick, foundation.

"Shopping." He shrugs.

"Correction…I'm shopping!" I laugh, reaching for the basket. "And you're browsing."

"Fine. Then I'm your personal chauffeur and professional basket holder," he corrects, pulling the basket away from me. "Have fun."

"You're crazy." I chuckle and stride over to the curly hair section, Caleb trailing behind me, pulling out his phone.

He snaps a photo and posts it on his socials, without me even telling him a thing this time. He's getting the hang of it.

My phone buzzes. I pull it out of my pocket and click the notification. The photo of his hand holding the basket with the bright colored swatches all over fills the screen, along with the caption:

This hand is reserved for @ameliacruztaylor only

I glance at him and burst out laughing as we get a few looks. "Great caption choice."

"Thanks, I worked really hard on coming up with that one."

. . .

CALEB

After dropping Amelia off, I make my way home. The patter of rain lightly splashes against my windshield, welcoming a change from the LA heat. I open my apartment door and slip off my shoes, ready to wind down for the night. I sink into the couch and flip on a few football games.

A few hours later, my phone buzzes in my pocket.

I pull it out and freeze at the name flashing on the screen. Thomas Hayes.

I hesitate for a second before answering, pressing the phone to my ear.

"What?"

"Is that anyway to greet your father?" He scoffs.

"Go on."

"Your play was a shitty move." His voice edged with disapproval, that I'm all too familiar with. "You risked it by nearing the sidelines."

"We won, so what does it matter?" I say, irritation rising as I switch off the TV.

"It matters because it was sloppy. The older you get, the worse you're playing because why did you hesitate in the fourth quarter, you know Carter was open—"

I clench my teeth, gripping the back of my neck.

"You keep playing this poorly, and you'll be just another quarterback whose success dies down before their thirtieth birthday. If you don't start listening to me, you can go ahead and kiss that success goodbye now."

I had a lot to prove throughout college. Living up to his expectations wasn't exactly easy. I've put in the work, but it's still never enough for him.

"I'm trying—" I start, squeezing my thumb hard, a small crack echoing in the silence.

"You think trying means shit?" he interrupts. "Stop playing house with your little girlfriend."

The line clicks dead.

My jaw locks, heat crawling up my spine. I should be used to this by now. I should be able to continue my night and brush it off.

But somehow, he's the only one who can really get under my skin. The only one who can make me feel like that little boy again, desperate for his father's approval.

He doesn't talk to anyone else but me like this. He's a great father to my sister, and a good husband for my mom, but to me? Tsk.

I shake my head, nostrils flaring. Before I know it, I'm in my car, heading to the one person who grounds me most.

23

AMELIA

A few hours and a bath later, my cuddly robe wraps around me as I sit in the bathroom sorting through all the makeup, hair care, and face masks. These are things Caleb refused to let me pay for. I kept telling him it was too much and that I wanted to buy them myself, but he just blocked my card and slipped his into the machine instead.

He's insane but also the best.

My phone buzzes. Caleb's name flashes on the screen as I answer, pressing the speaker button.

"Miss me already?"

Ripping open the sheet mask, I wait for him to speak. There's a brief silence.

"I do actually," he quietly says. "Can I stop by?"

"Now?"

His voice stammers. "Um…never mind. It's late, sorry." The rawness in his voice makes my heart ache. The only time he has ever sounded like that is when he was dealing with his dad… oh.

"No!" I say quickly. "Come over."

"You sure?"

"Yes, I'm not busy." I say, applying my face mask. Maybe him seeing me looking like a scary Michael Myers will make him laugh and feel somewhat better.

I change into some shorts and an oversized hoodie as I wait for Caleb to show up.

Thud

Thud

Thud

I jog to the front door, swinging it open, and my heart drops. He looks exhausted. Dark circles shadow his eyes, his hair is messily pushed back, and he's still wearing the clothes from earlier.

"Caleb." My hands reach out to his wrist, pulling him inside my apartment. "What happened?"

"My dad." He laughs bitterly. "Like always."

That's all I need to hear. I pull him close, then take his hand in mine as we settle onto my couch.

"You look scary." He pokes my face, forcing a smile. I can tell he's holding back.

"Don't I look cute?" I utter, chuckling.

He nods, tucking a strand of hair behind my ear. "Always."

"Now." I say, peeling off the mask and crumpling it in my hand, tossing it on the table, "What's going on?"

Caleb's body tenses as he stares out my window. "It's getting old. Constantly never doing anything right."

I lift both my legs up on the couch, crossing them as I lean back, listening to his words.

Hearing him speak like this feels like torture, he's always so bubbly and happy.

"When I got home tonight, he called," he squeezes his

thumb, making my chest tighten. "Letting me know how awful I was during the game"

My brows pull together.

There's a fine line between encouraging someone to do better and then it's whatever the hell his dad thinks he's doing. If he didn't stop, he would lose his son.

Sophomore Year High School, April 2014

We were all sprawled out across Caleb's bedroom after we celebrated his win. I was on the bean bag chair next to him, Tia was sitting way too close to the TV, I was afraid her eyes would get fried, and Amir was chilling right beside her.

"Caleb, come here," his dad called out from the living room. I watched Caleb rise, turning up the volume, as he squeezed his thumb on the way out. Tia glanced at him over her shoulder.

I sighed, getting up and 'pretending' to use the bathroom as I tiptoe down the hallway. I paused near the bathroom door, tilting my head, trying to eavesdrop.

"You may have impressed everyone else but you looked like a fool running down that field." He snapped.

I winced at his dad's tone, clinging onto the bathroom door frame as I listened. His dad never lets up on him, everything Caleb did had to be perfect in his eyes or it was no good.

"What do you mean? I scored the first touchdown even though Coach said—" Caleb's voice was quiet, laced with frustration.

"Who'd you rather listen to? Him or someone who actually plays in the league? His dad cuts in, scoffing.

I peeked my head further out, catching a glimpse of his dad, his face red. Caleb's jaw clenched but he stayed quiet.

"You'll be lucky if you get drafted at this rate. You think it'll be handed to you because you're my son? I don't give a shit if you scored your first goal, your form is lazy as hell."

Caleb's head drops as he nods.

"You're going to be like every other kid whose dreams are to make

it and end up failing instead. You'll just be a fucking disappoint and a waste of potential." He snaps, pointing down the hallway. "Now go to your room."

I gasped, tiptoeing back into the room as I sank into the beanbag, my stomach sinking along with it.

Caleb cracked the door open, squeezing his thumbs harder, his knuckles turned white. I watched him enter the room, looking like a boy who'd been crushed by his idol.

His eyes were dark as he sat beside me. I reached out, intertwining our hands, while his shoulders sagged in relief. I squeezed his hand, scooted closer, and rested my head on his shoulder as we watched the rest of the movie.

"I've spent my entire life trying to get his approval. I thought that once I went pro, he'd finally tell me how proud he is."

My heart breaks, feeling his pain like it was my own. "Look at me."

He finally turns his head, our eyes meeting. His filled with doubt and pain that he's been carrying for so many years.

"You have always wanted to go pro for yourself too, and you did. You have worked your ass off to get to where you are today. Your strength and determination are what got you in the NFL. Don't let him take that away from you."

"Fuck." He shakes his head, wiping unshed tears. "Sorry."

The last time I've seen Caleb even come close to crying was that day in high school. This is all built up and I'm afraid one day he'll break.

I reach out, my fingers brushing his cheek. "You've always inspired me, even as kids," I say. "I hope you know that."

He lets out a shaky breath, leaning in, pressing his

forehead against mine. Then he shakes his head. "Don't," he whispers, pleading.

"I mean it. It hurts me that you don't see yourself the way I do. When I look at you, I see a hardworking man who has never given up and has made every dream of his a reality."

"Not every dream," he murmurs, pulling back just enough to press a gentle kiss to my forehead. "There's still one more left."

In this moment, I'm feeling things I never thought I'd experience again, and that thought alone scares me...

Am I falling for my best friend?

24

CALEB

Driving over to Amelia's last night was definitely not on my to do list. It's not something I ever wanted her to see from me, but I had no choice. I'm so drained from hearing the same thing over and over from him and his fucking temper. I just needed to be near her, hear her voice…is that pathetic?

When she told me I was her inspiration, I almost told her that I loved her. I was going to confess, screw it, let it all out on the table, and accept the rejection. At least she would know.

Junior Year High School 2015

"Want to come to a pottery class with me after school?" I asked Amelia, watching her dig through her locker, searching for the scrunchies she always lost.

I shook my head, pulling out the spare I kept in my pocket, handing it over. "Here."

"Thank you! You always seem to have these, I'm starting to think you're stealing mine." She teased, slamming her locker shut, gathering her curls into a bun. "And, pottery?"

I chuckled and nodded. "Mhm. I've been going for a few months now."

She tilted her head, surprised. "Whaaat? You never told me that."

Yeah, I hadn't told anyone. Not even Tia. It was something I had kept to myself. It was my safe place. It was only a few blocks from my house, so I just booked classes online and walked there whenever I had time.

The reason I started was because my dad had been down my neck again, now that the season started again. I thought he was tough on me before, but now? It was worse, I'm almost a senior and coaches are actively scouting and visiting our school. It's intense and the pressure is real but my father isn't making it any better. I'm usually calm under pressure when he's not in my ear.

I understood why he pushed me to do better, I truly do. But I wished he would treat me the way other dads treated their sons. I saw other dads giving their sons high fives after games, ruffling their hair, a pat on the back. All I ever got was a "Do better next time." That was my gold star.

Was I a bad son? That's what I always thought. I always believed that was why he treated me this way. I was just a disappointment, I guessed.

"It's something I do that helps calm me down."

She didn't say a word, just silently understood me and pulled me into one of those hugs I'd never get over.

One hug from her felt like a whole pottery class. Suddenly, I didn't need to go anymore today.

She was always my safe space.

"Hayes, my office," Coach Banks calls out from the locker room door.

I toss my helmet in the locker, making my way over to his office.

He's sitting in his chair, leaning back, watching our last game on his computer.

I step inside, dropping into the chair I've sat in a million times, hearing the oh so familiar creak of the leather.

"What's up?" I say, leaning back trying to gauge his mood. I can never get a read on him. Is he pissed? Happy? The world would never know.

"Driftwear's hosting a celebratory event after the signing next week." Coach finally glances up, pausing the game. "Invite your girlfriend, they'd love to meet her."

I nod, thankful that we've made a good impression and squashed the rumors. I couldn't have done it without her, she made this possible for me. "Thanks for letting me know. I'll tell her."

"Mhm, now go shower. You fucking stink." He grins, gesturing me out of his office and I can't help but laugh.

> Question. Are you free next weekend?
> Driftwear's hosting an event to celebrate.

AMELIA
> Hmm, let me check my calendar.

My phone buzzes finally. This woman left me on read for an hour.

AMELIA
> I'm free. Sorry I thought I hit send. Got distracted by a cute dog video.

> Oh. I thought you broke up with me.

AMELIA
Don't worry, I will after the wedding. Lol.

I'm not looking forward to that.

25

AMELIA

"Who in the hell even decided that a chair should be called a chair? What if it was really supposed to be called a rug?" Maya groans, sipping her pineapple juice.

Maya, Tia, and I made plans to have lunch today at this new Filipino restaurant that opened up on Hollywood Boulevard.

"That's a solid question. Why is an orange an orange while a grape isn't called purple?" I question playfully.

"It just doesn't make any sense," Maya chuckles.

"What doesn't make sense?" Tia smiles brightly as she holds her purse rounding the table, pulling out the chair beside me. "Sorry, I'm a little late."

"It's fine. We were only talking about how things are named." I say, sliding the menu off the table looking at all of the different options. My mouth is beginning to water.

As lunch goes on, we gossip and chat about everything we can think of.

"So, how did you know he was the one?" Maya glances

up, leaning into the table. "You met him so young, how did you know that you'd end up marrying the guy?"

Tia's eyes lit up, just like always when Amir's brought up. He's genuinely one of the best guys I've ever met. He'd drop anything for her in a heartbeat. Once, Tia casually mentioned she wanted to go on a cruise vacation and what happened the following day? He booked a cruise to the Caribbean for her 21st birthday.

Tia sips her melon juice, leaning back in the chair. "I feel like our *real* relationship began when he started medical school last year. I always knew I loved him but our relationship was tested."

Maya raises a brow in awe. "Oh yeah, I remember you saying he'd come home late."

"Extremely late, he'd study all night at the library until like 9 p.m., then come back home and study more. It felt like we were losing the spark because of how exhausted he was, we barely had time." She sighs.

"But let me guess? He apologized and you two had late night sex?" Maya teases, eating a spoonful of sinigang.

I shake my head, twirling my pancit with my fork. "You would ask that."

She grins. "I've never experienced love like you two, so sue me for wanting to know the details."

Tia laughs. "One night we stayed up until like 3 a.m., and just talked like we used to. We communicated and came up with a schedule to make time."

"Oh," Maya says. "That's nice."

Tia smirks, rolling her eyes as she sips her juice. "And then we had sex. You damn perv."

There was this new exclusive nightclub called 'Eclipse' that just opened up downtown and it is invite-only. I haven't really spoken to Caleb about what happened with his dad but I won't bring it up unless he does. His dad's a sensitive topic and I never want to make him uncomfortable.

I've been staring at the mirror for the past two hours trying to perfect my curls and makeup. The two things I will forever take my time on if I can help it. My hair is looking voluminous tonight in its middle part.

Heaving a sigh, I run my hands down the smooth satin fabric of my light pink dress. It has a deep V-neckline that is making the girls look extra good tonight, sitting just right.

Maya picked it out.

Plopping down on my couch, I slip my white kitten heels on when a loud thud draws my attention.

Opening the door, my brows pinch in shock when Marcus is standing here, all six foot three with a black collared shirt revealing a quote tattoo on his chest, dress pants and a gold chain around his light brown skin. Goatee and dark black curls freshly cut. "You look great."

"Thanks, you too," I say, slightly confused.

"You're probably wondering why I'm here." He chuckles deeply.

"I am," I chuckle, leaning against my door. "I don't remember calling you for a ride."

"Lucky for you, I ordered us a limo. Wanna join?"

"Yes! But a limo?" I ask, leaving the door open so I can quickly swipe my keys and clutch off the table then lock the door, pulling it shut behind me. "Why so fancy?"

"The real question is, why not?" He teases, draping his arms around my shoulder as we walk down the hallway. "Let's go get your so called boyfriend."

Warmth floods my lower belly. Caleb being called my boyfriend doesn't sound as weird as I used to think.

We make it to the front lobby of my apartment, the sleek black Hummer limo parked in the drive-up area.

Maya pokes her head out of the top sunroof. "Damn. You look sexy!"

"No need to compliment. I know." Marcus winks at her as he approaches the door.

"I was talking to her," Maya says.

"Whatever you say." Marcus grins then whispers in my ear, "She's obsessed with me."

Turning my head towards him I press my lips together, patting his shoulder. "If that helps you sleep at night, I'll agree."

"Whatever, just get in." He rolls his eyes, opening the door. I climb toward the back with the two separate seats.

He follows, sliding into the long row of seats near the mini bar.

I whistle at Maya.

Jet-black hair parted in the middle, perfectly straightened without one hair out of a place, a crimson red strapless dress paired with a red bottom heel. She looks stunning.

"Thanks babe." She winks at me before leaning back, pulling out her phone.

As the limo pulls onto the highway, I reach across to grab a small bottle of vodka from the bar. It's been a while since we've gone out, and everything is going perfectly. Caleb's closing his deal, Soft Muse's engagement is at its highest in years, and I just got a raise. Time for some fun.

Fifteen minutes later, the limo rolls to a stop.

"We just pulled up. Hurry your ass down here," Marcus

speaks into his phone, Caleb's voice muffled on the other end of the line.

A few minutes later, the door slides open and my heart nearly stops.

Caleb's wearing a white button up shirt slightly undone, paired with black pants. His wrist covered with a simple watch, silver rings scattering across his knuckles.

He climbs into the van, his eyes locking onto mine. I shift in my seat as he got closer, his cologne hit me right in the face. It's so intoxicating, making my head spin like a carousel. Which is not good for me. I'm already low on iron as it is.

"You look beautiful," he says, his voice dropping an octave. He settles into the empty seat beside me, our knees brushing each other.

"Thanks," I say, turning to face him and lightly tug the lapels of his shirt. "I like this shirt on you."

His gaze drops to my lips and his phone blares, interrupting whatever he was about to say.

Clearing his throat, he reaches into this pocket, answering the call, pressing the phone to his ear. His smooth voice giving me a moment to collect myself.

Our next stop was Carter and Nico, a few of his football friends. I've never met them before but I've seen them on the field. They both climb into the van, with Carter heading straight for the seat near the bar. His messy blonde hair curlier than usual.

He wore a fitted forest green knit sweater that suited him nicely. He tipped his head greeting us as he got comfortable in his seat and Nico drops beside him.

"It's nice to finally meet the woman Caleb's been talking our ears off about," he smirks, meeting my eyes. "I'm Carter."

"Nico," he also chimes in, running his hand to fix his fluffy dark black hair.

I smile. "Hi."

Caleb hangs up the phone, and an idea pops into my head. We haven't taken any new photos since our fake dates, it'll be good to get some more buzz before the Driftwear event.

"Wanna take a photo?"

"I'm always down." He nods, already swiping the camera app open.

I scoot shoulder to shoulder into his personal space, prepared to take it.

He chuckles, shaking his head as a strand of hair falls perfectly against his forehead.

"What's so funny?" I huff, as a puff of air escapes my nose.

"I'd never be that far from my girlfriend."

"Our thighs are touching." I smack his thigh lightly, dragging my hand back to my own to prove a point.

The only way I'd get any closer to him is if—

"Sit on my lap."

Oh my.

"Only if you're okay with it." He adds.

"Yeah, how do you want me to…um…sit?" I ask, awkwardly. "Do you want me to sit higher up on your thigh? Edge of your knee? Or— "

My mouth stops moving in an instant, replaced by a quiet gasp. His left hand slides behind my back, his touch burning my flesh through the thin fabric of my dress, while his other hand hooks under my bare thigh, effortlessly lifting me onto his lap.

"Comfortable?" His warm breath grazes the shell of my ear.

"Mhm! Yeah!" I say, my voice higher pitched than usual.

The glow from his phone screen illuminates a soft light on his face, making him even more handsome. He adjusts the phone in his free hand, resting the bottom edge on his pinky, positioning us in the frame.

He grips my waist, and warmth spreads across my left thigh as Caleb places his veiny hand there, splaying his palm to fully grip it. It's such a small touch, but it feels like so much more.

Heat radiates from his palm, traveling through me in a way that makes it all the way to its *proper* destination. I've never felt *that* with him.

It makes me wonder what his hand would feel like on other parts of me, how they'd feel sliding slowly up my stomach to cup my breasts in his palms. He'd knead them just how I'd like it, rough enough to make me gasp and arch my back but tender enough to leave me aching.

"Fuck. Caleb, please," I'd whisper, my voice trembling with need. I can almost hear the low, guttural moan rumbling from his throat, spilling through his parted lips as he leans in, sucking my breasts, making my eyes flutter.

A sharp sting follows as his teeth graze over my nipple, nipping it gently, pulling a whimper from me.

"You like that, baby?" He swirls his tongue around it, making me curse under my breath as I nod desperately.

"Ready?" His voice pulls me back and I flinch.

"Huh? Oh yeah." I nod, trying to focus, tilting my head against his and stretch my lips into something camera-ready.

I seriously need to pop multiple ashwagandha gummies and calm the hell down. What is wrong with me?

He snaps the photo, and we both glance down at the

screen. I cringe almost immediately. Why the hell am I doing a thumbs up? That is so not real. I look like my father when we took that family photo at our barbecue last year.

I'm so nervous. It looks like we won the world's most awkward couple award.

And my face, do I always look like that? Why does it look so lopsided?

"We're supposed to be *madly* in love," he teases. "Not, whatever that is...a thumbs up, really?" Now he's full on laughing, his chest rumbling against my back.

"Excuse me." I shoot back a glare. "Let's just try it again."

"Aww, you look like your dad," he teases, gently squeezing my thigh.

Oh whatever.

Laughter erupts from the side of the van, loving every second of our bickering.

Carter turns his head, not doing a good job at hiding his annoying grin. "Let me see the photo, Hayes."

Rolling my eyes, Caleb leans forward, his hold on me tightening just enough to keep me from slipping off his lap to show the photo.

Such a traitor.

Marcus and Nico don't miss the opportunity to take a peek as well. Maya squats up to peer over and squints at the screen, and shocker, they all burst out laughing again, damn near shaking the van.

"What are y'all hyenas now?" I fold my arms.

"You look so cute." Maya teases. "I just wanna pinch your cheeks."

"Whatever, I'm redoing it!" A laugh unfortunately slips out before I could catch it. "Delete it."

"Try and keep the thumb down this time," he laughs.

"Just take the damn photo."

"Feisty."

Turning my head, I cup his jaw and guide his face toward mine until our eyes lock, lips just inches apart. "Better?" I whisper. "Do we look in love now?"

His eyes darken as he snaps the photo, gaze still locked on me. He doesn't check his phone. Not yet.

My fingertips linger on his jaw. Why can't I pull away?

"I don't need to check. I know I'm in love with you."

"What?" The word escapes me too fast.

"For the photo," he murmurs, giving my chin a gentle pinch before clearing his throat. "It looks like I'm in love with you for the photo."

Right, of course. For the photo.

26

CALEB

THE VAN APPROACHES THE ENTRANCE OF ECLIPSE. PULLING to a stop in front of the Valet parking area, a young man with a red vest approached our driver to take over, while another opened our side door.

Bright lights easily flood my vision as the cameras flash all around, surrounding us like a veil. Our names were being called from left to right. I turn, reaching for Amelia's hand as she steps out of the van onto the smooth red carpet beneath us.

"Amelia! Caleb! Over here!"

"Can we get a photo of the lovely couple!?"

"She must be a good shag in bed if you're with her now and not Vanessa Noles, huh?" A reporter sneers, holding up his camera. "Or is she just an easy lay?"

Anger fills me as I charge forward like a goddamn bull. "What the fuck did you say?"

The reporter's face falls as he lifts his camera higher, aiming it right at me. "It's a simple question—"

I cut him off, clamping my hand around the camera lens, forcefully shoving it down as he lets out a grunt. "You disrespect my girlfriend like that again and watch what happens. I dare you."

"Hey," Amelia tightens her hand around mine, tugging me toward the entrance. "Let's just go inside."

I glance down at her, my chest tightening with anger, but then I see the discomfort grow in her eyes as they lock onto mine. Shit.

A cameraman in the back had the balls to pipe up and ask it again, "Well, is she?"

Fuck it.

"Delete the footage."

"We, uh, we get paid for this. We can't do that," a journalist to my right says sheepish.

I ignore him and pull out my phone, opening the payment app. "Whatever you're getting paid, I'll double it."

A sharp inhale leaves Amelia, she yanks my arm damn near out of socket, forcing me to bend down, my face inches from hers as she glares at me. "Are you insane?" she hisses, her grip tightening. "You're not doing that."

A reporter speaks up from my left, aiming her phone in my direction. "I'll delete mine for $2,000."

I tap my phone against hers, the app instantly airdropping the money.

$10,000 later and all the footage has been wiped from every single camera.

Worth every damn penny.

I shove my phone back, and Amelia shakes her head beside me, mumbling something under her breath. I don't bother asking what.

I rest my hand on the small of her back, leading her

toward the entrance, as we walk past the velvet ropes and through the heavy black doors of Eclipse.

The scent of expensive liquor floats in the air and I won't lie…this place is practically the definition of sin.

My phone buzzes, and I pull it out to see a text from my soon to be brother-in-law.

> **AMIR**
> We're not gonna make it tonight. Tia's not feeling well so I'm gonna take care of her.
>
> What's wrong?
>
> **AMIR**
> Mostly likely dehydration. She doesn't want to stay home though lol
>
> CALEB ADDED TIA TO THE CONVERSATION.
>
> Stay your ass at home.
>
> **TIA**
> Boo. You whore.
>
> TIA HAS LEFT THE CONVERSATION.

Shaking my head, I murmur in Amelia's ear, "Tia and Amir aren't coming."

She pulls her phone from her small bag, and I catch a glimpse of her Kindle snugly tucked inside. Leave it to Amelia to bring a book to the club.

"Tia already texted Maya and I," she says, flashing her phone in my face.

So my own flesh and blood couldn't text me, but she could manage to send a group text. Typical.

And she called me a whore.

Best sister ever.

"Let's go hit the bar." Marcus nods toward the counter, where rows and rows of liquor glint under the lights.

He doesn't hesitate before draping his arm around my shoulders, dragging me along. My eyes meet Amelia's as she laughs and loops her arm with Maya's, the two of them following behind us.

We all gather by the bar, calling the bartender over, and no fucking way. You've got to be shitting me.

"Amelia?" The fucking bartender, the one who was flirting with her months ago is here.

"Yeah, Matteo right?" she says, smiling as her and Maya lean against the counter. "Surprised you remembered my name."

How could he? She's not forgettable.

I can't control what she does but in public she's my girlfriend and I'm not letting some douche who happens to have a damn British accent try to swoop in.

"How could I forget a stunning woman like you." Matteo says, reaching for her hand, parting his lips.

Oh for fucks sake, yeah, that's not happening.

Before he can so much as breathe on her, I step closer to the bar beside her and take her hand in mine.

I bring her knuckles to my lips as my eyes stay locked on his. "My girlfriend would like to order drinks. That's what the bar is for, right?"

Matteo blinks, retreating his hand. "Oh, my apologies. What would you like to order?"

"Uh, a tequila sunrise please." Amelia orders then glances at me with an expression I can't read.

"I'll have a shot of vodka, thanks," I say, a slight bitterness in my tone. I didn't mean to sound like an asshole, but I couldn't help it.

Matteo hesitantly nods and turns around to fix our drinks.

"You okay?" Amelia furrows her brows, looking up at

me with those deep brown eyes I love so much. Why is she so beautiful?

Fuck, would there ever be a right time to tell her the truth?

And the real question is, what scrap of our friendship would be left to salvage if she doesn't feel the same?

27

AMELIA

Three shots in and the dim room spins round and round. Maya and I are on the dance floor having the best time. Her hips sway and I rest my hands on them following her movements, swinging my curls around.

My mind drifts to Caleb. Ten thousand dollars. He paid that much to get rid of footage when all we had to do was post a few more photos of us to steer everyone's attention. Is he nuts? And on top of that…he referred to me as his girlfriend again, which was so freaking attractive.

The buzz from these drinks is swirling through my veins, and it's making me think of very bad things tonight. His arms, mouth, hands, hair.

My eyes start to weigh down, as I scour the place for Caleb in the sea of people.

Some guy approaches behind Maya drawing her attention to him, they start talking, and it looks like they're hitting it off.

So, I excuse myself and maneuver through the sea of celebrities and athletes, internally freaking out.

These are the people I've seen all over TV. Thankfully, I haven't run into any actors yet, but maybe that's a good thing considering my current state. I'd most likely make a fool of myself in front of my celebrity crush.

The music pulses through my body, making me feel alive as I finally catch the sight of Caleb sitting in the VIP booth with Carter, sipping champagne.

"There you are," I say, sliding into the booth next to him.

"Here I am." He smiles.

"I'm already ready to go and I just got here," Nico's voice catches me off guard as he walks up to the booth.

"Don't be a party pooper." Carter groans, tipping his champagne glass towards him. "Have a drink, man."

"Fine." Nico shakes his head but caves. "Need a refill?" He glances down at me with dark eyes that pierce right through me.

"No, thanks."

"Thanks for the offer." Caleb scoffs, while he leans back against the plush booth.

"Welcome." Nico grins, heading for the bar.

"I'm getting another drink too," Carter announces, slipping out of the booth to follow him.

And then there were two.

I cross my legs, angling myself toward him.

His gaze lowers to my bare thighs, lingering there for a second too long before his jaw clenches. Then, slowly, he drags his eyes back up.

"You're staring."

"Am I?" He exhales a quiet laugh, tapping his fingers against his glass.

"Mhm." I smirk, lifting my glass to my lips and peering at him over the rim.

"Don't do that."

"Do what?"

"Look at me like that." He leans in slightly, close enough that I catch the faint scent of alcohol on his breath. "Because I might get the wrong idea."

That was not what I expected him to say. At all.

Tilting my head, I let my gaze drop to his mouth, boldness oozing out of me. "Would that be so bad?"

His lips twitch.

"You didn't answer," I press, my pulse picking up speed.

His eyes darken, taking a swig of his drink.

I should look away. But I don't.

"You're drunk," he murmurs, fingers gripping onto his glass so tight, it could shatter.

"So are you."

A beat of silence.

My hand reaches up, cupping one side of his face, bringing him closer to me as our breaths mingle together. The smell of champagne and whiskey mixing together in perfect harmony.

This is so wrong, we shouldn't be doing this. We're both drunk and this will only lead to complications. He doesn't even mean it, but god. I want it.

He sets his glass down with a clink, his hand brushing against my thigh, so warm that it heats up my body.

"Tell me stop," he whispers, gripping the fabric of my dress.

"No."

"Fuck," he lets out a shaky exhale, leaning his cheek into my palm, emerald eyes locking onto mine, desperate. "What the hell are you doing to me?"

"I don't know," my lips hover near his, barely brushing

against the subtle warmth of his mouth as it sends tingles up my spine.

Our lips play a game together.

Teasing, lingering, drawing back.

And then the games stop.

His mouth crashes against mine, and I groan into the kiss, his free hand grips the back of my curls pulling me in closer, deepening it like he's a man starving.

I kiss him back just as hungrily, my hands sliding down his neck to his chest, curling my fingers to knot up the fabric of his shirt.

Our kiss is frantic.

My lips move urgently against his mouth, my tongue slipping inside, as he lets out a low growl. He tugs at my bottom lip with his teeth, breaking our kiss to skim his lips across my jawline, leaving me breathless.

My hands cup his face again, bringing him back to my lips, not wanting to stop. I moan into his mouth, as his hands slide up my thigh slow, tentative.

I pant against his lips, aching for more. Our tongues brush again, tasting the liquor, and intoxicating me more.

His hands slide higher, slipping beneath my dress, setting my skin ablaze. His fingers inch closer to my underwear…so close to where I want him most.

A loud crash of glasses breaking near the bar pulls us apart instantly. We both look at each other, breathing heavily, as reality settles in on what we just did.

"Shit." He rakes a hand through his hair, still catching his breath. "Amelia, that was—"

"A mistake," I blurt out. The words tasting sour on my tongue.

Why did I say that?

He doesn't answer right away, he just looks at me with those eyes that make me question everything.

"Right," he mutters, reaching for his drink again. "A mistake."

The hollowness in his voice makes my chest tighten. I want to say I didn't mean it, that the kiss felt right in more ways than I can count but the words are stuck in my throat.

We're both under the influence. He was caught up in the moment.

And me…I haven't let anyone in for a year. I'm terrified of screwing something up.

Kill me now.

The morning light shines through my blinds, and I groan, pulling the covers over my head.

"I need blackout curtains immediately," I mumble, my head once again feels like it's been smashed in by a brick as last night's events come crashing back.

Tell me to stop.

No.

What the hell are you doing to me?

Heat creeps up my face, and I twist, burying my face in my silk pillow, wishing I could take back what I said.

It was a mistake.

I blindly extend my hand, slapping it against the nightstand, and fumble around, hoping my drunk self was smart enough to plug my phone in.

My fingers brush against a nylon cable, and I sigh in relief when I realize the other end is connected to my phone. At least I did something right.

I exhale, sitting up against the edge of my bed, sliding

my feet into my pink fuzzy slippers I got from my dad for Christmas with the words "Best Daughter" written on the top of each foot. They make me smile every time I wear them. It's been months since I've seen my parents, so I can't wait for the Bahamas.

I briskly text the girls group chat now labeled:
`Chicks before dicks`
You can probably guess who decided to name it that.

> Tia, how are you feeling?

She answers in record speed, which probably means she's walking. She bought this under the desk treadmill so she can answer emails while she gets a workout in. Resourceful at its finest.

TIA
Better. Amir says I'm definitely dehydrated and need to relax... but I also need to workout.

Shhh. Don't tell him I'm on the treadmill.

MAYA
I'm sure he gave you a full body scan to come up with that analysis.

> Really? lol

TIA
Maya honey...can't you get your mind out of the gutter for one day?

You girls need to get laid.

> Hey! I didn't even say anything!

MAYA

I kinda did last night.

Hence the new group chat name.

> Aw man. He was cute, what happened?

MAYA

Couldn't make me come. He kept licking and flicking…and nada. Wasn't doing it for me.

I left in the middle of it. I got bored. Told him I had to feed my fish.

I think I left my lipgloss.

> MAYA LMAO
>
> You don't even have a fish tank.

TIA

Damn.

You created a villain.

MAYA

Stop. Now you're making me feel bad…for a man. Someone slap me out of it.

TIA

I'M ON IT.

My best friends are a mess.

As I finish getting ready for work, my phone dings on the table.

@calebhayes has tagged you in a post.

Clicking on the notification, it's the photo we took last night.

My pretty girl.

God, he's not making this any easier.

28

CALEB

LAST NIGHT WAS SUCH A BLUR. BUT ONE MEMORY WAS CLEAR as day, and it had everything to do with Amelia. The way she looked at me with those goddamn eyes, I get lost in. The way her mouth felt against mine. Her fingers clutching at my shirt like she wanted me.

It only took two words to shatter anything I thought was possibly real in that kiss. *A mistake.*

Today's finally the day I'd sign the contract for Driftwear, and I couldn't be happier. It's been a long time coming.

I walk into the conference room, in my suit and tie, pulling out the rolling chair, taking a seat. Our team lawyer, Daryl, Coach and a few men from Driftwear stride in with their manila folders.

"Just to overview everything, this will be a three-year contract with the possibility of renewal if all goes well." One of the men wearing a blue and white suit speaks up first.

"Caleb…" he gestures toward me. "… will be our

global ambassador and front cover for Rookie of the Year. Also wearing the new pieces from our new athleisure collection coming this winter."

Our lawyer nods, a firm smile spreading across her face. "It's official then."

They slide the contract down to me and I reach for the Driftwear pen they provided and etch my signature into the page.

It's official.

"Congratulations, Caleb," one of the Driftwear reps says. "We are so excited for this partnership."

After signing, I step out into the quiet hall and head for the parking lot. My first thought was to call Amelia but, I want my father to hear the accomplishment from me first.

I dial his number, listening to the dial tone.

"Caleb." He picks up, his tone flat.

"I, um, wanted to let you know that I signed the deal," I say, pulling out my keys.

"That's not something to be proud of. That was expected of you."

I pause, the excitement draining from my chest. Not even a congratulations. I don't know why I thought this time would be any different.

"You just better not fuck this up too."

The line goes dead before I can even answer.

I lower the phone from my ear and stare at it. The pride I felt moments ago is gone, replaced by a hollow ache I'm way too familiar with.

This isn't an accomplishment. It's an expectation. My phone chimes and my mom's name appears.

> MOM
> I'm so proud of you.

> Thanks mom.

MOM
> I'll talk to your dad. He's proud of you but you know how he can get and he only wants the best for you.

I snort. It's always the same excuse. He can say whatever he wants, treat me however the hell he pleases, and it's fine because he's incapable of showing "emotions."

To his own fucking son. Is it really that hard?

> No need, it's fine. I'll see you soon. Love you.

MOM
> Love you too.

Later that night, I put on my cologne, a black button-up with the sleeves cuffed, and black dress pants to get ready for the event tonight. I'm not as excited as I was earlier this morning but I get to see her, so that outweighs everything else.

I start the car, shifting the gear into drive, and head to her place.

I knock on her door a few times.

Silence.

Did she forget?

Knock.

Nothing.

Another knock, followed by three more.

The hallway was silent, the only sound coming from my knuckles tapping against the wooden door like a maniac.

Knock.

Okay, now she's scaring me.

Knock.

What if she's in the tub, and her goddamn Kindle fell in, and electrocuted her? Wait. Those are waterproof, right?

Kno—

"I'm so sorry!" The door swings open, and every single worry I just imagined vanishes in an instant. This woman will give me a heart attack one of these days.

"God," I exhale, my pulse pounding like a damn drum. "I thought something happened to you."

Instead of her laughing, I take a second to really take her in. She's wearing a champagne-colored dress that pools at her ankles, paired with white heels, stunning as always. But, beneath all of that, she looks burnt out.

"What's wrong?" I ask.

She grumbles, stepping aside to let me in. The moment I walk through the door, the state of her apartment speaks volumes…papers scattered across the kitchen table, her laptop overflowing with open tabs, and wired headphones dangling off the edge of the couch.

"Last minute work stuff." She chuckles. "Nothing I can't handle."

"Let's skip tonight."

"Not a chance." She shakes her head, adjusting my cuffs that came undone. "Work can wait."

Loud music thrums around us as we step onto the rooftop deck and we're immediately met with a giant Driftwear banner covering the entrance. As we move further inside, my teammates and I exchange nods and clap each other on the back.

"Our golden boy is here!" one of the guys calls out as he tips his wine in the air. "Congrats, man!"

"Yeah! Yeah! Yeah!" The words being chanted over and over again as the team looks my way.

A laugh slips out as I shake my head, these guys are a mess. "Preciate you all for showing out."

Marcus appears from the crowd, dancing his way over before his gaze flicks between Amelia and I. "You two want something to drink?"

"Not tonight." Amelia waves her hand dismissing him with a small laugh. "Too much work to do."

He tips an imaginary hat toward her. "Hard worker as always."

"You know me." She merely shrugs.

"Well, you two kids have fun." He says before sauntering off to mingle with the rest of the team.

Holding Amelia's hand, we make our way over to the bar, the shelves lined with the finest and most expensive liquor. They really went all out.

It feels strange to be celebrating…me.

"What can I get you two to drink?" A tall brunette approaches us with a small grin as we settle onto the stools.

Her eyes land on mine.

"Two waters please, thanks," I reply, slipping two semi wrinkled fifty-dollar bills from my pocket, dropping them into the tip jar, and taking a seat.

"Coming right up," she says with a suggestive tone. "You sure that's all you want?"

Amelia shifts on the metal stool as she snatches a cocktail napkin off the table. "Yup."

The bartender throws a glance her way before nodding and moving down the bar.

"You look upset."

"Nope." She shakes her head, crumpling the napkin in her hand. "I just think it's distasteful of her to flirt with you right in front of me."

"Flirting?"

We're plastered all over socials, so it's impossible for her to be working this event and *not* know I'm "taken."

Either she's been living under a rock or she simply doesn't care.

Amelia gives me an unamused look. "Don't play dumb."

I hold in a smirk, rubbing my jaw. "She was being friendly."

She lets out a dry laugh. "That wasn't *friendly*. That was *'if I wasn't working right now I'd be asking you to take me right on the table'* friendly," she says, adding air quotes to emphasize her point.

"Didn't know you were paying that close attention."

Her fingers pause, still gripping the napkin. "It was an observation."

The bartender returns, setting down Amelia's water first. A few buttons on her shirt now magically undone. "Here you go," she purrs, leaning over the bar enough to make sure I notice her cleavage.

Her gaze locks with mine again, as she lowers her voice. "Let me know if you need *anything* else. And I mean anything."

Amelia picks up her glass, taking a sharp sip, rolling her eyes. "We're fine. That's all."

The woman hesitates leaving for a second, maybe waiting for me to flirt back.

"My girlfriend and I are good," I say, reaching over to hold Amelia's hand that's resting on the table.

The woman's smile fades, but she recovers quickly with a tight nod. "Of course." She hurries off to serve the rest of the team.

The second she's out of our earshot, Amelia sets down her drink with a sharp clink. Then, with a dramatic flutter of her lashes, she mimics. *"Let me know if you need anything else."*

"It didn't sound like that."

"Then you need to get your ears checked," she mutters, tightening her hand around mine.

Is she…jealous? No. Impossible. She's my "girlfriend." Of course she'd be annoyed.

I trace my thumb over her knuckles, feeling the warmth of her hands. Strange heat creeps up my spine. I shift my gaze, desperate to find something else to focus on.

"Yo, what's up." Daren, one of the wide receivers, comes stumbling over draping an arm around my shoulder. I wasn't even aware he was behind me. "That bartender is hot as hell."

Amelia forces a smile, but it's so tight I swear I can hear her teeth grinding.

Daren turns back to me with a long groan. "Man, maybe I should go ask for her number," He nudges my arm before leaning down and whispering in my ear. "If you were single, would you?"

My body tenses and I feel Amelia's eyes on me, wondering what the hell our conversation is about before she glances away, checking out the event.

"No," I say cooly.

He snorts. "Why? She's not your type?"

My eyes land on Amelia, who's very much my type. My *only* type.

"I get it though, I wouldn't be looking either if Amelia was mine. She's looking sexy tonight," Daren slurs. "Maybe we can share—"

I clench my fists, shooting upright, looking straight into his eyes. "Lay off the fucking beer."

This guy's an idiot and drunk as hell tonight. Normally he's a chill dude, but right now, all I want to do is smash my fist into his jaw.

Amelia stands up, confusion written all over her precious face.

Daren stumbles away, going over to Carter and Nico, before calling out behind him. "Joking dude reeeelax."

"Hey, what happened?" she questions, looking up at me.

A few sharp clinks against glass draw our attention, over to Jackson Mitchell, CEO of Driftwear. He stands on the mini stage with a knife in hand. "May I have everyone's attention, please?"

We all gather, our eyes fixed on the stage. I reach for Amelia's hand, holding it as we shift closer.

"Partnering with Caleb Hayes is something we're incredibly proud of," Jackson says, gratitude and excitement lacing his words. "It's truly a pleasure."

Everyone claps and cheers, lifting their drinks in the air.

"Here's to a great long-term partnership," he adds, raising his wine glass. "Cheers."

"Cheers!" I shout with a smile.

Jackson steps off the stage and makes a beeline toward Amelia and I. "Caleb and Amelia it's nice to finally meet you both." He offers a hand.

"You too, sir." I say with a slight nod, meeting his handshake.

"Nice to meet you," her voice soft beside me.

"I'm glad that this worked out for us." Jackson says, taking a swig of his drink. "It was a tough decision and I don't want to dwell on it but that situation wasn't a good look for our brand." He pauses for a beat. "We wanted you as an ambassador but you know we have a zero- scandal policy."

"I understand," I say. "Thank you for giving me a chance anyway."

"Me too. It was nothing personal." He waves his hand dismissively. "Anyway, I won't take too much of your time. Congrats again and welcome to Driftwear."

He walks off, and the moment his back is turned, Amelia tugs my arm letting out the smallest squeal. "You did it!"

It wouldn't have been possible without her.

"We," I correct her, my fingers brushing the side of her jaw as I gently pinch her chin. "We did it."

Her eyes soften and a fire ignites in my chest. For the briefest moment I wonder if she's thinking the same as I am. If maybe, this is more than we've let on.

Or maybe I'm imagining it.

29

CALEB

Sᴇᴘᴛᴇᴍʙᴇʀ 1ˢᴛ

"Shit," I grunt as I line up behind Nico, hearing the deafening crowd in the air.

This is it. The Titans have been running their mouths all month with their trash talk. And now? We're face to face and they're good. Fast. Relentless. They know how to keep up with us, but we're not backing down.

No way in hell.

We're in the third quarter. I glance at the scoreboard and the score's 30-34, my pulse quickening. We can't lose this. Not now. If we do, I'll never hear the end of it, and worse, I'll let my team down. I'm not doing that. Not when we're this close.

Amelia's up there in the stands and that thought alone twists the knot in my stomach tighter. She's seen me play before, but this time it feels different, more intense.

The pressure builds, coiling in my chest as I jog backward, scanning the field. Carter's running his route and he makes a hard cut grazing the sideline, giving me a clear opening. But their defense is on my ass, closing in on me.

I fake a right to get some space, throwing the ball on impulse. It was a split-second decision, and I sling it almost 47 yards down the field. It's not my cleanest throw but it was all I had. The defense was too close and I needed to make something happen.

The ball spirals through the air as Carter jogs back, fingers stretching as he secures the ball.

I exhale as he bolts forward, pushing for extra yards. He's at the 30 yard line almost to the end zone.

A linebacker charges him, grabbing Carter by the collar and shoving him out of bounds.

Illegal fucking hit.

"Yo, what the fuck!" I shout, ripping my helmet off as I dart toward the sidelines, adrenaline pumping through my veins.

The refs need to call that, there's no way that was clean. Such a cheap shot.

My face twists in frustration as I approach the referee glaring at him as he deciphers what to do.

The whistle blows.

"Penalty Titans. Illegal tackle," the ref announces, his voice cutting through the chaos.

I look over at a pissed-off Carter, who's already on his feet, wiping his jersey and shaking off the hit.

"You good?" I slap him on the back as we all gather around the huddle.

"He's lucky I'm in a good mood or I'd bash his fucking face in," Carter mutters, leaning into the circle, fired up.

I'm right along with him. This is the energy we need, though. I'm heated.

I pull my helmet back on and look up at Coach, who's

even more pissed off than Carter, His face is flushed, veins prominent and popping out his neck as he yells at someone. Then, he locks eyes with me and hand signals for Play 27.

Quickly, I flip my wristband on my left arm for reference, checking the play call.

"Time to whoop some ass." Marcus grunts, stepping into the huddle.

"Alright. East right slot, X-lock, clamp south, Y-dagger, run past three. Let's go!" I clap my hands. They nod in sync and we break from the huddle, sprinting back into formation.

I take my position behind center, calling the cadence, as my pulse is thundering in my ears as I snap the ball. I drop back, my eyes sweeping across the field.

Marcus is running his route, cutting left toward the sideline.

The Titan's cornerback is closing in on him fast, but I know Marcus has the speed to pull this play off. He's at the ten-yard line, almost there.

I pull my arm back, launching the ball as it cuts through the air and Marcus leaps up, catching it before the cornerback gets him.

He secures it tight in his arm, then uses his free hand to shove the defender off, creating a bit of space. With a quick pivot of his foot, Marcus does a spin before they collide.

He sprints the last few yards toward the end zone.

Weight slams into me from the right side as I'm slammed into the turf, my left shoulder and helmet digging into the grass. A sharp pain shoots up my arm and I grunt as the linebacker sprints off down the field.

But I don't even care about my shoulder, I need to know if we won.

I push myself up, wincing at the throb, clutching my

shoulder tight. When I glance up, the LED scoreboard changes.

36-34.

The crowd's cheers grow loud as I spot Marcus on his feet, doing a backflip, smashing the ball into the ground.

We won.

Tia and Amelia hurry toward me, slipping past the cameras and reporters. Amelia reaches for my arm gently, and I flinch at the sting.

"Are you okay?" they say in unison.

"You need to get this checked out," Amelia insists.

"I'm fine."

It's nothing major. I've taken worse hits before, even though this still hurts like a bitch. They'll wrap my shoulder up, and by the wedding, I'll be fully recovered.

"Don't try and be all macho about it," Tia scolds, folding her arms. "You're not missing out on Bahama fun with a broken shoulder."

"It's not broken."

Tia jabs a finger into my injured shoulder. I hiss through clenched teeth, cursing under my breath and clutching it tighter.

"Still not broken?" she mocks.

"Where's Amir? I prefer him over you." I grumble, rolling my eyes.

Tia and Amelia walk me over to the sidelines as the medic waits for me.

Before I follow her inside, a smile tugs at my lips as I glance down at Amelia. "Nice to see you worried about me."

"I always do."

"Maybe you can kiss it to make me feel better?" I tease, half-hoping and half-begging.

She lets out a laugh, severing eye contact and fumbles with her jersey.

My jersey.

She doesn't even know what she's doing to me.

I want to tear it off her. My grip tightens around my shoulder.

I don't know how long I can keep this fake dating shit up.

Later that night, I'm icing my shoulder when I check my phone and see a text from Carter in the group chat:

BROMANCE

Marcus and Carter came up with that last year. I've changed it multiple times and so has Nico, but somehow it keeps coming back.

> **CARTER**
> That dipshit scratched the hell out of my neck.
>
> **MARCUS**
> Poor baby.
>
> NICO HAS LEFT THE CONVERSATION.
>
> **CARTER**
> The fuck.
>
> CARTER ADDED NICO TO THE CONVERSATION.
>
> **NICO**
> We don't care.

CARTER

I hope your bruise takes forever to heal.

Take that back.

CARTER

Marcus is the only real one in this lame group.

Go back and watch Twilight. Because I know that's what you're doing right now.

MARCUS

I'm loving this.

NICO

Bye.

CARTER

nothing's wrong with twilight.

MARCUS

You're watching it without me?!

30

AMELIA

Sᴇᴘᴛᴇᴍʙᴇʀ 21ꜱᴛ

"Who's ready to party?" Tia bursts into her living room, a white Bride to Be sash draped over her white lace dress that stops right above her knees. Her rhinestone headband with a veil attached reflects off the light as she flashes us all a grin. "Wooooo!" She raises a tequila bottle in her hand like a trophy.

After weeks of planning with Maya and having several meltdowns over setting up the games, decorations, and RSVP invites, the hotel suite we booked for Tia's bachelorette party is all ready to go.

Amir whistles as he steps up, taking Tia's hand and giving her a small twirl. "Look at my beautiful fiancé."

Caleb leans back against the couch beside me, his black button-down shirt exposing his chest as his silver necklace dangles lazily against it.

My eyes linger for a beat too long. My feelings haven't faded one bit no matter how much I hoped they would.

We haven't had the need to prove to the media anymore

now that he's signed and I'm so ready to get to the Bahamas already just to have an excuse to hold his hand… or do anything, really.

Maya pulls out her phone, tapping the screen to order us a ride.

"Don't get too drunk tonight. Flight's at 8 a.m.," Tia scolds, her eyes locked on her brother.

Caleb's brow furrows, crinkling his skin. "Why are you looking at me?"

"Because you sleep like you're a dead man," she retorts dryly.

I stifle a laugh. "She's not wrong."

"Always on my sister's side." He rolls his eyes, giving my thigh a quick squeeze.

"Us girls gotta stick together." I shrug in defense.

"Don't worry, we won't be late, babe," Amir says to Tia.

"Our ride's here!" Maya calls out beside me, dragging her luggage. "Time to ditch you men." She heads out the door, patting Amir on the shoulder before looking up at him. "No offense."

"Offense very much taken." He shakes his head letting out a throaty laugh. Then turns to Tia, pressing a kiss to her lips. "See you in the morning, I love you."

She pouts. "I love you too."

My eyes soften as I witness how in love they are. I've always loved their relationship. The gentle touches, the way he cares for her, and wants to make her genuinely happy. It stirs something inside me.

It makes me want to believe in love again. Maybe putting your heart out there again isn't so bad because sometimes, you gotta meet a few frogs before finding your prince…or so I've been told.

And I've already kissed a human form of a frog. That has to count.

Animated movies please, don't let me down.

We check into a fancy hotel near LAX, grab our keycards, then take the elevator up to the 20th floor. As we roll our luggage down the luxurious hallway, Maya slides the keycard into our door. "Prepare to have fun tonight, my queen," she grins, holding it open for Tia and me.

"SURPRISE!"

Blair and Skye, Tia's other closest friends, pop out from behind the couch just as I wave my hand over the fancy light switch.

Tia lets out a scream, clutching her heart before bursting into laughter. The king suite is all decked out in yellow, pink, and shimmering decorations. Balloons floating all the way to the ceiling, and in rose-gold letters the word **BRIDE** hangs over the couch.

We step further inside, closing the door behind us as Tia takes it all in with wide eyes.

In the main bedroom, cream satin robes hang neatly on a rack, with a table filled with face masks, games, cute glasses, and…sex toys.

"I can't believe you guys did this!" Tia throws her arms around Maya and me in a tight hug before spinning around, hugging the other girls. "You guys are so sneaky."

Her eyes land on the purple dildos, pink vibrators, and a blow-up sex doll neatly arranged on the glass table beside the bed. She freezes. "Really guys?"

Maya smirks. "It wouldn't be an iconic bachelorette party without some fake penises."

"I second that," Blair chimes in, pointing a finger in the air. She's a wildcard like Maya, hilarious and always down for a good time. I've met her a handful of times, she seems sweet.

Tia picks up a dildo, poking it a few times before laughing. "They're so squishy."

I laugh. "We're gonna have lots of fun."

Maya loops her arm through mine. "Now, should we start with cock…tails," she deliberately drags out the word, "or dive straight into the games?"

"Both." Tia and Skye say in unison.

"That's what I'm talking about." Maya heads straight to the speaker, connects her phone, and hits play.

"S&M" by Rihanna fills the room, officially kicking off our wild night.

A few hours in, and a few drinks later we're all sitting on the bed, robes on, with our face masks, sipping cocktails through a yellow penis straw.

If my mom saw me right now, she'd have a panic attack…and put me on a three-way call with my Lola.

"Alright, babe, next game is Truth or Shots." She sets her cocktail down, grabbing the deck of cards. "It's simple… answer honestly or take an insane amount of shots back to back." She grins, shuffling the deck. "First victim is obviously the bride."

Tia takes a slow sip, with a groan. "Oh, I can't wait to hear this."

Maya picks a card, her eyes beaming up as she dramatically clears her throat. "Where's the wildest place you and Amir had sex?"

Skye and Blair squeal, huddling together as they sip.

"We're starting off with the heavy questions I see." Tia looks up, deep in thought. "Okay let me think."

"Damn, so it's been more than one place?" Maya laughs, clearly impressed as she sets the card down.

Tia smirks, reaching for it and fiddling with the card. "Our sex life is important to us."

Blair raises her glass. "Amen!"

Tia finally answers, lowering her voice. "Storage closet."

I choke on my drink. "What?!" I raise a brow, offended that she never told me this valuable information.

Skye's eyes widen, leaning in, clearly invested like we all are. "Wait, a storage closet? How did that even happen?"

Tia shrugs, her grin widening. "Well, we were at one of his med school conferences last year and it just happened."

"Uh…uh." Maya shakes her head, disapproving the lack of detail. "Don't skimp on the details."

Tia laughs, and flings her card at Maya. "We were just talking and mingling with his colleagues. He saw an empty closet and we joked around with the idea. But then we thought, why the hell not?"

We all ask a few more questions around the group when Tia suddenly gasps. "Wait, can I borrow someone's phone? I want to take a picture of us before I forget! My phone's in my bag and I don't feel like getting up."

The girls all search the bed for their phone, but I kept mine tucked into my shorts under the robe.

"Here." I unlock my phone, open the camera app, and pass it over.

"Lifesaver." Tia's expression brightens as she angles the phone up. "Okay ladies, let's all get in!" She beckons us closer, adjusting the frame. "Say cheese."

Snap

Tia looks down at the photo, her face easing as she hands my phone back. "I'm having so much fun. Seriously, thanks for planning all this." She smiles, then gestures toward Maya. "Okay, let's hear more dirty questions."

I glance down at the photo briefly before shoving my phone into my pocket.

Maya shuffles the cards, pulling one out and grins in my direction. "Ooooh, this is a good one, ready?"

"Bring it on."

"What's your sex fantasy?"

You're kidding. I really don't feel like getting plastered tonight. It's either expose myself or throw up later.

I think I'll expose myself.

"My sex fantasy is that..." I begin, feeling my cheeks warm. "I've always wanted to have sex in front of a mirror or recreate a scene from my favorite movie."

"Naughty girl." Maya teases. "Can confirm. Mirror sex is the best."

Tia raises her glass. "Cheers to that."

"You can!" Blair hypes me up, taking a sip of her drink. "You just gotta tell him."

"Pass those notes to Caleb. I'm sure he'd love that." Skye chuckles, poking my arm.

Why does the thought of me and Caleb having sex sound so thrilling? I wonder what he's like. Rough? Gentle? A sinful mix of both?

God, my mind's spinning with a million thoughts.

Tia and I make eye contact and she shifts uncomfortably, definitely not a topic you want to hear about your brother.

"I'm sure he would." I awkwardly laugh, wiping my hands dry against the silk robe desperate to get the topic off me. "Shall we move on to the next question?"

Maya rests a hand on my knee, giving it a light squeeze that helps calm my racing thoughts. "Skye...your turn."

As the night goes on, our eyes grow heavier as the cocktails catch up with us.

We tell Tia to get some rest in the main bedroom while the rest of us clean up the room, throwing our trash away, getting ready for our flight in the morning. Skye and Blaire have a later flight than us so they're taking care of the rest of the room and they'll be staying in the king suite with Tia.

Maya and I exchange a quiet goodnight with them before heading down the hall toward our own room, the hotel hallway quiet as we roll our luggage.

After getting unready and winding down for the night, I lie in the shared room with Maya, who's already curled up in her bed, as the quiet hum of the air conditioning and her deep breaths fill the space.

I reach for my phone, swiping up on my family group chat text.

> **MOM**
> Have a safe flight tomorrow baby girl. We can't wait to see you.

> You guys too. Thanks <3

> **DAD**
> Can't wait to see you tomorrow.

> **MOM**
> Night honey. Mahal kita.

> Love you both.

I swipe out of the group chat, and Caleb's name is at the top of my recents, but I don't remember texting him at all tonight. Frowning, I click on his name.

A voice memo? When did I send him that? It's only ten seconds long. Maybe I sat on my phone or something.

An hour ago…hmm. I press play.

"My sex fantasy is that…"

Muffled noises.

NO.

"I've always wanted to have sex in front of a mirror or recreate a scene from my favorite movie."

Oh god. This is not happening. Thankfully, he hasn't seen it yet.

No biggie. No reason to get all worked up. Don't panic.

I'll just hold the message down to delete it, but just as my finger hovers over the screen—

Seen. And minutes later…

Incoming call from Caleb.

31

CALEB

Our bachelor party consists of me, Marcus, and a few of Amir's friends from med school. Pretty chill night here at the house, which was exactly what he wanted.

We are deep into our poker game when I reach for my beer, taking a small swig. I shuffle the cards in my hand, checking my deck. King. Jack...

My phone lights up on the table, breaking my concentration. I glance down. The airline sent a check-in notification, and there's also a new text from an hour ago.

New message from Amelia

I set my cards face down and tap on the notification, seeing a voice memo. It must be important, maybe she needs me to drop something off at the hotel.

Excusing myself from the table, I swipe my deck of cards before Amir tries to cheat...again. I walk into the kitchen, pulling out the stool, taking a seat. I raise the phone to my ear as the voice memo automatically plays.

"*My sex fantasy is that...*"

Muffled noises follow. What the hell is this?

"I've always wanted to have sex in front of a mirror or recreate a scene from my favorite movie."

Holy shit. I swipe out quickly. That was clearly not meant for me.

The faint noise of poker chips clanking against the table grows distant. I adjust in the stool, dragging a hand down my face, inhaling deeply. I should just let it go. Pretend I never heard it.

Wait. My read receipts are on. Shit. Well, there goes that plan.

Marcus walks into the kitchen, looking my way curiously. "Everything good?"

I nod. "Yeah, I'm just gonna make a quick call. I'll be right back."

Marcus smirks. "A call, huh?"

I roll my eyes, already knowing where his mind's at. "Not the kind that starts with the word booty."

"No judgment." He puts his hand up in surrender. "Enjoy your *call*."

Shaking my head, I head toward the back, sliding the screen door open, stepping onto the patio. The cool air hitting against my skin as I slide the door shut behind me, pacing the wooden deck as I call Amelia.

The phone rings. Once. Twice.

She picks up and starts rambling "Um…hi. So about that text, let's just pretend you didn't hear any of that—"

I take a quick peek through the screen door, making sure no one's coming outside.

"You know," I lower my voice, "if you wanted to bring a fantasy of yours to life, all you had to do was ask."

"Oh," she says shakily.

"And for the record, I like a woman who knows what she wants."

I let the silence stretch.

"Goodnight, Amelia."

I end the call before she can respond.

Sliding my phone back into my pocket, my heart starts pounding against my ribcage. Was that stupid of me to say? Jesus.

When I step back inside, Marcus steps out of the kitchen looking at me. "You lost by the way."

Rolling my eyes, I walk back with him to the pool table, taking my seat. "Deal me in."

One minute, I'm unwinding in bed, replaying last night's conversation with Amelia on a loop, and the next, my alarm is deafening in my ears, reminding me that we have a flight to catch.

I hardly got any sleep. Between Marcus giving me shit later on for stepping out the game for my "booty call" and my own damn thoughts refusing to keep quiet, I might've drifted off for maybe three hours, if that.

The LAX terminal is crammed, like always, people rushing with their luggage, flight announcements echoing overhead, and people waiting in line for their coffee. I make my way toward the gate with the guys, adjusting my backpack over my shoulder, rolling my suitcase behind me.

And that's when I see her. Amelia, standing near the beam seating, as she rolls her luggage closer to her leg, hair gathered in a messy bun with two curl pieces cascading down, stopping right above her brow.

She looks up, her eyes meeting mine. And just like that, I'm fully awake.

"You look awful." Tia gloats, walking up to me, looking all refreshed like she just got a facial.

I stare at her, then press a hand to my heart. "Thanks. You really know how to make my morning so much brighter."

"Anytime." She strolls off, looping her arm through Amir's, leading him toward their seats.

Amelia keeps sneaking glances at me but says nothing, and she keeps fidgeting with the edge of her sleeve. Is she embarrassed about last night? I hope not.

An hour goes by with me sitting behind her in these uncomfortable airport seats and all I've been doing is listening to Maya and Marcus argue about whether they'd rather live on Earth as giants or miniature-sized people. My brain is going to fry if I have to hear Marcus say, "But if you're a giant, you're just gonna crush every person in sight," for the tenth time.

I turn my head, catching a whiff of her strawberry perfume as I lean back slightly, lowering my voice as I murmur near her ear. "So...in front of the mirror, huh?"

She freezes. I lean back further, stealing a glance at what she's doing, and notice she's reading a physical book this time rather than her Kindle.

She exhales deeply, slipping a bookmark between the pages, and my chest tightens. It's the same pink one I gave her back in high school.

"What?" her voice trembles as she turns her head slightly toward me. Her glossy lips hover dangerously near mine.

"You want to watch yourself?" I say, staring at her lips. "Is that the only reason?"

I don't know what's gotten into me, but I'm done

playing it safe. I'm fed up. It's time I step up and prove I can be the best damn boyfriend she's ever had.

The flight announcement blares over the intercom.

"Good morning, passengers. This is your boarding announcement for flight 1924 to the Bahamas. We will now begin priority boarding."

I stand up, rounding the seats, reaching for her suitcase. "After you," I gesture for her to go first.

She offers a nervous smile. "Thanks." As she steps toward the boarding agent and scans her ticket, I trail right behind.

The roar of the jets reverberates through the air as we step onto the plane, greeted by the flight attendants.

I fall in step behind her down the aisle as she slides into the window seat. After adjusting our bags in the overhead compartment, I take the seat beside her.

A few hours in, a flight attendant walks by, handing us ginger ale and crackers which are the only two things I actually enjoy about flying.

"What's your book about?" I glance over at the cover, tilting it slightly with my finger to sneak a peek at the back.

"Since when do you care about what contents are in my book?" She laughs.

My mind flashes back to that day, her reading that book on the way to the cake testing.

"Since I realize how filthy those books you read actually are," I murmur, though I'm fighting a grin as I take a sip, staring at the flight map on the monitor.

"Define filthy." Her gaze shifts, and I can feel it burn into the side of my head. I refuse to look at her yet. "Because I assure you, that was the tamest part of the whole book."

"Is it now?" I turn my head to meet her eyes.

She goes back to reading as a slow grin curves her mouth.

Hours pass, and as the final minutes count down, the plane begins to descend. Amelia leans toward the window and raises the shade.

Sunlight spills in, casting a warm glow across her skin, as she takes a moment to admire the island and the clear blue water, rippling.

"It's so beautiful," she says, smiling at the view.

"Yeah, it is," I reply, though my gaze isn't on the island.

We step out of the shuttle van, and the photos didn't do this place justice. Towering palm trees surround the entire hotel, the entrance is lined with water and smooth stone pathways and large boulders. Everything about this place feels calm, like a bubble of pure bliss, far from the chaos of LA. I roll my suitcase, following the others inside.

"Welcome to Paradise Island." An older man calls out from behind the front desk. "Let me get you guys checked in so you can soak up every bit of sun we have here in the Bahamas!"

After we check in and grab our key cards, we head toward our rooms while everyone else splits up to do the same. Amelia lags behind, dragging her suitcase as if it weighs a hundred pounds.

"Need help back there?" I grin, as the wheels of her luggage skip against the carpet.

"No," she huffs.

"I bet you wish you had your High School Musical suitcase instead."

"Yeah, yeah." She retorts, yanking her suitcase again over the carpet.

I chuckle, stopping in front of our room as she pulls the keycard from her pocket and slaps it against my chest.

"Ouch." I place my hand over hers, mock-wincing as I take the card. "That's gonna leave a bruise."

"It'll match the one your shoulder." She can't hide the smile tugging at her lips and I'm glad to be the one who pulled that string. "Just open the door. I need to pee."

"Wouldn't want to keep you waiting." I laugh, swiping the keycard, watching the light flash green, followed by a beep.

I walk in first, taking in the room. A mini bar, couch, sleek bathroom, and a beautiful window view of the ocean. And then my gaze lands on the bed.

As in a singular bed.

"Wait, what?" Amelia steps in behind me, yanking her suitcase fully inside just as the door slams shut with a loud clunk. She scans the room, then stares blankly at the bed confused. "Where's the other one?"

I raise an eyebrow, scratching the nape of my neck, joking. "You don't see it?"

"I'm serious."

I flop back onto the mattress. "Well, at least it's comfy?"

She folds her arms. "Call the front desk."

"I got it." I nod, stretching out on the white sheets before reaching over for the phone, pressing the front desk button.

I hear the faint sound of the bathroom door closing as Amelia runs to go pee and the call connects.

"Hey, there seems to be an issue with our room. We booked two queen beds."

"I am so sorry for the inconvenience," the man says, his

voice sounding a little flustered. Clacking from the keyboard is all I hear.

"Unfortunately, we're now fully booked."

Shit.

I glance up at Amelia who's just emerged out of the bathroom, blissfully unaware of our current situation.

"We can offer free breakfast vouchers for your stay if that would help? Give me one moment." He puts me on hold as the sound of the automatic bad quality elevator music fills my ears.

She catches my eyes, mouthing, "What did they say?"

"They're giving us free breakfast vouchers because they have no other rooms left."

"Wait." Her eyes light up, like a kid on Christmas morning. "Breakfast vouchers?"

I laugh at the way she geeks over food. "Yeah, for the *whole* week."

Her mouth folds up and twists as she considers the options.

"Hang up," she says eagerly. "Tell them it's fine."

"So now you're okay with sharing the bed with me as long as food is involved?" I smirk, feigning offense.

"As if you'd want to share the bed with me anyways," she counters, setting her suitcase down on the floor.

"I wouldn't have complained."

The elevator music stops and the man asks me if I would like to accept his offer. "Appreciate it. We'll take those vouchers," I say before we hang up.

Amelia claps quietly as she steps over to the mirror, fixing her bun.

"I could sleep on the couch." I offer.

She follows my line of sight and laughs pointing at it. "You wouldn't even fit."

"Trust me, I'd fit."

"Um." Her throat bobs as she swallows. "It's fine, uh, just promise me, you won't hog the blankets."

"Sorry princess, that's one promise I don't know if I can keep."

She groans. "You seem more insufferable than usual today." She kneels down, flipping open her suitcase to unpack.

"It's part of the Bahama charm."

32

AMELIA

The other wedding guests, including my family, arrive tomorrow which means we have the entire day to relax and take it easy.

Tia texted the group chat earlier that we're all meeting for dinner tonight in a few hours, so in the meantime I'll be hitting the pool.

After changing into my pink two-piece bikini I pull a few face framing pieces from my bun, sliding my sunglasses up and slip my sandals on. I step out of the bathroom and look over at Caleb, who's scrolling on his phone waiting for me.

"Ready?" I ask.

He barely glances up at first, still focused on his phone but when he finally does it feels like time has slowed down significantly. His eyes rake over me boldly starting from top to bottom like he's memorizing every inch. It makes me feel a little nervous, but excited. I'm not used to him looking at me this intently, especially half dressed.

Lying under the blazing sun with my Kindle in hand, feeling the warmth seep into my skin is exactly how I want to spend the rest of my life.

Palm trees sway lazily around us, drinks are being served, and the lounge chairs are so comfortable I could sleep here all night. I might just ditch Caleb later and do exactly that.

I tilt my head just enough to peer over the top of my sunglasses, glancing toward the pool as Caleb steps out, water streaming down his rippling abs, glistening in the sunlight.

His broad shoulders somehow look even more defined than before. The injuries have subsided, leaving only a small bruise.

Woah.

"Water feels good," he says stepping closer to me as water continues to drip, torturously slow.

I hum, pushing my sunglasses back up with my finger. "Oh yeah?"

"Take a swim with me and put your filthy book away for a minute," he teases as his eyes glint with mischief.

Heat rushes to my skin. "Caleb!"

"Joking. Come on," he grins, reaching for my hand, helping me up. I quickly toss my sunglasses onto the lounge chair as we make our way to the steps of the pool.

I dip my toes in the cool water, but it's the feeling of his hand resting on my lower back that makes me shiver.

He steps down, guiding me with him, and we fully emerge into the water up to my hips just as 'Boom Clap' by Charli XCX blares from the speakers, filling the air.

We both swim to the far end of the pool, where it's

quieter and more secluded, surrounded by boulders and more palm trees. I close my eyes for a moment, letting the sun warm my face as I shift slightly, searching for a comfortable spot while the water gently laps against our chests.

My eyes snap open.

His leg brushes against mine under the water, sending a rush of heat through me. I glance at him but he's not looking at me, he's just taking in the view.

His leg brushes against mine again, and I let out a soft laugh. "We're practically alone over here and you're still taking up space."

A quiet chuckle rumbles from him. "You're the one who keeps moving."

The only sounds are the gentle ripple of water and faint music drifting through the air.

His lips curve into a playful smile as he shifts in front of me. "Feel good?"

I lean back against the edge of the pool, resting my elbows on the concrete, watching him float closer. "Yea…"

He's right in front of me, so close I can't help but glance at his lips, my breath growing shallow. My arm almost slips off the edge, but he's quick, wrapping my legs around his waist to steady me.

His hard body presses against my chest, igniting something deep in my core. I instinctively wrap my legs tighter.

I'm trying not to get carried away, but it's hard with him so close…his presence is overwhelming.

His hands settle on my thighs, burning against my skin as they slide upward, reaching for the strings of my bathing suit. I swallow, trying to steady my breath.

He rolls the strings between his fingers, each movement making my pulse race.

I bite my bottom lip, forcing myself to stay calm, to not give too much away. Then my brows furrow when his voice slices through my jumbled thoughts.

"Maybe we should head back," he says with a smug grin, pushing himself up from the pool, his swim trunks hanging dangerously low on his hips. "Don't wanna be late for dinner."

My jaw drops, watching water droplets trail down his taut back as he leaves me here, breathless.

God.

"I still can't believe my little sister is getting married this week," Caleb says reaching for his menu. The resorts' restaurant is so elegant and classy, it has wraparound sliding doors that let the cool breeze sweep in, it's literally the perfect romantic scenery.

He flips through the menu, looking over at me briefly.

Amir smiles warmly, resting his arm behind Tia's chair rubbing her shoulder, kissing her temple. "I'm lucky," his voice light. "Unfortunately that just means I'm stuck with you," his eyes landing on Caleb.

Tia laughs, swatting at Amir's chest. "He's not that bad."

Caleb raises a brow, shocked that Tia defended his honor. "What do you need?"

Tia rolls her eyes and I can't help but laugh at their bickering. "You know what, I'm never defending you again."

"He is that bad." Marcus quietly chuckles as he steps toward the table taking a seat by Caleb.

"You saved me a seat, how kind of you." Marcus nudges Caleb's arm laughing as he takes a seat beside him.

Maya strolls in wearing a sheer black cover-up. "Hey, hey, hey!"

"Uh oh, here we go." Marcus rolls his eyes. "Loud mouth is here."

Maya plops down beside me and glares at him. "You're just mad that I got a room with a balcony. Don't be jealous."

"So, how do you feel about being a soon to be wife?" I glance over at Tia, smiling.

"Counting down the days," she says, taking Amir's hand.

"It's crazy that it's been a goal of mine to marry her and now it's actually happening," Amir adds.

Love is such a beautiful yet complex concept. There was a time when I thought I had it all figured out, and truly believed I was experiencing it. I even imagined myself marrying Jared last year. But, ever since he cheated on me, it's been nearly impossible to look at any connection with an open eye.

Now, I can't help but jump to the worst-case scenario over every interaction. Every gesture. Every word. I always feel like every conversation is laced with ill intent and that they don't really mean what they say. It's just a game for them. That's why I never think too hard if a man flirts with me, I always push back in the end. I've never gotten closure from my breakup and the more I think about it makes me wonder if I let my anger get the best of me. Did I shut myself off from healing properly?

That's why my feelings for Caleb, however uncertain, are so terrifying. We're still caught up in this whole fake dating scheme, and what if everything between us has only ever been part of the act?

We finish up our last bites of dessert, Tia groans, leaning back in her chair unzipping her shorts. "I'm beyond bloated."

"Agreed," I say.

"Ready to go to bed?' Amir laughs, reaching for the check the waiter left a few minutes ago and sliding in a hundred-dollar bill.

"Mhm. I am going to slip into a food coma any minute now," Tia says.

Maya and Marcus mumbles something that sounded like a 'me too' as they reach for their checks, jotting down tips.

Caleb reaches over, sliding the check toward him, and my hand shoots out landing on top of his "That one's mine."

"I know," he says casually, scribbling with his pen a tip before slipping his card inside.

"You always do this."

"You should know this by now," he grins, handing the check to our waitress. Then his gaze locks onto mine, making my heart skip several beats."When you're with me, don't bother bringing a wallet."

Caleb and I head out the restaurant, automatic door glides open as the cool breeze sweeps in carrying the ocean scent our way. The gravel crunches beneath our feet, and I look up at him to ask a question that's been sitting on my chest for weeks. "Have you spoken to your dad lately?"

Caleb deeply exhales. "Not since the Driftwear event."

Figures. I'm just nervous about seeing him tomorrow. I just hope, for Tia's sake, his dad doesn't start any problems.

"Do you plan on talking to him tomorrow?" I waver.

He huffs out a dry laugh, squeezing his thumb again that makes my heart ache. "Honestly? I'd prefer not to, but I will for Tia."

Entering our hotel room, he kicks his shoes off and takes off his jacket, leaving him in a plain white t-shirt. I slip off my sandals and look over at him sitting down on the couch scratching his eyebrow, annoyed.

"He doesn't get it at all," Caleb mutters as his voice is thick with frustration. "He doesn't get how he fucked up my childhood."

My entire chest tightens knowing I was there with him through it all and I hate how I didn't stand up for him. It makes me want to claw at my insides. He does so much for people and what does he get in return? His dad telling him how much of a disappointment he was at age thirteen. He's always trying to please everyone and it's time for him to get the same treatment.

My eyes soften, and I settle beside him, squeezing his arm gently.

Our eyes lock, and the longer I look into his, the more I realize something's changed. I think I'm in love with my best friend and I can only hope maybe he feels the same.

Then he softly grips my chin. "You always do that."

"Do what?"

"Look at me like I matter," he murmurs. "Like I'm enough for you."

Silence.

"Because you are."

Love feels like a myth to me. A fluke. It's something

that's wrapped up in a pretty bow, but the moment you unwrap it, all that fills it is lies. But God, when I'm around him, it's like unwrapping that same box and finding it full of hope, promises, and happiness instead.

I'm in the middle of brushing my teeth when Caleb walks in, shirtless, and I freeze mid-brush.

"Mind if I brush too?" he asks, stepping closer. His forearm brushes against mine, sending a trail of goosebumps up my arm.

My eyes travel down his body through the mirror. He's only wearing a pair of grey sweatpants slung low on his hips, V-line on full display tonight. Damp fluffy hair, and black-framed glasses. My gosh, does he workout with the Avengers or something?

I continue brushing. "Not at all."

He grabs the toothpaste and with one precise squeeze, drags a line of minty blue paste onto his brush. As he brings it to his mouth, our eyes meet in the mirror. Heat rises in my chest as I try to focus on my own reflection.

He grins. He freaking grins.

Shortly after brushing, he leans over the sink to spit, his eyes still locked on mine. I should be grossed out, but why does that only turn me on? He finishes and flips down the faucet as he grabs the floss.

A few seconds later I finish brushing and turn the water back on, sneaking glances at him like I'm a freaking creep. I don't even realize how long I've been staring until he tosses the floss into the trash and jerks his chin toward the sink.

"Water's running."

And just like that, he strolls out, shutting the door behind him. He's gotta stop doing that to me. I can't take it. Seriously, how does he manage to make every mundane task so attractive?

It's so not fair.

33

CALEB

As Amelia finishes up brushing her teeth, I grab my backpack from the desk, unzip the front pocket, pull out a small bag I brought to fix up the pillows, and slip on a shirt.

The water shuts off and she emerges out of the bathroom. Her curls are piled up in a pineapple bun, skin glowing, lips glossy and full. She's wearing black mini shorts and a white tank top that clings in all the right places.

Her gaze drops to the bed. "That wasn't there earlier."

I shrug.

She runs her fingers along the smooth satin pillows. "Why in the world did you pack silk pillowcases? I have my bonnet."

"Options. At least now you have a bonnet *and* silk pillowcases."

"Thanks, you're not wrong. I need a new bonnet with a tie, though. The one I have now ends up halfway across the room by morning." She laughs before climbing into bed, dramatically building a pillow wall.

"Is that really necessary?" I chuckle as she perfectly aligns it in the middle.

She smacks the middle to fluff it out a few times. "Yes. I don't want those dogs anywhere near me." She points at my feet, playfully.

"Very funny." I wave her off. "And my 'dogs' are neatly trimmed, thank you very much."

I switch off the light, leaving the room dim, and crawl into bed near the window. "Switch sides with me."

"What?" She flattens the pillows with one hand, glaring at me. "No. I'm comfortable already."

"Please?"

"Ugh, why?" she groans. "You're already over there."

"I need to be by the front door."

"What difference does it make?"

"Because unless a man wants to climb up 180 feet to break in, at least I'll see them first."

"Why assume it's a man?" she counters.

"Because men are the worst."

"Not all of them," her eyes soften, before caving in. "Fine, but I'm too lazy to get up and—"

"Just get over here." I chuckle, reaching over the pillow wall. My hand finds her slim waist, and I tug gently only for her to land right on top of me. She sucks in a sharp breath, her silky thighs now straddling my hips, eyes wide as we both freeze.

I could make a joke like I usually do, at least it won't be awkward for her but the air shifts into something more tense as my chest rises and falls slowly, each breath deeper than the last.

The silence between us lingers, and I can't help but notice the little things, how a few loose curls rest against her forehead, the gentle flutter of her lashes, the slight part of her lips.

And her scent...it's different tonight. Usually, it's strawberries. But now, it's something warmer. Sweeter.

Vanilla.

Jesus.

If I thought strawberry smelled good, this is heaven. The scent wraps around me, pulling all my focus.

Then she presses her hands on my chest like she's about to push herself off but her hips shift just enough that I can feel the pressure of my length against her through the thin fabric.

"Oh," she mumbles so faintly I almost miss it.

Shit, that feels good.

She starts rolling her hips again, hesitant, unsure. It's slow like she's testing me...or herself. Each shift makes it harder for me to stay still.

She rocks her hips again, just lightly, and if she doesn't stop, I might come like this.

I shake my head, resting my hands firmly on her hips. "What are you doing?"

Her eyes widen again, embarrassment written all over her face and I curse in my head.

"Oh my god," she stammers, trying to scramble off me. "I don't know why I did that—"

"No," I say, my voice husky. "If you're gonna do that, don't hold back. Put all your weight on me."

I ease her hips fully down so she feels the outline of my hardness.

She lets out a quiet moan and the sound alone sends a rush of heat straight to my cock...it's so hard, it borders on painful.

"What do you want, Amelia?"

She bites the inside of her lip, looking everywhere but at me.

I bring one hand from her hip to the nape of her neck, tilting her head down until she has no choice but to look into my eyes. "Look at me and tell me what you want."

I barely recognize my voice. It's rough and desperate. Because I am.

She hesitates for a moment, then without my guidance, she rolls her hips on her own.

"Shit," I whimper. "You're still not telling me, princess."

I have never fucking whimpered a day in my life.

"Right now? I just want to continue this," she whispers.

"Want me to be quiet?"

She nods, slow and uncertain, like she's afraid that if I speak, it'll shatter whatever this moment is.

I'll shut up. She can take whatever the hell she wants from me, until my very last breath.

Sliding my hands back down to her sides, I memorize every curve and dip before gripping her hips tightly again. I gently rock her back and forth over my aching length, slower.

She can feel all of me. I know she can. Her fingers fist the material of my shirt as she rubs me, picking up speed.

Heat floods in my stomach, and I can feel myself getting harder with every roll of her hips. She wants me to be quiet but I don't know how much longer I can hold back.

"Ah," she exhales, a breathy groan slipping past her lips.

She rests her forehead against mine, our lips inches apart as she rides me harder. I can tell she's getting close by the way her breathing changes.

My chest rises and falls rapidly as she takes what she

wants and I thrust my hips, pressing harder against her core, holy fuck.

"Oh my god," she whines.

Her hands grip my shoulders as she moves faster, pushing us further to the edge. Our breathing grows heavier until we're panting, she moans louder, her back arches, and I know she's about to come.

The shrill ring of her phone cuts through the moment, shattering it into a thousand pieces.

Amelia startles, her body jerking in shock as she climbs off of me faster than I could blink. I frustratingly turn my head to glance at her, already on the other side of the pillows, her breath still uneven as she clears her throat, reaching for her phone on the nightstand to check who's calling.

The screen lights up against her flushed face, before she presses it to her ear.

"Tia...hey yeah the caterers will um, be there tomorrow," she answers, her voice shaky.

I groan, scratching my eyebrow before letting my head fall back restlessly against the pillow, closing my eyes.

Cockblocker award goes to...

34

AMELIA

The sun shines through the curtains of our hotel room and I stir.

Something warm wraps around me, pulling me in closer, and it feels so good. I blink slowly, my brows pinching together as I peek down and see brown floppy hair, a white shirt, tanned arms, and biceps filling my vision.

Oh my god. Caleb's cuddling me.

His arms drape over me, resting against the curve of my waist, and the faint scent of him drifts through my nostrils, comforting in ways that makes my pulse flutter.

I can't help running my fingers through his hair, feeling each delicate strand slide between them. His grip tightens around me, sending a jolt of electricity through my body.

"Mmmm," he groans, half-asleep.

My hands still.

"Don't stop." He nestles into me more.

This moment feels like second nature to me as my fingers move on their own, slipping through his hair, scratching his scalp as he stirs and moans, last night flashing through my mind.

Look at me and tell me what you want.

What possessed me to do that? I feel like I'm going insane with how he makes me feel. Every word, every touch, every look.

I want him.

But could I really have him? How complicated will that be? Could you imagine me saying "Oh hey by the way ever since we kissed my feelings for you have changed. I know this is all fake but maybe me and you could be more?"

I'd sound insane.

"Keep touching me." He stirs, burying his face in my neck as his lips brush my throat, lower heat pooling in my belly.

Okay I have to get up. I can't stay here. We have so much to do to set up for our guests and I can't afford to lose focus.

"Caleb," I murmur.

He groans, holding me tighter, squeezing me in a way that sends a signal straight down to my core. No. No. Not the time.

"Hey," I whisper-yell. "Time to wake up."

He finally rolls over to his side, and I suddenly feel cold, the warmth of his body slipping away.

"Yeah?" His morning voice low, deeper sending a little shiver down my spine.

He blinks up at me, his eyes still heavy, then sits up against the headboard, stretching his arms behind his head. His muscles flex, and the veins in his forearms are so prominent that I can't look away.

"Last night was something," He says lazily, turning his

head to meet my eyes. "Got a little carried away...didn't we?"

The air between us thickens faster than cornstarch in boiling water, and I swallow hard shifting uncomfortably in bed as I rub the back of my neck. "We did...um I hope things won't be awkward between us but——"

"We can just forget about it, yeah?" he sighs, rubbing his jaw.

Forget about it? My stomach twists as I try to keep my face neutral. He's brushing this off like it was nothing. But it meant something to me.

That was only a fun night for him. Nothing more.

My shoulders sag, feeling a sting in my heart. "Right. We can forget about it. Cool."

"Come on," he says, reaching out to pinch my chin. "Let's go be the best couple we can be."

I scan the outdoor venue Tia and Amir booked for today's event, making sure everything is running smoothly. Rock boulders surround a small waterfall, and purple jacaranda flowers are in full bloom all around.

All the guests are showing up today and I'm praying to avoid the relationship topic now that Caleb's my date but knowing his Aunt Barbara...I don't think that's happening.

Maya and I move between the tables, placing the cute yellow menus as the caterers set down the plates and utensils.

"Thanks guys. You're really helping me out," Tia groans, making her way toward me, exhaustion etched across her face.

"That's what maid of honors are for," I grin. "Now go

away. Just greet everyone up front." I give her a playful nudge.

"Don't ruin your manicure." Maya laughs, shooing her away. "We got this."

Later that afternoon, we see all of her family arrive, glancing around the venue and greeting Amir and Tia up front. Then I spot my parents.

"Show time," I murmur at Caleb behind me as he gently kneads my shoulders.

"Hi, anak!" Mom squeals, running up and wrapping me in a tight hug.

I exhale a deep breath, feeling her warmth, realizing how much I've missed her.

"Wow. Ang ganda mo!" I blatantly admire my mom, taking in her teal maxi wraparound dress and shoulder length brown hair speckled with caramel highlights. "I love this new color on you."

She tosses her hair over her shoulder dramatically. "Salamat, I wanted to try something new."

Dad then steps up, his deep brown skin glowing, looking sharp as ever in his suit as he pulls me into a hug, giving my shoulders a firm squeeze. "You look beautiful."

"Thanks, dad." I smile warmly.

"Kamusta ka na Mrs. Taylor," Caleb's voice behind me, warm. "Mr. Taylor, great to see you again."

Hold on, since when did he know Tagalog?

He steps around me, giving my mom a hug first. She squeezes him so tight he might just pop, before she pulls back as he and my dad hug.

"When did you start learning?!" My mom asks.

He lets out a small chuckle. "Ilang buwan na," he says, pausing to rub the back of his neck. "I'm trying."

Okay wait…his pronunciation is actually so good.

"Nonsense. You're a natural," my father corrects him, as Caleb gives him a firm handshake. "You already know how to respond. That's amazing, son."

"Thank you." Caleb's eyes gleam, the look in them showing that he feels like he's done something right. This is how he should always feel.

"Let's go find the soon to be married couple!" my mom exclaims.

"Yes, let's go." My dad reaches for my mom's hand, leading her in. "We'll see you guys later."

Facing Caleb I look up into his eyes curiously. "So you've been learning Tagalog." I state.

He peers down at me, the sun shining behind him creating a warm glow around him. "Yeah."

"You never told me."

"Wanted to surprise you." He grins, slowly slipping his hands into his pockets. "Did it work?"

"Oo," I smile, saying yes in Tagalog.

An hour later I'm holding a glass of Moët champagne, chatting with Marcus when my eyes flick toward the arched flower garden foyer.

Caleb's parents. Crap.

"Want my champagne?" My eyes anxiously lock onto Marcus as I quickly pass him the glass, a little splashing over the top.

"I won't turn it down," he says, taking the champagne from me. "Why are you in such a rush?"

"Caleb's parents just got here." I jerk my head toward the entrance behind him.

He peers over his shoulder. "Shit."

"I'll catch up with you later okay," I say before scurrying off toward Caleb before his parents get to him, my heels nearly sinking into the grass.

I crash into Caleb, latching onto his arms as he looks down at me, confused. "Need me to carry you?"

"No," I chuckle. "But ask me again at the end of the night and my answer might be different."

"Caleb," his dad's voice startles me, and we quickly turn to face him. I straighten my posture. "Amelia," he smiles, but it's so small you'd need a magnifying glass to see it.

Thomas and Christine Hayes.

Caleb's almost a carbon copy of Thomas, just a smidge shorter, maybe by an inch. His short grey pompadour is perfectly styled, his goatee neatly trimmed. He's wearing a navy-blue suit tailored to fit his broad shoulders.

"Mom, Dad!" Tia shrieks from behind me, rushing forward with Amir giving them big hugs.

Christine tugs Caleb and Tia into a soft hug, rubbing their backs up and down with her pointed French tip nails. She murmurs something in Caleb's ear that I can't quite make out. It makes him smile, causing a ripple effect onto me.

"Hi, sweetie," Thomas says, pulling Tia into a hug as Caleb withdraws, his expression tightening.

I notice his tenseness, his shoulders taut and jaw clenched. Without thinking, I slip my hands around his waist, snuggling into his side. Small gesture but his body loosens up a fraction.

"You two seem serious," Thomas comments, glancing down at my hand around Caleb. "Thought it'd be over by now."

"Don't say things like that," Christine chides, tucking a strand of blonde hair behind her ear. Her blue eyes bore into her husband's sharply.

"What, honey? I'm honest. Never pictured him as the

settling type at this age. That's all." He shrugs, his emerald eyes flickering between Caleb and me.

"And why not?" Caleb retorts, snaking his hand around me and rests it on my hip. "You don't think I'm capable of committing?"

"No, it's not that." Thomas laughs bitterly. "I'm just curious why you're busy flirting instead of focusing on your career. You don't want too many distractions, right?"

I'm standing right here. Seriously? I want nothing more than to curse him out, to let him have it for once. I clench my jaw so tight, I'm almost certain there's a gigantic vein about to split my forehead in half.

"My relationship doesn't interfere," Caleb scoffs. "And if you're gonna stand here and insinuate that Amelia's a distraction to me then you're out of damn mind."

"Dad?" Tia's face falls, her nostrils flaring. "Seriously?"

Amir looks between all of us, scratching the back of his head, as he pulls Tia closer to him.

Thomas looks at Tia and sighs. "Can't I ask a simple—"

Christine starts to speak but Tia beats her to it, voice fiercer than I've ever heard it. "It's none of your business what Caleb's doing. He's a grown man and more than capable of being in a relationship and focusing on football. Just because you couldn't doesn't mean he can't. You're lucky Mom even got back together with you. You're being an asshole Dad," she snaps, stepping closer to her father.

"Tia, stop. It's fine," Caleb shakes his head, but she narrows her eyes at him.

"I wasn't finished." She snaps, turning back to her dad glowering. "This is my wedding week. You're here to support me and Amir, and this is the first thing you do? If you can't keep your stupid comments to yourself and can't respect that, don't bother staying. I'll personally book you a flight back."

Silence. The only sounds are distant chatter fading into the background and the wind rustling through the palm trees.

In all my years of knowing them, Tia has never raised her voice at either of her parents. She's always been their princess.

I remember when she couldn't get an appointment with a popular nail tech that does all the celebrities' red-carpet nails, so he paid triple the price to secure a booking last minute.

Thomas' expression falters, caught off guard by Tia's outburst. He presses his lips into a fine line and pinches the bridge of his nose.

"Let's just enjoy the wedding, okay?" Christine says solemnly, trying to ease this unwanted tension.

"Yeah and while we're at it, how about we avoid this bullshit all together? Don't bother speaking to me from now on." Caleb stares at his father before slipping away from my arms, stalking toward the main office of the venue.

"Caleb!" I call out, reaching for his arm but he's out of my reach.

Tia's eyes start to glisten.

"Sweetie—" her dad starts.

"No. You've done more than enough, just um... find your seats." She sniffs trying to hold it together, gesturing toward the tables.

Christine reaches for her daughter, squeezing her shoulder. "I'm sorry, baby." Then leads her husband through the venue.

"Come here," Amir says, smoothing back Tia's hair and kissing her forehead.

I squeeze Tia's arm. "I'll find Caleb, okay?"

She looks at me, offering a small smile that doesn't quite reach her eyes. "Thanks."

"Of course." I rush out, hurriedly following him inside while I squeeze myself between tables.

Maya grabs my arm gently. "Woah, woah, what's going on? Why's Caleb so pissed off?"

"He, uh, ate something bad," I lie, terribly.

Caleb doesn't really talk about how strained his relationship is with his father. Only Marcus and I know outside of Tia and his mom. It's not something he goes telling people unless they happen to overhear an argument. It's not my business to tell.

Maya raises a brow, clearly seeing through the lie, but she doesn't push. "Tell him to drink ginger-ale," she says. "Hope he feels better."

Entering the cold air-conditioned building, my goosebumps rise, and the workers I spoke to when we arrived are still sitting at the front desk.

"Have you seen a tall, brown-haired guy come through here?" I ask, motioning the word tall with my hands.

One of the ladies nods, gesturing to the waiting area. "He headed down that way toward the restrooms."

I say a quick thank you, quickening my pace down the hall. There's a waiting area next to the bathroom with a few brown chairs.

"Caleb?" my voice echoes throughout the quiet building, my heels clacking against the tile.

He rises from one of the chairs, turning around to meet me. "Sorry for storming off like that, I just had to get some space."

Shaking my head, taking his hand in mine, I rub my thumb against his. "Are you okay?"

"I am." He exhales. "I'm just tired of having the same conversations. It's exhausting."

"I know." I sigh, cupping his jaw, tilting his head down as I rest his forehead against mine, standing in the comfortable silence.

Words aren't always necessary, it's being with one another that truly makes a difference.

35

AMELIA

I WANDER OUTSIDE, TENDING TO MY MAID OF HONOR DUTIES as I make my way toward the arch flower garden foyer to check for any more arriving guests when Marcus rushes up to me out of breath, clamping his hands down onto my shoulders.

"Um, hi."

"Hi." His eyes dart around frantically, like he's searching for an escape route. Then, without any type of warning he twists me around, steering me back the way I came.

"What are you doing?" I ask, baffled.

"I just wanted to hang out with you over there."

I halt. "Okay, what's going on?" I turn around to face him as suspicion is creeping in and then I see *him*.

Jared is here, with Kim.

Marcus groans, kneading my shoulders chastely. "Was trying to save you from seeing him but I failed."

That's sweet.

Marcus continues to swiftly steer me through the tables, weaving through everyone until we reach Caleb.

"Code red," Marcus spews out, stopping me abruptly behind Caleb like I'm a car.

Caleb's at the table, focused on organizing the games on the iPad Maya handed him. The ones we'll be playing as part of the wedding festivities later today. He pauses, locks the tablet and gets up. His eyes flick to Marcus then down to me. "Code red?"

If I know Marcus at all, he's definitely rolling his eyes. "Code red as in jackass is behind us somewhere."

Caleb's muscles tense.

"I can handle myself, you know?" I scoff, even though I appreciate the heads-up.

"We know," Marcus and Caleb say in unison.

Marcus spins me to face him, his voice perfectly dipped with sarcasm. "Have I ever told you how much I hate that jackass?"

"All the time."

"Okay good. Just double checking." He plasters on the fakest smile known to man before walking off.

"How you feeling?" Caleb asks, searching my face.

Honestly, I thought I'd feel doleful seeing Jared again. It's the total opposite, actually.

A part of me will always be curious as to why he made his decision. He told me briefly back in LA but it didn't make any sense.

I always knew you weren't mine.

Like what the hell? All four years I was with him. I never swayed, never batted an eyelash at another man. It was only him. I kinda wish I knew what he meant by that.

"Honestly? I'm more than fine."

"Good." Caleb grins. "I want to be the only one on your mind baby," he cups my face pressing his lips on mine.

My heart stumbles at the sound of Caleb's voice calling me baby. Did he mean to say that? I lean in to kiss him again, chasing the warmth, but he pulls back.

Then I hear a familiar voice.

"Hey," Jared's voice cuts through from behind me.

Oh. That's why. The fantasy bubble I created now cracks into tiny pieces. I swallow down the lump in my throat. It's humiliating how fast I was ready to believe it was real, that for a second I believed he felt something for me too.

"Oh hi," I mumble back to Jared.

Beside me, Caleb's hand brushes my lower back ready to give his Oscar worthy performance as my boyfriend.

"It's nice seeing you two again. You guys are seriously the cutest." Kim beams, giving a small wave. "I've been dying to know how he asked you out? I hope I'm not too forward but I'm such a hopeless romantic."

Caleb and I should've prepared flash cards because I have no idea how to answer this question. I don't want to make it over the top…maybe I can tweak a scene from a movie and pray she doesn't catch on.

"Actually… we used to go to Manhattan Beach all the time as kids." Caleb says, breaking up my thoughts. My head snaps up at him.

That place holds a lot of memories for us. There were times I just couldn't focus studying at the library or at home. I needed to get away, so we'd pack a picnic basket and stay out there all evening until the sun set.

"We used to go there all the time and one night, I don't know, I just couldn't stop staring," he adds and my pulse races with every word. "Never could get her out of my head."

His gaze drops to mine. "I knew she was the one I wanted to be with since then. I'd be an idiot to let her slip from my fingers any longer than I already have. I'd regret it for the rest of my life. I just never had the courage to ask her to be my girlfriend until recently."

"Awww," Kim coos and grips Jared's arm. "Stop. That's adorable. You two are so getting married next."

Caleb's eyes are still on mine, unwavering, and goosebumps dance across my skin despite the warm breeze outside. He seems so sincere, it almost feels true. And for a split second, I let myself bask in it.

"Yeah, he's the best." I say, my eyes softening.

"Take care of her. She deserves the world," Jared says.

"You don't have to tell me that." Caleb tucks my hair behind my ear, his fingers lingering on my jaw. "I know."

My breathing grows heavier before I sever our eye contact and look at Kim. I'm not letting myself get sucked into this fantasy any longer than necessary.

"Right." Jared clears his throat. "You always did."

Amir's mother calls out to Jared, her voice excited. "Get your butt over here, nephew!" Kim and Jared both excuse themselves from us as they walk over.

"I don't know what you saw in him," Caleb says as his fingers trail up and down my sides.

"You don't see it?"

"No. He has the looks I guess, but so do I," he jokes.

"Who said you had the looks?"

"Your body did last night," he murmurs low, kissing the top of my forehead. The faint scent of his cologne wraps around me as he brushes past.

Blood flushes to my cheeks.

Maya begins banging the microphone with her palm to see if it's working, it blares with a screeching sound. "Sorry guys, Testing. Testing."

She finally speaks into it, beckoning everyone over to find their seats. "Time to play The Couples Quiz! We need someone to ask each pair a set of questions to test their compatibility!" She adds excitedly, standing on the flat wooden platform to oversee everyone.

I sink into my seat next to Caleb, my attention locking on her.

Across the yard, my parents are seated with Caleb's parents chatting about who knows what. Thomas is smiling wide though, I wish he'd stay that way when talking to his son.

"I'll ask!" Caleb's Aunt Barbara walks up to Maya as her dark brown bob and floral dress sway to grab the microphone.

Dear lord.

"Perfect." Maya hands her a flashcard.

Marcus brings out two wooden stools placing them down beside each other, then sets a dry erase marker and board on top.

"Okay each pair will come up and Barbara will ask a question while the couple writes down their answers for each other," she instructs, talking with her hands. "Whoever has the most points will win...um...nothing but at least you had fun," she quickly smiles.

Sounds easy enough.

Stepping off the stage, Maya walks past all the participating pairs, handing out a sheet filled with the questions.

Maya leans down whispering in my ear, "You and Caleb better win."

"I thought this wasn't a competition?"

"It's not, but you better get more than him," she whisper-yells, shooting a glare at Jared.

"Will do my best." I grin, taking the pen from her.

The first couple to play by force are Marcus and Maya. Tia wanted them to participate in the game instead of being the coordinators, even though they're definitely going to lose.

"If they could have dinner with any fictional character, who would it be?" Barbara asks.

They start writing, and Maya's face betrays her because she has zero confidence in what he just wrote down.

"Flip!" she calls out.

They flip their boards and I stifle a laugh.

"Jessica Rabbit." he jabs a finger at her board. "Best answer you could've given."

Maya on the other hand snaps, looking at Marcus's board. "Sebastian? As in the fucking crab?"

Marcus grins, erasing his board.

Barbara lets out another small laugh. "Language!"

"Shit." Maya slaps a hand over her mouth. "I'm so sorry."

Everyone chuckles.

"What's each other's favorite hobby?" Barbara continues.

They both jot something down quickly.

"Flip!"

Marcus turns his head, leaning down to read her board. "Oh, you got jokes, huh?"

Getting ghosted by every woman he talks to.

Maya starts erasing her board, crossing her legs. "I mean, it's something that happens often, so I assumed you were doing it on purpose, no?"

"Or maybe you're jealous you're not the one I'm flirting with." Marcus teases, then flips his board over.

Getting on my nerves.

Maya rolls her eyes. "Original."

As the questions went on the worse the board answers became. They ended up scoring a 5/10 on compatibility. Those points were given as a courtesy.

Maya and Marcus find their seats bickering like an old married couple as Barbara calls the next pair. "Caleb and Amelia, you're up next!"

Caleb rises from his seat, holding his hand out for me and I take it as we walk across the grass and sit on the wooden stools.

My eyes scan the venue, but Jared's intense stare makes me uneasy. Why is he looking at me so hard?

She asks the first question. "Who's the better cook?"

I write down my answer with this almost dried-up marker, then hold the board against my chest, waiting for Barbara.

"Flip!" she says.

Both of our boards reveal his name.

I burst out laughing. "I'm gonna learn! Frozen pizza is getting boring."

Caleb smiles, gripping the edge of my stool, sliding me across the wooden platform next to him with ease, kissing my temple. "I'll cook for you, don't worry about it."

My stomach twists in knots, god he's really good at this.

Barbara chuckles, asking the next question. "If your partner could eat one snack forever, what would it be?"

He lets out a throaty laugh already writing down his answer before she even properly finishes the question.

I take a second shaking the marker to get some more ink, writing down mine.

"Alright, flip those boards!" she twirls her finger, gesturing to us.

Caleb flips his first.

Nougat cocoa + Leche flan

I grin, leaning in as I murmur quietly. "I think you know me too well at this point, is there anything you don't know?"

"No." He meets my eyes. "I remember every single detail regarding you."

I swallow hard, his gaze dropping to my lips, before I clear my throat and flip my board.

Halo-Halo.

My mom shouts from the crowd to Caleb. "I know that's right!"

"You've got me hooked, Mrs. Taylor!" Caleb shouts back.

After we finished all of the questions, we won the compatibility test with 10/10 as well as Tia and Amir.

As everyone goes back to chatting, Barbara comes up behind us as Caleb and I start to stand.

"Looks like the next couple to get married is you guys," she whispers in a giddy way. "Are you two thinking that far ahead?"

My body goes rigid as we turn toward her.

"We haven't talked about it, but if he popped the big question…I wouldn't say no."

Caleb steps behind me, loops his arms around my waist, and plants a gentle kiss on my neck that sends my pulse into overdrive. "I'd get on one knee right now, if I could."

I'd love for him to get on his knees too…

Oh, get a grip, Amelia.

"Look at my boy all grown up." Barbara pinches his

cheek. "I'm happy for you two. Me and your uncle are just like y'all. Can't keep our hands off each other."

Caleb's hands still on my waist, as his chest vibrates against my back. "Information we didn't need to know."

She waves him off with a chuckle. "Oh hush, that's a good sign you two are in love. When you feel like you can't be away from the other too long, missing their warmth. It's a good feeling. Hold on to that, alright?"

My gaze warms as she squeezes my cheek, and I can't help but smile as she heads toward her husband.

"And now what do you really think about it?" Caleb says turning me around by my hips to face him.

"Of marriage?" I hum, pushing my curls behind my ear, I'm starting to get over stimulated with all this lovey dovey talk, sweat is starting to gather at the back of my neck.

Caleb pulls out a scrunchie from his pocket, handing me it.

"Thanks." I take it, flipping my hair over and twisting it into a messy bun, pulling a few strands loose to frame my face. "And, I do believe in it. I think it's a beautiful way to show how committed you are to someone." I bite the inside of my cheek. "Seeing my parents happily married makes me want that someday."

"Whoever wins your heart is one lucky man."

Those words catch me off guard and my eyes snap to his just in time to see the faint twitch of his lips.

"Yeah, hopefully they don't think I'm too much." I admit, letting out a weak puff of air past my lips.

"It'll never be too much for the right person. Trust me, princess."

A few days pass and one of the things on Tia's itinerary is paddle boarding. I didn't complain about it but in my world, I belong on solid ground only. Am I a scaredy cat? Yes.

"So, let me get this straight, I'm supposed to balance myself on *that?*" I ask the instructor, Luka, one more time, squinting my eyes toward the skinny ass board hanging on the rustic shop wall. "It's quite small don't you think?"

He shakes his dark hair, amused. "No, but don't worry, I'll be with you every step of the way."

"And if I fall?"

"Then I'll catch you or at least save you from drowning," he says with a wink.

Oh. He's flirting.

"No need. I've got her." Caleb holds my hand, gently leading me toward the other gear.

Thirty minutes later we make our way to the beach while the rest of the family sits comfortably nearby, phones in hand and ready to film an embarrassing video of us if we fall.

How sweet of them.

"So, hold the board near the edges, kneel down to stand up, and when you get in the water, rise with your chest." Luka instructs as we practice on the sand first. "Keep your knees, elbows, and waist slightly bent and have your feet facing forward."

I follow his directions exactly, bending down as Luka moves behind me making sure my hands are in the right position.

Heat spreads through my body, and it's not from the sun, nor from Luka, but from Caleb. He's watching me or correction... staring.

Arms folded, head tilted, analyzing my every move. His gaze feels like it's burning right through my bikini.

Caleb takes long strides toward me, tucking the board under his arm, holding the paddle in one hand. Luka must notice as he backs away almost instantly to go help Tia and Amir.

I squint up at Caleb, the sun in my eyes doing nothing to hide the ridges of his muscles on full display. His sunglasses push back his hair, and a few brown strands fall across his forehead. He looks as handsome as ever.

He ducks down to my eye level and swiftly takes off his sunglasses. Then he places them on my face, his fingers brushing my temples as he adjusts them so they're not crooked.

"He keeps hovering around you like a damn mosquito," he mutters, rolling his eyes.

"Jealous?"

"Yes."

Before I can process how quickly he answered, Luka claps his hands. "Alright it's time to get into the water. Carefully attach the leash to your ankles."

The words barely leave his mouth before Caleb's on his knees, taking my leash, securing it around my ankle with ease.

My core pulses (completely against my will) and is definitely getting the wrong idea about him being on his knees. Dang it.

He peers up at me fastening the straps, his thumb grazing my ankle before pulling away. "There." He then briskly fastens his own.

We step into the cool water, the sound of our family and friends cheering us on drifts from the beach. Ignoring the noise, I set my board down and steady myself, climbing on and settling into a kneeling position.

Gripping the paddle, I plunge it into the water, propelling myself forward as I edge deeper into the waves.

I bend my knees and use the board for balance as I push myself up to stand. I wobble, muscles trembling as the board rocks beneath me, but I force myself to find balance and stand tall.

"I did it!"

"You always can," he says, paddling in small motions beside me.

We paddle around for a few minutes, getting the hang of it, then a small ripple throws me off balance, water almost splashes all over me but thankfully I catch myself.

"Careful." Caleb's eyes rake down my body and my breath stutters. "You're gonna get wet."

I tsk, murmuring to myself. "Too late for that."

36

CALEB/AMELIA

CALEB

My sister's sitting along the water, looking deep in thought as her fingers tremble. I tilt my head, confused, walking over to her.

"Hey, you good?" I lightly smack her arm, dropping down beside her. "Where's Amir?"

"He's returning the paddle boards." Tia says inhaling a deep breath. "I'm just thinking about the wedding. I want it to be perfect."

"And it will be," I reassure her.

"For how long though? How long until dad makes you want to pull your hair out?"

Tia never fully understood how much our father's words truly affected me growing up, and how much it still does even though I try to brush it off.

And honestly, I don't want her to. There's a reason for it.

She sees him in a way I never could. To her, he's the man who showed up to every field trip with packed snacks, took her on shopping sprees when she brought home a good report card, who beamed with pride when she got into college. That's the dad she knows. The dad I wish I had.

I rest a hand on her shoulder, giving it a gentle squeeze as my expression grows serious. "He knows how much this means to you. He won't mess it up again."

"Yeah, I guess." She offers a fragile smile as tears well up in her eyes.

"Stop doing that."

She sniffs, blinking with unshed tears. "I'm not doing anything."

I reach out, brushing my thumbs against the corners of her eyes. "No crying shit during your wedding week."

Later that night, we're back in the hotel room after a long day at the beach. I'm so ready to crash out if only Amelia would finish in the bathroom. She's been in there for what feels like hours.

"You almost done?" I call out from the couch. "Are you doing a 50-step skin care routine?"

"Impatient now, are we?" She snickers, the bathroom door muffling her voice. Then she slides the door open and her face is covered white with tiny black dots.

"What the hell is on your face?" My brows furrow, walking inside the bathroom toward her to inspect it. It smells like cookies and cream. "And is that a spatula?"

She looks at me like I asked the dumbest question on earth as she waves it in the air. "It's called a silicone brush applicator," she says matter of factly.

"Looks like a spatula to me," I roll my eyes, poking at the other clean end.

"Fine," she laughs, turning toward the mirror again, spreading out the white mask on her chin. "It's a spatula.

BUT silicone brush sounds so much more sophisticated don't you think?"

Her words sort of fade as I admire her.

"And second, it's a cookies and cream pore detox mask."

I have no clue what that is but she could talk me through her entire skincare routine and I'd pull up a chair taking notes.

I step back, resting my hands behind me on the white porcelain tub, still looking at her through the mirror. "What does that do exactly?"

"It helps with the blackheads." She meets my eyes, chuckling with her mouth open so it doesn't disrupt the cream. "Can I please put it on you?"

I knew I'd end up wearing it, it was only a matter of time.

"Let me shower first, then you can do whatever you want to me." I hold her gaze, reaching behind me with one hand to grip the collar of my shirt.

I pull it over my head before tossing it onto the gray wooden floor.

Her eyes travel slowly down my chest to my stomach, igniting something deep and fervent within my gut.

"Okay," she says before scurrying out of the bathroom.

Ten minutes later, her alarm buzzes outside the door while warm water streams down my body. I pop open the top of my shampoo bottle just as a soft tapping sounds at the door.

"Caleb?"

"Yeah?" I reply, squeezing the shampoo into my palm.

"Can I come in for a second to rinse it off?"

"I'm kinda busy," I say, running shampoo through my hair as it lathers.

The shower is frosted glass so she wouldn't see anything but I wouldn't mind if she did.

"Only for a few seconds and I'll be out." She groans through the door. "My face is cracking as we speak."

I can't help but shake my head and laugh. "Door's open."

"Thanks," she answers as the wooden door slides open, letting in a cold breeze as I close my eyes, washing my hair.

Her footsteps tap against the floor as the faucet begins to run for a few minutes before she leaves.

After finishing up, I crack open the glass door reaching for the white towel hanging on the hook. Wrapping it around my waist, tucking it in securely, as I step out.

The bathroom door is half open, so I pad over to close it. Just as I reach for the handle, it slides open and something smacks me square in the chest.

Or rather someone.

"Shit," I whisper, gripping the fabric tighter as my towel nearly comes undone.

"Sorry!" she blurts out, pressing her hands against my damp chest. "I heard the water stop running... I just needed to grab my phone."

I love when she touches me.

"I'll let you finish," she stammers, realizing her hands are still on my chest as she yanks them away like she was about to get burned. Then she quickly turns around to leave.

"Didn't you need something?"

"Oh," she lightly smacks her forehead as she freezes. "Right!" She steps closer, her pajamas brushing against my chest, sending a wave of warmth through me.

She snatches her phone off the counter and slams the sliding door shut behind her.

I unwrap my towel, slipping into my plaid bottoms and grey shirt.

"Do I have to do anything before the mask?" I call out, glancing at the serums and moisturizers perfectly lined up against the mirror.

"Wash your face with that cleanser." she shouts back. "Green bottle on the right."

I follow her directions, then slide the door open until it bounces against the hinge, seeing her sprawled out on the bed waiting. "I'm all yours."

AMELIA

I'm leaning against the sink as he towers in front of me, bending down just enough so I can brush his thick hair back. I start applying the mask to his forehead, the thick cream sliding smoothly across his skin.

He closes his eyes, humming

"You like it?" I chuckle.

"Mhm."

I continue, applying the cream in light strokes to coat every inch but a stubborn strand of hair keeps falling in his face. I blow on it gently, but it refuses to budge.

I huff, setting the container and brush down, then spin around to dig through my makeup bag.

"What happened?" He pouts, opening his eyes as I turn back to face him.

"Wear this." I fight back a grin as I hand him a fuzzy fuchsia headband.

"First a face mask and now this?" He complains but takes it from me anyway, slipping it over his head.

"You look adorable." I tease, reaching up to gently rub the fuzzy fabric.

"I'm not supposed to look adorable."

"Too late." I grab my spatula again, dipping it a few more times into the container as I cup one side of his face. "Bend down a little."

He listens, lowering his head to my level until he's so close, I can feel his breath ghost against my skin.

Then, in one swift motion, his hands grip my hips and hoist me onto the counter. My breath catches in my throat, my legs parting on instinct, making space for him to step between them.

"Better?" he asks, tilting his head.

"Uh…yeah." Much better if I'm being honest.

He plants his hands on either side of me, caging me in so I can finish.

His lips hover close, and a slow heat spreads across my cheeks. The closer I am to him, the harder it is to resist wanting to kiss him.

"We should take a picture together," I say, swiping the last bit of cream onto his other cheek as it starts to dry. I grab my phone and set the timer. "Proof that you're still a good boyfriend," I tease.

This is my poor excuse to get even closer to him and that's all I want right now.

"I definitely don't want to disappoint," he chuckles, before gripping my hips and lifting me off the counter. Then he grabs his phone, handing it to me. "Want to do the honors?"

I nod. Turning around and facing the mirror. "Let's do a mirror pic."

Caleb's expression shifts, playful but a hint of something else I can't pick up.

"Where do you want me?"

"Wrap your arms around my waist and kiss my neck,

check…whichever one you want."

There's a slight hitch in my voice as I say it but I'm using this to my advantage while I battle with this ongoing war with my feelings. His hands on me have become my new favorite thing. Any time he's near me there's this electrifying feeling I can't ignore.

It's never enough.

"That I can do." He moves slowly, snaking one hand around my stomach, pulling me against his chest, his heart beating steadily against my back.

He lifts his free hand, gently sweeping my curls off one shoulder and draping them over the other. I swallow hard as butterflies stir in my stomach.

I point the camera toward the mirror trying to focus, but he's making it impossible to think straight.

Through the mirror, I watch him get closer to my neck, smudging some of the mask off, and making me giggle.

"Like this?" His lips linger on my skin, searching for the most sensitive spot below my ear.

"Yeah, perfect."

I exhale a deep breath, pressing the shutter button, but I don't know if he notices because he lingers a moment too long.

My heart pounds wildly in my chest, as his hands slip beneath the hem of my shirt, tracing the bare skin of my waist.

I stare at him through the mirror. When his eyes lift to meet mine, they're dark, pulling me deeper into the shadows.

His lips brush over my pulse, trailing hot, feather-light kisses up my neck before his teeth gently nip my ear. A low moan escapes me.

I flush my back into him, desperate for more friction,

anything. I spin around, fingers trembling as I grip the hem of his shirt, pulling him closer.

He cups one side of my face, his thumb tracing my bottom lip before tugging it. I part my lips, leaning in, craving the kiss.

The loud alarm blares, yanking us out of the moment. His fingers flex at his sides. "Fuck…" he curses under his breath.

"I'll let you wash your face." I blurt, snatching my phone off the counter and rush toward the bedroom, closing the door behind me.

I crawl into bed feeling Caleb's warmth lingering on me and I bury my face into the pillow, groaning.

This is driving me insane.

37

AMELIA

THE NEXT MORNING WE'RE ON A FERRY TO HARBOUR Island. It's been an hour, and I totally underestimated how sick the sea would make me. The only good thing to come from this is that we're going to see the famous Pink Sand Beach.

Maya and Marcus are knocked out. Amir and Tia are cuddled up. Caleb and I sit in the back while the rest of our family and friends fill the seats up front. My mom strolls over, wearing the largest wide-brimmed hat I've ever seen.

"Honey, you okay? You look a little dull," she says, settling on the other side of me. Her hand comes up to press gently against my forehead, her touch warm and soothing as she studies my face.

"The ocean and my stomach aren't exactly best friends right now," I groan, clutching my belly.

Tia glances my way, unzipping her yellow bag as she rummages through it.

My dad approaches from behind my seat, smoothing

my hair back, completely flattening the curls at the top but I don't mind.

Tia rises, walks over, and plops down on my lap. She cups my face in her hands and shakes my head side to side a little too fast. "You cannot get sick on me! Not this week," she exclaims.

"Really, Tia?" Caleb says, rolling his eyes as his sister manages to make me ten times more nauseous.

My stomach churns like butter and the world tilts sideways on its axis. I glare at her, swallowing down the nausea curling low in my gut. "And you just made it worse. Thank you so much for that."

"Sorry," she grimaces, pulling her hands back and glancing guilty between my parents. "Morning, Mr. And Mrs. Taylor."

My dad shakes his head with a chuckle, while my mom lifts Tia's legs to drape them over hers. I'm forever grateful for the relationship we all share.

"I want to curl into the fetal position and have someone roll me off this damn ferry."

"Can't do that. I'd miss you too much," Caleb murmurs, pressing a featherlight kiss to my temple. "I'll be right back." He adds with a small wink before wandering off.

He's playing the perfect boyfriend. Every small gesture makes me forget we're not actually together. The light touches on my back, the kisses to my forehead, the way he says things messes with my head. God, I feel pathetic.

It's not even new. He's always been sweet to me. But now? Now it makes me want to jump his freaking bones.

"We can't toss you off because we need you to sing Karaoke on our wedding night." Amir jokes from his seat.

"I think your ears will bleed if I do that."

"Lucky for you…you have me," Tia pulls out a new mini bottle of Pepto Bismol from her bag. "Sorry for making you feel worse but this will make up for it."

"Thanks. I didn't even know they made mini's." I let out a weak cackle.

She unscrews the cap, raising it to eye level, pouring the bright thick liquid to the line. "Drink up."

She hands it to me, and I chug it down in one swift gulp.

"Here," Caleb says quietly as he approaches, holding an ice-cold water bottle and hands me a pack of pretzels.

"Thanks baby—" the words slip out before I can stop. My eyes widen, panic growing. Desperate to cover it up, I start coughing obnoxiously, snatching the pretzels from him, the crinkle loud in my hands.

I'm beyond horrified. Why does the word baby feel so natural coming out of my lips? I never said it to Jared when we were together.

He doesn't say anything as he uncaps the water bottle and lifts it to my lips. I swallow the cool liquid, feeling the burn of Caleb's gaze on me.

"Welcome baby," he grins, sitting beside me as I take the bottle from him.

Pins and needles prick beneath my skin as my face flushes with heat.

My mom shoots me a look that says, *"When's the wedding?"*

She's been rooting for Caleb and me for as long as I can remember. He is quite literally the perfect man.

"He's good for you," my father whispers in my ear before him and my mom walk off to their seats and now I can't stop smiling like an idiot.

There's a flutter in my chest and I take another slow slip of water. Then I close the top and lean my head back against the seat, it's a little uncomfortable but I'll manage.

Caleb slips his arm around me, gently angling my head to rest on his shoulder. A light kiss presses to my forehead.

I close my eyes, nestling closer as his heartbeat thrums steadily against my ear, and it's the most comforting sound I've ever known.

"It's so beautiful here," I let out a content sigh, sitting on my knees as the pink particles slip through my fingers.

"Isn't it?" Tia says, tracing the sand.

"We should plan another trip here."

"I'm so down for that." Maya agrees, laying back to get a tan.

"You've always loved the beach," a deep voice behind me makes my body stiffen. My stomach coils into a perfectly tied knot as I glance over my shoulder and there he is.

Jared. His girlfriend's MIA today, she decided to sit this one out because she wasn't feeling well.

Maya glares up at him, and sits up. If looks could kill... he'd already be zipped in a body bag.

I stand up, dusting the sand off my white cover-up skirt.

"Can I talk to you?" He asks.

Tia shakes her head, eyes flicking between me and Jared. "Maybe you shouldn't."

"Yeah, go back on the ferry, see how your little girlfriend's doing," Maya snaps. "Get lost at sea while you're at it."

"Look, I just want to speak to Amelia real quick, that's all. I swear I'm not here to start anything," Jared says, rubbing the back of his neck.

I heave a sigh.

I can't avoid him forever. Maybe talking to him is what I need to close that chapter before I even consider telling Caleb how I've been feeling.

"It's fine," I say softly, glancing at my girls. "I'll catch up with you two later?"

Tia nods, but Maya on the other hand, shoots Jared a death glare. Tia gently shoos her away as they stroll toward Amir, Marcus, and Caleb near the umbrellas they set up.

Jared and I walk along the water, in silence for a few seconds. It's funny how once upon a time I was so in love with this man.

"Sorry. I'm a little nervous right now." He clears his throat. "We haven't talked like this, alone, in a while."

Wow, such an incredible observation Sherlock Holmes.

"Anyway, I wanted to say again that I'm truly sorry for what happened between us, there's no excuse for what I did."

The memories flood back to me again in an instant. Vivid and sharp. His phone lighting up. The text messages. The sinking feeling in my chest that made me feel like I was being weighed down by the ankles.

I bite the inside of my cheek, meeting his gaze. His eyes are familiar, warm, exactly like they used to be and it makes me wonder why he ruined us?

"I've always wondered if I was the problem." My voice is low, almost fragile.

"No." His eyes glisten with remorse. "God, no."

"So why did you do it?"

He reaches out to lightly touch my hand, and I flinch, not expecting the contact. But I don't pull away… not yet.

"I was so stressed with work and I felt like our relationship was…" he exhales, giving my hand a light squeeze, "losing its spark at the time."

Ouch.

"And you didn't think to talk to me about it? Give us a chance to figure it out? You just decided to cheat?" Anger boils in my stomach, but I try keeping it at bay.

"No!" He lazily tilts his head forward, frustrated. "I didn't mean to—"

"Who was she? Was it Kim?"

He shakes his head quickly. "No. It was just some random girl I met at a bar. Amelia I promise that month, I didn't feel like myself." His eyes lock on mine so intensely, it's like he's trying to etch his words into my memory. "I never meant to hurt you, us, I regret it every day since," his voice raw. "I loved you, you know that."

I swallow hard, tears threatening to spill. He loved me. Yet, he still did what he did. How could I believe anyone else after this?

"I always knew you weren't really mine." He steps closer, his presence looming over me as our hands remain in each other's.

Those were the exact same words he threw at me back in LA.

"I saw a future with you. Why the hell do you keep saying that?"

"You may have seen a future with someone else," he corrects me. "That's why I'm not surprised."

"Surprised?"

"You and Caleb. He's looked at you the same way since

I met you. He's been in love with you since high school, and it's about time he finally admitted it."

Time slows…Loved? Since when has Caleb ever looked at me in any way in high school? We were always friends, strictly platonic. There were no moments in school or even in college where he has ever flirted with me or insinuated at anything more. He was just being kind.

"It never bothered me because you never reciprocated it," he continues, gently rubbing the back of my hand. "But remember when he bought that wireless heating pad and brought it to school because your stomach had been cramping all week? I didn't even think of that. When we first started dating, I felt like the world's shittiest boyfriend. I couldn't compete with him."

Memories tumble back in… every moment Caleb was protective, attentive, always showing up without being asked. But as quickly as the thought comes, I try to shake it off. That's what best friends do, right?

"It wasn't a competition. You were still my boyfriend, Jared."

"I know that and I'm a piece of shit for what I did to you." His voice cracks. "It just got harder for me to accept that he's the one you were always meant to be with. I was selfish. I'm glad you two found each other, but I'm sorry I hurt you along the way. I hope we can someday be friends again."

I nod solemnly, a quiet weight settling in my chest. I don't think me and Jared could ever be friends anytime soon but for the sake of Tia and Amir, we can be cordial moving forward and grow from this.

"Thanks for giving me the chance to talk to you again." He gives my hand one last squeeze before walking away.

This was the closure I've been needing. It doesn't erase

the pain he caused me, but it's something I've been longing to hear.

Could Jared be right? Has Caleb loved me all along… and just been too nervous to admit it?

Should I be the one to tell him first?

38

CALEB

We've spent practically the entire day under the blazing sun, my muscles now heavy with exhaustion. Before calling it a night, we decide to take advantage of happy hour, savor a few drinks that warm my chest, and enjoy a late-night swim.

"I'll get us another round." I push back my chair.

"I'll come with you," Maya says, rising before I could say anything.

"Can I tell you something?" she says, her eyes burning into me, as we approach the bar. "You're an idiot."

"That's exactly what I love to hear when I'm talking to a friend," I say dryly, glancing down and meeting her stare, which may or may not be freaking me out. Why is she so scary?

"Any person with eyes can see how pathetic you are for her," she says bluntly and my brows furrow. "You look like you were about to commit murder earlier."

It killed me to watch Jared reach for her hand, to see

them that close again. I wanted to rip him away, to protect her, to stop him from hurting her again.

"It's called pretending." Lie.

"No, it's called you being a fucking moron." She rolls her eyes, as the bartender approaches. "It's really painful to watch."

"Six Bahama Mama's please." She smiles sweetly. A whole different look than the one she's been giving me.

"Look, I don't know what you *think*, Maya, but it's all fake. Amelia knows that too," I say once the bartender leaves. "This is all for show. Once it's over, we'll go back to what we've always been." Painful lie number two.

I still want to talk to her about how I feel, but I'm scared to risk stirring up something complicated, especially with my sister's wedding just around the corner.

"Oh that's how you're going to play this? I see." She grins, shaking her head. "I don't know why you won't admit it to her. I see right through you. Your emotions are like a glass window."

Note to self: add Maya to the list of pain in the asses.

Marcus jogs up, water dripping off his curls. He glances down at Maya. "Don't stare too hard."

She rolls her eyes. "There's not much to look at."

He doesn't try to repress his grin.

"He won't tell Amelia how he feels," she groans. "And it's genuinely pissing me off now."

"Oh sweet child, let's all have a chat." Marcus flashes me a mischievous smile that looks scarily similar to Maya's as he intertwines his hands, like he's some love guru.

"Look, my only concern is that I don't want to risk losing her." I sigh. "What if she doesn't feel the same way?"

"At least you tried," Marcus counters.

"Do it soon, or it might be too late. She might find someone else…" Maya says, searing the thought into my brain. "…kiss someone else, and you'll just have to sit there and watch her fall in love with someone new *all* over again."

"Damn it." I squeeze my thumb, fear swirling in my chest.

"You'll thank us later." Maya chuckles, leaning against the bar as she grabs a few of our shots from the bartender.

Marcus lingers for a moment, his expression grim. "If you're serious about her, if you really love her—"

"I do."

"Then it's simple. You've got two options here."

"I'm listening."

He lifts a thumb. "Option one: Tell her how you feel before we fucking leave. If you don't, you'll lose out on the best girl out there. This is the closest you two have ever been. You really gonna let that slip by?"

"And the second option?"

He lifts his pointer finger next. "The second option is realizing that you have no other choice but to do the first option."

"You know, there are a few moments where I genuinely feel annoyed by you." I stare at him deadpanning. "This is one of those moments."

Fuck. They're both right.

Wedding bros

> **MARCUS**
> Is it wrong if I hook up with one of Tia's bridesmaids?

AMIR

yes.

> Yeah.

MARCUS

Oh ok.

> Dude.

MARCUS

Relax. I haven't done anything.

AMIR

I swear if you manage to break one of her friends' hearts…

MARCUS

You have no faith in me.

> I wonder why.

AMIR

You'd sleep with any woman who even looks at you. I don't want any drama.

MARCUS

No fun.

AMIR ADDED TIA TO THE CONVERSATION.

TIA

Don't even think about it. My friends want love. LOVE.

MARCUS

ok. sorry.

<3

> 🍆

> That's all you're doing tonight Marcus.

TIA

EW GROSS.

TIA HAS LEFT THE CONVERSATION.

> Oh shit I forgot she was in here.

MARCUS

🫳

AMIR

This is why I'm the one who's getting married.

AMIR HAS LEFT THE CONVERSATION.

39

AMELIA

Look, I don't know what you think Maya but it's all fake, Amelia knows that too.

This is all for show, once it's over, we'll go back to what we've always been.

That's what I overheard when I went up to the bar to grab a few extra napkins last night. I've been so conflicted about my feelings, believing Jared when he said Caleb always loved me, but now my questions are finally answered.

He's my best friend, and that's all there is to it. I shouldn't be upset. This is what we agreed on and he's not doing anything wrong. He's simply playing his part in this whole thing. Guess I fooled myself into thinking something had shifted for him, but it was only me all along. My mistake.

I groan, putting my emotions on the back burner and slip on my silk pink dress and heels for the night.

Caleb and I walk into the banquet hall for the rehearsal, and most of the guests are already here. We take our seats at the end of the long white table, decorated with vases holding single roses and candles neatly arranged all around. Everything looks beautiful in the dim lighting. A few minutes into the rehearsal, once everyone has arrived, Maya and I exchange a glance, silently preparing to make our toast.

"We'd like to make a toast to the lovely couple." Maya and I stand up, both clinking our glasses.

"Yes!" Tia squeals, clapping as she leans against Amir. "My girls!"

"It's been an absolute honor for us to be your best friends, let alone being your maids of honor. It's been truly a blessing to witness a love like yours." I beam softly.

"You two have been through so much together, with eight years on your belt and many more ahead. I wish I met you guys back in high school, but I'm forever grateful for the present." Maya adds, a gentle smile pulling at her lips.

"We love you both. Cheers!" Maya and I say simultaneously.

Tia and Amir echo together. "We love you too!"

"Oh my god, we love you all!" my mom shouts across the table, making everyone burst out laughing as glasses clink together.

"We love you, Mrs. Taylor!" Tia and Amir laugh, their hands intertwining.

We all chat and talk around the table, enjoying our pastas, per Tia's request and everyone starts spilling about love and how they knew it was real for them. I'm grateful no one's glanced at Caleb and me.

"So…" Barbara prods gently. "When did you first realize you loved her Caleb?"

Of course we weren't going to get out of this conversation that easily.

Jared's eyes find mine instantly and I choke on my pasta, hurriedly washing it down with a small sip of chardonnay.

Caleb leans forward, placing his hand on my thigh beneath the table, and warmth spreads across my cheeks. "Well, as a teenager, I was always anxious about certain things. Still am, if I'm being honest." He chuckles under his breath.

I glance at him, wondering where he's going with this.

"She's just always had this way of grounding me with a simple look. It's like she knew what I needed before I could even process it myself. She'd pull me into hugs, hold my hand, look at me like I matter."

My heart pounds against my chest.

"She makes me see things in a different light. She listens without judgment, makes me laugh on days I forget how, and reminds me that I'm more than enough…that I've done something right in my life."

His eyes find his dad, a flicker of emotion sailing through them before he looks away.

"And I have done something right, because loving her is the best thing I've ever done."

Jared nods at me with a knowing look, like he was right about what he said on the beach. Kim dabs at her eyes with a napkin, and the whole table falls into a hush, wrapped in quiet awe.

Until Marcus pipes up, "Kiss! Kiss! Kiss!"

"No, we don't have to," I say, shooting him a glare until he bursts out laughing.

"Kiss. I won't live forever to witness this love," Barbara adds dramatically, clutching her heart.

Oh god. Could she be any more dramatic?

Caleb and I lock eyes, and my stomach flutters.

"Cover your eyes," my mom laughs, throwing her hands over my dad's face.

This is so awkward.

Then Caleb cradles my face, his thumb brushing along my cheekbone. He leans in and kisses me in a way that makes my head spin.

The room erupts in cheers and glasses clink all around, but my mind is consumed by how he tastes and how he always holds me like I'm the most important person to him.

We pull back, breathless, and he rests his forehead against mine. The room fades into the background, and for a moment, I let myself forget this is all just an act because I know it won't last forever.

I open my eyes and find his gaze already holding mine, soft and full of something I can't quite place. How I desperately wish this were real. To believe we might be more than just a fleeting moment that will all end tomorrow night.

His thumbs sweep over my cheek before he leaves me with one final, lingering kiss.

As the night goes on, Caleb and his dad head outside to grab a few karaoke machines for us. They've been gone for quite a while now…I step out into the hallway, faint arguing drifting near the elevators. Curious, I move closer to the noise and recognize Caleb's dad's voice.

"You're being pathetic right now. This puppy love shit won't benefit you in the long run. You need to make it into the Super Bowl and your head is all over the damn place," Thomas says, his voice cold.

Caleb's snaps. "I'm the happiest I've ever been, and all you care about is football! I love it too but Jesus, can't you relax and get off my fucking back!? If anything, Amelia's the one motivates me to do better. At least she believes in me. What the hell have you ever done for me?"

His dad's face falters for a second, then hardens. "You're not being the son I raised right now. I thought you'd be better than this—"

"Oh, fuck you!" Caleb's voice echoes down the hall.

What the? I finally step forward, anger and frustration boiling to the surface, and I snap, letting all hell break loose.

"Sorry if I'm disrespecting you, Mr. Hayes," I snarl, unable to hold back. "But I don't care anymore. You're using Caleb as your crutch, and treating him like he's your personal punching bag. You retired from the NFL already, stop projecting your insecurities onto him!"

Thomas's jaw tightens, and just as he opens his mouth to speak, I cut him off again.

"And for the record, Caleb got here all on his own. He's worked so damn hard to be where he is today, and you're a terrible father for never loving him like a son. All he's ever wanted was to feel loved by you, to hear that you're proud of him." My chest rises and falls rapidly. "I've had enough of hearing you shit on him. He doesn't need you. He never has."

Caleb steps in front of me, blocking his dad's view. He cups my face. "Amelia, it's fine. Just go back inside."

"No."

Thomas exhales sharply, dragging a hand down his face. "I'll go," he mutters, his voice edged with frustration. He presses his lips together, and if I'm not mistaken, a flicker of guilt slashes across his face as he grabs the two karaoke machines and heads back toward the wedding rehearsal room.

Caleb sighs as he caresses my jaw. "You didn't have to do that. It's not your problem."

"I know." I chew the inside of my lip. "I'm sorry if I overstepped."

"Never apologize," he says, low and firm, threading with something raw. "You mean everything to me. I hope you know that."

I do. But not in the way I wish he did...

Tia's wedding rehearsal ended and Caleb and I take a late-night stroll. The music fades from the lobby behind us as he swings the doors open, and the cool night breeze brushes against our skin. The sun is setting fast, turning it into a deep purple hue, casting a soft glow over the resort.

He guides me down the steps toward the empty pool area, which was closed off for the night, and with a gentle pull, he leads me behind the palm trees and into an empty cabana, drawing the curtains shut behind him.

Leaving us alone, with only the dim lights peering through the thick fabric covering us.

"This resort is truly beautiful," I say.

"Not the only thing," Caleb murmurs, tucking hair behind my ear.

"You don't have to do that anymore." I say, inching backward.

"Do what?" His brows knit together, confused.

"Pretend."

His eyes darken as he echoes, "Pretend."

"Yeah, the wedding's tomorrow. We've pulled it off and can stop now." I swallow hard, holding his gaze. "Just like I heard you say last night, we can go back to what we've always been. Friends."

"You really think I've been faking it all this time?" His

voice cracks with a mix of anger and desperation that cuts right through me like a blade. "Is that what you believe?"

"That's *exactly* what I believe." I sigh, my heart sinking at how final this sounds. "And I'm telling you now, we can stop. It's over."

I take another reluctant step back. Every instinct screams to close the distance, to feel him near me again, but I can't. As much as every part of me aches to tell him how badly I want him, I won't let myself fall deeper. Not when I know he doesn't feel the same.

The silence is thick and suffocating, broken only by the rustling of palm trees and the steady thud of my heartbeat pounding in my ears.

"And what if I don't want to stop, huh?"

My breath catches in my throat and I freeze. His words hit me like a punch to the gut.

"What if I told you I've been in love with you since high school?" His gaze pierces mine as his hands grip my hips, pulling me flush against him. "And not a single fucking day goes by that I don't wish I was yours?"

My knees nearly buckle, the heat between us so undeniable I can barely keep myself steady.

His lips graze my cheek, planting a delicate kiss. "Does this feel fake to you?"

I can't think. His body pressed against mine feels solid and warm. My breathing growing heavier by the second.

"Because I promise you, it never was for me." His lips drag lower, brushing the side of my neck, and my core pulses in response.

"And the things I want to do to you are far from friendly," he breathes, each word trailing fire as he presses a final kiss to the hollow of my throat. "Tell me," he murmurs against my skin with a wicked grin, "do friends kiss like we do?"

No. Definitely not. My brain scrambles to keep up, everything's happening so fast, so intense. I can barely think straight.

"Answer the question," he commands. "I need to hear you say it."

I bite my bottom lip, the word slipping out in a shaky whisper. "No."

"Well now you know," he exhales, barely holding himself together. "I'm in love with you."

I suck in a sharp breath, my heart hammering against my ribs.

I always believed I'd never love again, that diving too deep with someone wasn't worth it because I didn't have the strength to try. For so long, I kept my heart locked away, hidden in a box I didn't dare to open. I never realized Caleb held the spare key.

"Please say that again," I plead, desperate to hear him repeat it.

He hovers over my mouth. "I've always been in love with you."

Before fear can make me pull away, like it always does, I finally whisper the four words lodged in my throat.

The words that will change the course of our friendship forever.

"I love you too."

His lips crash into mine.

It's far from gentle, it's raw and hungry. Heat floods through my body as his blunt nails dig into my hips.

God, I never want this to stop.

40

CALEB

The resort is quiet tonight, just the faint ripple of water from the pool nearby, and standing in front of me is a beautiful woman I've loved for years...who actually loves me back.

She tugs me by the tie toward the lounge couches, breathless as she pulls away from our kiss. "I want so much more but I'm a little nervous," she admits with a quiet laugh.

I tilt her chin up, lips grazing hers in a promise. "Do you trust me?"

"Yes." She says, her pupils widening.

The moment the word leaves her lips, I press a quick kiss to them, then step back a few feet to secure the curtain flaps of the cabana, sealing us inside. I loosen my tie, slip it over my head, and let it fall carelessly to the floor.

I unbutton my shirt slowly, one at a time, my gaze locked on hers. "Take off your dress."

She swallows, reaching behind to unzip it just enough

for it to loosen. It slips down an inch before sliding gently from her shoulders.

While I watch her, I pop the last button free and shrug off my shirt, letting it fall beside my discarded tie.

She tugs at the hem of her dress, shifting her hips so the fabric slides down, just barely grazing her hardened nipples.

"That's it," I rasp. "Keep going."

The crisp clink of metal cuts through the air as I unbuckle my belt, yanking it free and letting it fall with a thud.

Her dress pools at her feet and my breath catches. God, she's stunning.

My eyes drink her in. Every. Single. Inch.

"God, this is insane." She laughs nervously, eyes swirling with adrenaline. "What if someone catches us?"

"Then we'll just have to be quiet."

Sinking to my knees in front of her, my hands grip her waist as I press slow, lingering kisses up her stomach, my tongue tracing a path that draws a low hum from her lips. When I look up, her eyes meet mine…wild, mirroring my anticipation.

"Can I?" I beg, my fingers skimming the waistband of her underwear.

"Yes."

A slow grin tugs at my lips as I hook my fingers inside the fabric, sliding it down her thighs in no rush. When I finally see how wet she is, my gaze darkens and I toss the soaked panties aside.

"Sit on the couch."

She obeys, settling into the cushions while her eyes never leave mine. I take off my pants and boxers, revealing myself completely.

Her gaze drops to my length, hard and aching for her. And the look on her face nearly undoes me on the spot.

"This is what you do to me." I admit, lowering into the couch across from her, my hand trailing down my chest before curling around my cock.

Her breathing turns shallow as she presses her thighs together.

"Touch yourself."

Her gaze flickers between my hand and my face. "You want to watch?"

"Please." The word leaves me without any damn shame. I don't care how pathetic I might sound right now.

Her hand drifts lower, fingertips ghosting down her stomach. My breath catches the second she reaches her core, and all I can do is watch... entranced.

"Look at my pretty girl." I sit up straight. Stroking. "Lift your leg up for me."

She listens, placing her black high heel on the couch. "Should I take off my—"

"No." I shake my head. "Leave them on."

She shudders at my command, as her fingers move in slow circles against her slick center.

"Does that feel good?" I whisper, pumping myself at the same pace she's moving, never breaking eye contact.

"Oh god. Yes," she pants.

"Shhhh." My jaw clenches as I lean back, taking in the way her thighs begin to tremble, her chest sinking in with uneven breaths.

"Slide a finger in."

Her middle finger easily slips inside, drawing a low moan from her sweet lips.

"Another."

She gasps as she slips in another.

"Now fuck yourself."

She sucks in another breath, as she begins to pump her fingers.

"Faster."

Her eyes flutter shut, rolling back in pleasure, as she picks up speed.

"Eyes on me baby," I stroke myself faster as she opens her eyes. "Now, imagine that's my cock sliding in and out of you until you come."

A warm glow spreads across her face, and she picks up her pace even more at my words. Her fingers work faster, and she's so goddamn wet, squelches fill the thick air along with our labored breathing.

"You're perfect," I pant, feeling my abs tighten as I twist and stroke myself. "I've waited so long to see you like this."

"Caleb," she utters a soft moan, her hazy eyes locked onto mine as she spreads her legs wider, opening herself to me so I get the perfect view of her wet core.

She digs her heels into the cushion as she sits up and I can tell she's almost there. "God—" her words cut off as her body goes still.

"You're close, aren't you?"

She nods frantically, her lips parting in a breathless 'O' shape.

"Come for me."

She clamps her eyes shut, arching her back as a sharp gasp spills from her lips, her body writhing against the couch as she fails to keep quiet. She pulls her glistening fingers out, rubbing her clit to ride out her orgasm.

Holy shit.

"God, Amelia." I pump myself faster, the sight of her shaking pushes me over the edge.

A deep groan rumbles in my chest as I release, my body

taut with waves of pleasure crashing through me. I lean back on the couch for a moment, my mind reeling from everything that just happened tonight.

She blinks up at me, breathless, and lets out a airy, dazed laugh.

Then I glance around the quiet cabana before stepping to the nearby towel rack. I clean myself off, grab a fresh towel, and sit beside her, pressing it gently to her skin, letting the moment settle around us.

"How are you feeling?"

"Perfect," she murmurs, amusement flickering in her eyes. "I can't believe we did that. Seriously, someone could've caught us."

"It would've been your fault, you weren't exactly quiet." I tease, my knuckles gliding lightly down her arm.

"Neither were you," she sighs, nestling into me. Her warm skin luminous under the dim light of the cabana.

I pause, my heart thudding faster. "I know it's probably a little late to ask this, but...does this mean we're dating now?"

She giggles. "God, yes. I'd love to be your *actual* girlfriend."

Warmth floods my chest.

"Then I'm all yours."

41

CALEB

I'M IN A SUIT AND TIE, FEELING ALL SUAVE WHEN I WALK into Amir's room as he gets ready for the big day. "Tia's a lucky woman." I tease, walking up to him and fix his tie.

"Man, I've been waiting for this moment forever," Amir says, shaking his head with a laugh.

"Yeah, it's been a long time coming. Feels like yesterday you were trying to date my damn sister," I say as I smooth down his tie.

"Braces and all," he says with a grin, patting my shoulder.

"How did you know she was the one?" Marcus asks, adjusting his collar in the mirror.

"Well, there was this one time we went to that karaoke place downtown. She was singing her little heart out." His eyes soften, like he's reliving the memory. "She just looked so happy, so full of life, and it hit me… if I never got to witness that again… I don't think life would be worth it."

That's exactly how I feel about Amelia.

"Damn. That's cute." Marcus chuckles.

Amir's lucky to be with my sister, she's one of the best women I know. But Tia's lucky too, because I know he'd drop everything for her in a drop of a dime.

After my talk with Amir, I walk outside to the vineyard to get myself situated.

"Caleb!" Tia shouts, her flowy white dress billowing around her.

"What the hell are you doing walking around here, he might see you," I groan, jogging toward her.

"Hi to you too," she beams.

"You look beautiful." I chuckle. "But seriously you can't be out here wandering around."

"Thanks… I just needed to talk to you," she peeks over my shoulder before dragging me into the empty corner tucked away.

"About what?"

"I want you to know that whatever you decide to do with Amelia after this, I'm 100% on board. I mean, my opinion doesn't really matter, but I know how you are, always trying to look out for my feelings and all that blah blah blah."

"Oh, about that—"

"Like, I literally don't care at all. I don't know how Amelia hasn't picked up on the signs, but we all see it. She's also extraaa happy today, so…maybe shoot your shot."

I bet she is. After the night we had, I'm fucking ecstatic.

"Well—" I try to tell my sister but she won't stop talking.

"Lately, you have been so obvious. It's like you're her little puppy dog," she laughs, ruffling my hair. "It's cute seeing you in love."

"Well, thanks for that." I mumble, brushing my hair back into place. "Your wedding photos are gonna look like shit with me in them."

She rolls her eyes. "Seriously, you need to stop being so scared all the time about the what if's."

"Amelia and I—"

She pulls me into a hug, cutting me off for the umpteenth time. I hold her tightly, resting my chin on her head.

"Tia! Get your butt over here," Maya scolds, holding Tia's veil. "Amelia's ready to do your hair!"

"Okay, I gotta go before she kills me before I can walk down the aisle. Love you lots!"

"I love you too." I laugh to myself as she rushes off.

They're a handful.

The outdoor speaker begins playing the harmonies of Here Comes The Bride. White and saffron flowers are splayed along the grass, perfectly aligning with the pathway. Our family and friends…along with Jared are seated in the white chairs, the gentle breeze blowing through, carrying the scent of the ocean. It's such a beautiful day, and that's when my eyes lock onto the most beautiful woman I've ever laid my eyes on.

Her curls are defined all the way down to her waist, a small yellow flower tucked behind her ear, wearing a yellow silk bridesmaid dress. I can't take my eyes off of her.

The sun beams down on her, warming her complexion even more, and the heat sneaks up to the back of my neck. I tug a finger into my collar, feeling it tighten as if it's suddenly too small.

Tia starts slowly walking down the aisle in her wedding gown, the delicate fabric trailing behind her, and she looks absolutely stunning. She catches my eye, flashing me a warm smile and my eyes begin welling up.

Seeing my baby sister marry the man of her dreams is an overwhelming feeling I wasn't expecting. I glance over at Amir waiting for her, and he's already tearing up, never once taking his eyes off of her.

"You may all be seated," the officiant announces. "We are gathered here today to celebrate the beautiful love between Amir Anderson and Tia Hayes."

Amir and Tia take each other's hands, gazing deeply into each other's eyes while I keep sneaking glances at Amelia. Her gaze softens as she watches the ceremony.

As they exchange their formal vows, my sister's eyes begin to water. She turns around, reaching out to Amelia, who gently hands her a folded piece of paper.

"Amir, you've been the light in my life for many years now," she sniffs, looking back and forth between him and the paper. "I honestly don't know what I'd do without you by my side."

Amir inhales deeply along with her, rubbing the back of her hand.

"I'll always love you and you've taught me what it means to be truly happy," she smiles, a tear gliding down her cheek. Amir quickly swipes it away with his thumb before he begins to share his vows.

"Tia, you are my entire world. There's never a dull moment with us, and I can't thank you enough for sticking by my side through medical school and putting up with my crazy schedule."

"Just like how we have a flight to another conference in a few weeks," she teases.

We all chuckle.

"Exactly. You make everyday worth it," he adds, finishing his vows. "'I'll forever love you and I promise to keep your heart safe."

Their voices fade into the background as my gaze lands on Amelia again. She's standing not even five feet away from me but even then, it doesn't feel close enough.

Hours pass as we all mingle, celebrating and dancing. Tia and Amir booked the reception at the Grand Salon which is a fancy theater styled room. It has white and grey walls, glittering chandeliers, and more than enough space to dance and frolic.

Marcus is in the middle of the dance floor, jamming to "I Wanna Dance With Somebody" by Whitney Houston. A classic.

"Now this is a wedding reception!" Tia shouts, raising her champagne glass in the air as she sways to the music with Amir and Maya.

"Alright, I wanna slow this down for all my couples out there. This one's for you," The DJ says as he types in his computer. "Congratulations Amir and Tia."

"I Gotta Be" by Jagged Edge begins playing.

"May I have this dance, beautiful?" I ask, offering my hand.

"Always." She smiles, intertwining our fingers. I bring her hand close to my chest as I lead her to the dance floor.

I rest my forehead against hers, as I wrap my arms around her waist, pulling her in. Our bodies sway to the music in perfect rhythm.

"I love you," she whispers.

My heart is in her hands, it always has been. She owns me in ways she may never fully understand. In this lifetime, and the next, it's her. There will never be anyone else.

"I love you more."

42

CALEB

"POTTERY 101. LET'S MAKE SOME CUPS." THE INSTRUCTOR, Cecil, laughs in front of Amelia and me.

We got back to LA a few days ago and the first thing I wanted to do was book a private pottery class for our first of many dates. And I want to recreate her fantasies tonight if she'll let me.

Cecil hands us our aprons, before walking over to the table to get our materials ready.

I pull the apron over my head, reaching behind to tie it when I feel her hand rest over mine, swatting it away.

"Let me do it," Amelia says, grabbing the strings, securing it tight enough that I let out the most dramatic cough.

"Calm down back there, you're going to suffocate me," I joke.

"I'm sorry!" Her hands quickly scramble with the strings loosening it and I turn around to face her.

"I'm joking, baby." I say with a grin, grabbing the apron from her arm and slipping it over her head. I spin her around, moving her hair to one shoulder as I tie the strings.

Reaching into my pocket, I pull out a scrunchie and hold it up. "May I?"

She nods, smiling as she sinks onto the stool beside me. I step behind her, gathering her curls in a loose pony, and tie it off to keep it out of her face.

"Do you think of everything or what?"

"I try my best," I reach down to bring her knuckles to my lips. Hopefully soon, this same hand will be wearing a ring.

"Okay! Let's go ahead and begin sculpting," Cecil says, taking a seat in front of us at her own pottery station. "First things first, keep your chest low and rest your elbows on your knees." She gestures towards the ball of clay on each of our wheels. "Press the pedal slightly on medium speed, then release. Wet your hands, rest your non-dominant hand on the outside, and use your opposing thumb to apply slight pressure to stabilize it."

We follow her directions, pressing our hands into the malleable clay. The instructor guides us as we press our thumbs into the center, creating a deep hole to begin shaping.

This part is my favorite, it's calming and it reminds me that we all start from nothing, what matters is how we shape ourselves, how we mold our lives into what we want them to be.

We have the power to start over, again and again, until we get it right. It's never too late.

I may have waited too long to tell her how I felt, but I don't regret a single second because everything led us to this moment.

Cool, wet clay seeps between my fingers as I carefully

work it, but my attention keeps drifting to someone more important. I glance over at Amelia, watching her lean in, completely absorbed.

She dips her sponge and hand into the water, squeezing it onto the clay as she smooths the edges. She's a natural. Her lips press together and I can tell she's forgotten I even exist right now.

I'm so mesmerized by her that I don't realize my own clay collapsing beneath my hands. "Shit," I murmur, watching as the clay slumps into a flat mess on the wheel.

Amelia laughs loudly, glancing at me while she continues sculpting her clay. "You okay over there?"

"Just peachy," I tease.

As we continue shaping our clay, Cecily announces that she's heading to the back office, giving us some alone time. Taking full advantage of this moment, I rise from my stool dragging it across the tile floor before placing it behind Amelia. I take a seat, resting my chin on her shoulder. She hums, tilting her head just enough for me to press scattered kisses down the side of her neck.

"Having fun?" I murmur between kisses.

"Yeah, this is nice. I've missed doing this with you."

I kiss my way up beneath her ear, my hands grazing her wrists while my thumb circles gently over her skin.

"Can I please ruin this?" I whisper, my lips grazing the shell of her ear before nipping her lobe, sliding my hands closer to her sculpture.

She doesn't answer with words, she doesn't have to. She takes my hands in hers, pulling me flush against her back as she intertwines our fingers together, not caring about her clay. Our hands move together, deliberate and unhurried, as the clay seeps between our fingers.

"I'm living my Ghost movie fantasy right now," she chuckles under her breath.

"You like the idea of me being behind you?"

Her breathing shifts as I brush my lips along the curve of her jaw. I press closer, my chest molding to her back as our hands keep moving in the clay. The wheel spins beneath our fingers, but all I feel is her. Her body. Her touch.

"Mhm," she says, voice unsteady as she glances over her shoulder. "You're good with your hands."

I smirk, capturing her bottom lip between my teeth. "You should see what they can do in the bedroom."

A storm brews behind her now darkened gaze, like she's seconds away from pouncing. Fuck, she's pretty.

She shifts, pressing her back against me just enough for her ass to graze my already straining cock through my jeans. I dig my fingers into the clay, my control slipping.

"Care to demonstrate?" she murmurs giving me those unmistakable fuck-me eyes. Similar to that night we shared back in the Bahamas.

Gripping the edge of her stool, I spin her to face me, the clay long forgotten as she lifts her foot off the petal. I scoot in between her legs, hands gliding up her thighs against the apron. Her breath stutters when my fingers trail higher, inch by inch.

"You sure?"

"I want you, Caleb. Now."

That's all I need to hear.

"I'm ready to pay!" I call out to the instructor.

She bursts out laughing, swatting my thigh. "You're insane."

"Only for you."

43

AMELIA

Life has a funny way of giving you what you need instead of what you think you want. For so long, it felt like me versus love, when really, love had been on my side all along, just waiting for me to stop being so stubborn and let it in.

It's always been him.

After Caleb hurriedly paid for our class, our instructor let us place our poorly made and squished clay sculptures on the shelf to air dry, so we can pick them up next week.

He wastes no time following behind me as I unlock my front door. The moment it clicks shut behind us, his fingers hook around my belt loop, tugging me against him.

"I want you to remember something," he murmurs.

"Remember what?"

"I'm a gentleman and I fully respect you."

My head tilts in confusion. "I know that."

"Good because the way I want to make love to you tonight isn't the best representation of that."

Holy shit.

His hands slip under my ass as he hoisters me up. My legs instinctively wrap around his waist as he claims my lips in a deep, heated kiss as he stalks toward my bedroom, kicking the door shut behind him.

He pulls off his shirt and leans down, planting kisses along my jawline. His tongue flicks out, leaving a burning trail down to the hollow of my throat.

"Caleb," I whisper.

"Yes?"

"What's your fantasy? You know mine. It's only fair."

His eyes darken and shift into something dangerous. "My fantasy is seeing you on your knees with your mouth wrapped around my cock."

Oh. My. God. The mouth this man has is enough to put me into cardiac arrest.

Without saying another word, my fingers tug desperately at his belt, fumbling slightly as my heart pounds against my chest.

Then he slides off his pants leaving him in only his boxers and my eyes drop to the bulge straining against the fabric. I'm both nervous and unbearably eager.

With a sharp exhale he shoves his boxers down, tossing them aside, freeing his hard cock.

His entire body looks sculpted to perfection.

Lowering to my knees, I wrap my fingers around his length. The heat of his skin singes against my palm as I look up at him and stroke, slowly.

"Shit." He pants, gripping the base of my ponytail tightly. "Open your mouth."

The command in his voice makes my core ache and needy. He doesn't have to tell me twice.

My lips part as I take in just the tip, swirling my tongue.

Then I envelop him fully, feeling him hit the back of my throat, making me gag.

I look up at him, locking eyes as I suck slowly, wanting to savor every inch. He thrusts his hips gently, and I rest my palms against his thighs to steady myself.

"Please don't stop," he whimpers, thrusting faster, fucking my mouth until drool runs down my chin.

Every nerve in my body ignites, my drenched underwear clinging to me, desperate for him to fill me. I circle my tongue around the head, tasting his pre-cum, and moan.

Pulling back, I focus on the tip again, stroking him with both hands. His head falls back, chest heaving.

"Fuck. I can't take it." He bends down, devouring my lips in a fierce, desperate kiss.

I grin with pride just before he lifts me off the ground and guides me to my mirror.

This is what I've been craving. Someone who isn't afraid to take what they want.

He tugs my jeans down with rough urgency, and I step out, kicking them aside as he strips off my sweater, exposing my already peaked nipples.

"No bra?" He groans, spinning me around to capture one nipple with his mouth. His warm tongue circles it as he cups my breasts, squeezing and kneading.

"Oh," I moan, my eyes fluttering. I need him. I can't wait anymore.

He starts to pull away to grab his jeans from the floor, but I grip his arm.

"Wait," I say. "I'm on the pill, if you're okay with that."

"I've been tested. I haven't been with anyone." He spins me to face the mirror, pressing close behind me, his thumb tracing slow circles on my hips. "I want to feel you. All of you."

"Please."

"Don't take your eyes off us," he commands, his breath grazing my ear. "I want you to watch me fuck you."

The moment I nod, he grips himself, positioning at my slick center. He slides against my slit, slowly, until I'm trembling beneath him.

Then he eases the head of his cock inside me, inch by inch, stretching me until I gasp.

God.

He gives me a moment, letting me adjust, before pulling back and driving balls deep inside me.

"Fuck!" My palms slam against the glass mirror for balance as my breath catches in my throat.

"You're so tight," he groans, kissing along my neck. His grip tightens at my hips, and he begins a rhythm, pulling out and thrusting back in, harder, deeper, until stars dance behind my eyes.

The force of his brutal thrusts draws sharp cries from my lips, and I lower my head, overwhelmed.

Caleb's hand tangles in my hair, tugging until I'm forced to meet our reflection.

"Keep watching," he coos. "Look how pretty you are."

"Oh shit," I pant, eyes fixed on our bodies in the mirror. I've never felt so alive.

My hair's disheveled, eyes glazed over, and sweat slick on my skin. God, we look so good together. His eyes are dark, filled with pure lust. "Harder."

He obeys, his pace ruthless now. One hand reaches around to press low on my stomach, the pressure making my whole body pulse.

"You like this, don't you?" he taunts, lips brushing my shoulder. "Watching me fuck you from behind."

All I can do is nod and whine. His other hand slides up to cup my breast, teasing and pinching my nipple. I'm so close to coming… it's too much.

"You feel so fucking good," he hisses, frantically pounding into me.

"Oh, God!" The pleasure hits hard and fast, white-hot and blinding. My legs quiver, as I glide my fingers down the mirror, smudging it as the shockwaves take over me.

"Come inside me," I plead, pushing my hips back, chasing every wave of sensation I can pull even though I could cry from the immense pleasure.

His eyes screw shut, and with one powerful drive, he groans loudly as he releases, burying my neck with kisses.

I lazily collapse, feeling boneless against the glass as he curses, both of our bodies going rigid.

Then he scoops me up and carries me to the bed.

He disappears into the bathroom, returning with a cloth to clean me up. I lie back, smiling and completely worn out.

"You're smiling pretty hard," he teases.

"Because that was the best sex of my life." I say, still trying to catch my breath. " Like, life-changing."

He chuckles breathlessly, leaning down to kiss me. I tug him down beside me until we're both laughing and tangled up in the sheets.

There's nowhere else I'd rather be.

44

CALEB

Waking up with Amelia in my arms is what I imagine heaven would be like. I slip out of bed slowly, careful not to wake her, and head to the kitchen to scramble a quick breakfast. Once everything's ready, I place it on a tray and carry it back to her room.

She's sitting up against the headboard, rubbing her eyes, her curls are a little messy, looking so sexy and serving as a clear reminder of what we did last night.

I chuckle, placing the tray on her lap. "Morning, sleepy head."

"Mmm, morning." She smiles sleepily, picking up her toast. "Thanks, I could get used to this."

"I'll gladly do it."

I glance at the clock and sigh. "As much as I'd love to stay and eat breakfast with you, I gotta go. First shoot with Driftwear's today."

Her brows lift and her eyes gleam. "That's today? How exciting! Are you ready for it?"

"Yeah, but I'd much rather lie here with you," I say, my voice dropping as I frown.

"Me too. And I feel bad you didn't get to eat."

"Maybe I can later?"

"That can definitely be arranged."

I'm about to kiss her, but she pulls back, covering her mouth. "I have food breath!"

"I don't care," I pout. "Oh come on, you're really gonna make me go to work without a kiss? That's bad luck."

"Go." She cups my face, pecking me before nudging me away. "Before Coach kills you for being late."

I take the same hand she nudged me with and kiss her inner wrist. "Fine."

Reluctantly pulling away, I slip on my clothes.

"I love you," she says amused, taking a sip of her orange juice.

"I love you too," I toss her a wink, then jog back to steal another quick kiss.

I'll never get enough of her.

Once the photoshoot wraps up, Marcus approaches, an energy drink in hand and an obnoxious smirk on his face. He slaps me on the back. "You look oddly refreshed this morning." He narrows his eyes. "You're practically glowing."

I shake my head, shoving him back. "I just got a good night's rest."

Marcus gives me a side eye and raises his brows, his grin growing extremely wide. "Mhm... good night's sleep my ass." He pauses dramatically, then switches to the worst

British accent I've ever heard. "But I digress. I shall not question you further."

Carter and Nico follow behind him, their eyes full of the same mischievous gleam. I can already sense where this is headed. "Don't start." I warn, before they have a chance to speak.

But who am I talking to again? Right...these idiots. Still, I gotta love them. They came to support me during the shoot and are treating me to lunch for our cheat meal.

I won't be too hard on them today.

"Maybe Amelia can introduce me to some of her friends?" Carter teases.

Nico shakes his head with a small but barely there smile.

I can't help but grin and nod, feeling like I won the damn lottery. This is everything I've ever wanted, and somehow, by the grace of God, Amelia wanted me too.

She is my home. Wherever she is, that's when I'm the happiest.

It's been officially a month since Amelia and I started dating, and tonight she wanted to cook with me for our date. So, I stopped by the grocery store on my way back and picked up some pasta for her, knowing it's one of her favorites.

I watch as she stands near the stove in nothing but my oversized t-shirt and the sight already has me going feral. It looks fucking amazing on her.

I sneak up behind her and scoop her up effortlessly onto my shoulders as she presses her thighs against my face.

"Oh my god!" She squeals, gripping my hair and clinging to me like a koala.

"I've got you," I laugh, feeling her shift as she settles on my shoulders. She peers over my head, her face inches from mine as she tries to look into my eyes.

"How are we going to cook like this?" She chuckles, her voice laced with amusement and curiosity. Her legs tighten around me and a shiver runs down the back of my spine.

"You know how," I say, my hands sliding up and down her thighs, giving them a light squeeze. Her legs are so smooth it makes me want to linger and kiss them, but I try to focus.

"Oh, this'll be so fun," she giggles once she registers what I mean. Then she fully locks into character, channeling Remy from Ratatouille as she tugs my hair and bosses me around the kitchen.

Her laughter is infectious as she pulls me toward the cabinet. I reach for the noodles and the creamy Alfredo sauce as she takes charge.

It's beyond sexy when she takes control and tells me what to do.

Our final task is sliding the garlic bread into the oven. After setting the timer, I gently place her back on her feet in front of the kitchen counter. Six minutes left and counting.

"I wonder what we can do to pass the time," she grins, looking up at me with mischievous eyes, the kind of look that lets me know we're both on the same page.

"I have an idea." I lift her onto the counter, gripping the back of her neck to tug her closer, sealing our lips together. Her fingers trace along my jaw, igniting fire in my chest as she angles her head and deepens the kiss.

I slide my tongue along the seam of her lips and she

parts for me, meeting my tongue, and I'm rewarded with the sweetest moan.

She lifts her hips, tugging her shirt and I eagerly help pull it off her, lazily tossing it to the side.

She's wearing black panties and a matching sheer bra where I can see her perfectly taut nipples and the sight sends a message straight to my cock. Her breasts press against me and my hands roam her supple body, gripping her hips as I tug her to the edge of the counter. "So perfect."

She exhales a shaky breath as I nudge her thighs apart, my fingers brushing dangerously close to where she needs me most. I meet her gaze, the hunger in her eyes a perfect reflection of my own.

"Fuck, you're already wet."

She groans as I tease her center with light strokes, barely touching her but it's enough to make her squirm.

"More..." she breathes, shifting her hips forward.

I obey, adding more pressure as my fingers begin to circle her clit, picking up speed.

A strangled moan breaks free from her lips as I push her underwear aside, and easily dip my middle finger inside her. Her breathing grows labored, turning into a rapid pant.

Music to my ears.

"That's it baby."

Her eyes clamp shut, and I know she's seconds away from coming. I slip a second finger, curling them just right to hit the spot that makes her body spasm.

"Oh my god," she stutters, riding my fingers as I lick a slow trail from her throat up to her jaw.

"You're so beautiful," I rasp against her skin before nipping her earlobe. "Let me feel you."

She clenches her walls around me and I know she needs

more so I pump in and out of her deeper and faster until she's gripping anything within reach, knocking over the kitchen utensils as they clang to the floor.

"Keep riding my fingers like that. Don't you dare stop."

She grinds faster. "I'm coming, ah-" she cries, gripping my wrist, keeping me in place. Her body tightens around my fingers one final time before she convulses, pleasure washing over her.

She slumps back against the counter, shuddering, completely wrecked. I've never seen anything more beautiful.

Just as the oven beeps, I pull my fingers out and suck them clean, eyes never leaving hers.

"Dinner's ready."

45

AMELIA/CALEB

"Let's go, Vipers!" Fans chant all around the stadium, vibrations rumbling through my chest and beneath my feet as we sit in the suite Caleb insisted we watch the game from.

This is the last quarter and only two minutes remain in the game. It's a close call right now with the score at 20-23. The Vipers are behind but anything can happen and it's making my palms all clammy.

Amir stands up to get a better view of the game. "Oh shit, look at Marcus."

We all stand up, our eyes glued to the field as Caleb throws a perfect 50-yard pass just as he is about to get tackled. Carter, Nico, and Marcus bolt for the ball, but Marcus gets there first and just as he's about to catch it, he gets tackled hard to the ground.

"Come on, Marcus," I murmur quietly. "Get up."

As the players help him off the ground, Marcus clutches the ball tightly as the speakers go crazy: "The ball is secured!"

"Yes!" Everyone screams his name, knowing Marcus and Caleb just brought the team closer to an easy touchdown.

Marcus pushes himself up, limping slightly toward the sidelines with help from the trainers. He can't help but flash the crowd with his signature grin.

There's a slight pause in the game for Marcus to get settled and I see Caleb jogging over to check on him.

Maya scoffs as she walks away toward the snack bar, relief apparent in her tone.

As the game resumes, the ball is back in Caleb's hands, and everyone's on the edge of their seats. They're so close to the end zone, at the ten-yard mark.

Caleb scans the field one last time, looking for an opening. It looks like he's going to throw the ball but he can't afford to. He quickly tucks the ball and bolts forward, shifting his feet, dodging the oncoming defense.

The other players try to tackle him, but Caleb's quick on his feet, bulldozing his way through. He's nearly at the end zone... oh god, my heart is pounding.

The speaker shouts, "Caleb Hayes ran through and scored the winning touchdown, securing victory for the Vipers!"

The stadium roars and the stomping continues as we all chant. I stand up, cheering so loud as I watch Caleb's team lift him in the air before putting him down to celebrate.

We make our way out of the suite and I jog across the field. "Congrats!" I squeal, jumping into his arms. He catches me with ease, his hands gripping my ass as he lifts me, hooking my legs around his waist and kissing me in ways that I'll never grow tired from.

Flashes from cameras go off as reporters start shouting questions, congratulating him, and calling us a cute couple.

"Told you, you're my lucky charm," he says, smiling against my lips.

"Oh yeah? Good, because you're stuck with me." I chuckle, using my thumb to wipe my gloss off his lips, before he sets me on my feet again.

He grins, tugging the hem of his jersey. "Keep this on later."

"I will."

Caleb then freezes, his eyes shifting behind me. I glance over my shoulder.

Thomas Hayes.

My stomach drops, and I step back hitting Caleb's chest with a small thud. Feeling awkward about our last encounter.

Thomas nods toward me. "Always a pleasure."

"Hi." I let out a nervous laugh but I can feel Caleb stiffen behind me.

His arm wraps around my waist. "Father," he says, his tone cold.

"May I have a word with you, son?"

The tension is so thick between them and I don't want to leave him but I also want to give him space to figure out what he wants for himself.

"I'll meet you in the lobby, okay?" I turn to face him, lightly grazing his arm.

After a moment of silence, he nods reluctantly, pressing a kiss to my forehead before I scurry off.

I'm praying something good comes from this.

CALEB

"Amelia's changed quite a lot since she was a kid," my father starts, stuffing his hands into his pockets.

We're in the press conference room before interviews begin so he's got exactly thirty minutes to say whatever he needs to and then I'm out. I'm not exactly in the mood to go through this constant cycle with him.

"What is it now? Here to critique my throw again?" I retort, ignoring his remark. "Knock yourself out, you've only got thirty minutes."

"That's not why I'm here, Caleb."

I fold my arms over my chest. "Or was I too distracted during the winning touchdown? Which one? It's always the same shit."

"I'm not here for any of that. I want to apologize," he says sternly, meeting my gaze.

I stare at him and blink, thrown off guard. This man rarely apologizes, I think I've heard him say the words "I'm sorry" a handful of times and those were always reserved for Tia and my mom.

Never once directed at me, not even when I needed it. Those two words probably could've fixed a lot of things as a kid, maybe I wouldn't have felt so worthless to him.

"I wanted to push you because that's what I thought would make you the best. It's what my father did to me as a child. He never let up, waking me up at 5 a.m. every day to practice, yelling in my face to go over plays. It didn't matter if it was snowing or raining or if I had an injured foot and I hated him for that. Never gave me the time of day unless it was on his terms. I swore if I ever had kids I'd never be like him, but here I am doing the same thing to you," he says sheepishly. "Your mother convinced me to go to therapy, once we got back from the trip."

I let out a hollow laugh. "And you think telling me that changes anything?"

His shoulders tense.

"All those times you called me pathetic, a disappointment, and a failure?" My voice hardens. "Do you know how many times I've wanted to hear you say that you were proud of me?" My chest heaves as all the emotions come crashing in. "I didn't deserve half the shit you gave me. I was just a kid trying to be enough for you. I never had a fucking father. So don't come in here acting like you've changed."

A tight knot forms in my chest.

"I deserve that." He nods, pressing his lips together. "I wasn't a father to you."

I scoff under my breath. "And even then I'd still look up to you. It feels like I'm chasing something I'll never get and all I've ever wanted from you was to love me like a son. That's it."

The words spill out of me and I can't stop them. I've waited so long for him to treat me like the son he once held, the same one he stood beside, smiling as I blew out the candles on my sixth birthday. But, I can't fucking remember any of it. Only the photos prove it ever happened.

Because by the time I was old enough to hold a ball in my hands, everything went downhill. There wasn't any more love after that. All that was left were expectations. Yelling. Drills and critiques. And utter disappointment.

Sports were the only thing that ever mattered in his eyes but as I stare into them now... for the first time I see something different.

Regret.

He exhales, dragging a hand through his graying hair. "I can't change the past. But I want to do better and I will do better if you allow me. I want to be a father to you again. I want to tell you I love you and how proud I am of you." He pauses for a second. "Because I am. I always have been, even if I had a shitty way of showing it." He shakes his head. "Not once did I tell you how well you were doing. How that throw you made against the Titans was one of the most impressive passes I've ever seen in my career." His throat bobs as he swallows.

My fingers twitch, squeezing my thumb in short pulses as I hear him say the words I've longed for. Every night, I'd come home from school wishing he'd give me something as simple as a damn high five for winning a game.

"But more than anything, what I'm most proud of is the man you've become. A better man than I ever was." He meets my gaze, his eyes glossed over, pulling a chord deep inside me.

I swallow hard, hating how tight my throat feels. I should be angry and I am. But God, the kid in me has ached to hear those words for so long, it physically hurts.

"You can hate me. I get it and I don't expect you to forgive me overnight or ever, but I will prove it to you," he says hoarsely, voice thick with emotion. "I'll let you get back to it and give you space. But I mean it, Caleb."

My jaws tighten as I grind my molars together watching him slip out the door, leaving me here in the overwhelming silence as I process what the hell just happened.

46

AMELIA

"How was the talk with your dad?" I ask, tracing lazy patterns on his bare chest as we lie under the sheets of his bed after we both freshened up after the game.

Taking showers with him has easily become my new favorite thing. I'd love to do it everyday if I could. But I need my alone time and space to do my "everything" shower routine. Him seeing me shave… everywhere is not ideal for me.

His fingers begin toying at my hem under the covers of the extra jersey I found in his closet.

"It was a lot," he sighs, his chest sinking under me. "It was like seeing a different person. He told me he loved me and was proud."

My heart aches. I twist under his arm, cuddling him as I continue to trace along his chest, feeling his steady heartbeat beneath my fingertips.

He stares at the ceiling, his fingers brushing against my thigh. "I don't know what to do. Part of me wants to believe it and the other half is saying not to give a shit and keep my walls up."

"It's okay to feel that way," I whisper, glancing up at him. "You don't have to do anything until you're ready."

He nods, pressing a kiss to the crown of my head.

"And you don't have to have all the answers right now. Take it one day at a time, and see where it goes, because you're allowed to feel anger, sadness, bitterness, all of it. It's time to take the same advice you gave me months ago."

"You're right." He cups my jaw, his thumb rubbing my bottom lip. "Maybe I should try therapy? Talk it out with someone?"

He continues tugging at my bottom lip like it's calming him.

"I think that's a great idea," I whisper, pressing a kiss to his thumb. "And if you want, I'll help you find a therapist."

He leans in hovering over my mouth, as heat pools in my lower stomach. "What would I do without you?"

I grin against his lips, teasing. "Mmm, you'd probably be with some random girl, still partying all night, just lost."

He smirks, pinching my sides, making me squirm until I'm rolling over in his bed.

"Oh is that what you think, huh?"

I laugh uncontrollably as he keeps tickling me, gasping when he ends up on top of me, his elbow resting beside my head. "Caleb!"

He looks down into my eyes, his teasing fading into something softer. The warmth of his breath fans over my lips as his fingers trail slowly down my neck making me shiver.

"You're wrong," he whispers. "I wouldn't be with some random girl. I'd spend all my time searching for you."

I swallow. His fingers continue their slow descend down my throat.

"You always know what to say."

"Because it's the truth." He leans in, pressing a lingering kiss to the corner of my mouth. "You think I wouldn't find you in this lifetime or the next? You're incredibly mistaken. I've always been yours." I slide my hands up feeling the dips of his abs beneath my fingers as he hisses. "You've got me hooked around your little finger."

His hands disappear under the jersey and the second he touches my center, he freezes.

"You're not wearing—"

Yes. I purposely didn't wear any underwear tonight. Sue me. I've grown so comfortable with Caleb when it comes to sex and he has made me feel so beyond wanted, like every little thing I do turns him on.

He groans as he gets out of bed, dropping his sweats and boxers. My eyes trail down his body, watching his back muscles flex, and all I can think about is running my nails down them. Leaving my mark.

"Come here."

"Yes, ma'am." He grins getting back on top of me, his hardness pressing against my stomach.

Bunching the jersey up to my waist, he lifts one leg over his shoulder, gripping my ankle tight.

Teasing me, he drags his cock up and down my wet slit, each stroke drawn out until my breath comes in shallow pants.

When he flicks my clit with his tip, my voice catches, hoarse. "God."

"My jersey looks good on you," he whispers against my leg, gnawing like he's starved. Then he reaches behind him, snatching up a pillow. "Lift your hips."

I do as he says as he slides the soft satin pillow beneath my lower back.

"Comfortable?"

"Yes."

"Good." He kisses my leg again, then slams into me in one swift motion, burying his cock inside. He's so deep in this position, that I let out a loud strangled cry as my hands dig into the bed sheets.

His free hand slides up my arm, weaving our fingers together before pressing them firmly down on the mattress to keep me in place.

"You love when I fuck you like this, don't you?" he groans, pulling out all the way and thrusting back in.

There's something about me wearing only his jersey while he's completely naked, pounding into me, that's driving me absolutely insane.

And the way he talks to me… God, he talks dirty and praises me all at once.

I whimper as he thrusts harder and faster, making me arch my back and suck in a deep breath. I can't last much longer with the pace he's going. "I don't know if I can—"

"You can take it." He leans down, kissing me with everything he has as he stretches me, our bodies flush together. "You can take every single inch."

My vision becomes hazy as I see double of him from the overwhelming pleasure. Every time he slides in and out, I feel myself drifting further into a daze. My orgasm brews and he notices, his mouth falls open as he grips my leg tighter.

"Shit," he grits through his teeth.

"Oh my—" My words cut off as an explosion erupts within me. It's such a euphoric feeling, one I know I'll never get enough of. He moans and continues slamming into me and I clamp my legs shut at the intensity. I am so sensitive but I don't want him to stop.

He presses our hands further into the mattress, hovering his lips over mine. "You can do one more for me, can't you?"

Oh, fuck.

He takes his hand off my leg, spreading me open and reaches down between us circling my clit at an intense speed with his skillful fingers, and my vision goes white.

My breathing becomes more jagged as another orgasm threatens to wash over me. My chest rises and falls in quick motions and I swear my heart nearly stops.

He's fucking me in an erratic way and I'm teetering over the edge, unable to control the moans pouring out of me. I'm probably saying words that aren't even in the English dictionary.

I clamp my eyes shut as I feel myself about to come again and I take a deep breath.

He halts, pulling out of me and takes his hand away with a stupid grin on his face.

I pant as he edges me and delays my release.

"Look at me."

I lazily open my eyes and his gaze is locked on mine with fire in them.

"Good girl." Then he rams himself all the way in, stretching me all over again.

His hands move faster over my clit, rubbing it over and over as he fills me. "You look so goddamn pretty."

One more movement and I'm a goner.

His breathing picks up, and I know he's close too. He leans down again, crashing his lips onto mine as he buries himself inside me.

"Yes!" I cry in ecstasy as my whole body shudders and contracts beneath him.

'Fuck," he moans.

I can't hear anything but the pounding of my heartbeat in my ears as he gently plasters onto me and I cling to him.

I'm still struggling to catch my breath when he props himself up on elbow, brushing strands of my curls from my forehead, stuck to my skin with sweat.

"I can't move." I let out a weak chuckle.

He huffs out a laugh and kisses my lips before getting off me to go to the bathroom. I take that opportunity to sprawl out like a starfish and stare at his ceiling in a complete and utter daze.

God, I'm so in love with him.

47

AMELLIA

4 MONTHS LATER

    Caleb should be back home from his therapy session in a few minutes and I'm pacing around our apartment like a mad man, yeah our apartment. He asked me to move in with him and I couldn't be happier. Sleeping beside him every night has been my new favorite thing, even if it takes me fifteen minutes just to wake him up in the morning.

    He truly sleeps like a dead man.

    I'm so proud of him, he's been feeling so much lighter and the relationship between him and his dad has improved so much.

    But today is his 25th birthday and I really want to celebrate with him alone before we have his huge party later tonight.

    The jingle of keys snaps me out of my thoughts and I hurriedly grab the cake from the fridge, snatching up the lighter and sticking the numbers 2 and 5 on top.

    "Hey, princess." He opens the door, shutting it behind

him as he stalks toward me. "Aw, you didn't have to buy me a cake."

"I wanted to." I chuckle, then he cups my face, kissing me in a way that'll never grow old. "Make a wish."

Caleb closes his eyes and blows out the candles. When he opens them, he smiles as his gaze locks on mine. "You're here. All my wishes have already come true."

This man never fails to give me butterflies.

"Happy Birthday handsome," I say, looking up at him. "I love you."

"I love you too," he murmurs as he takes the cake from my hands and sets it on our diner table, some whipped cream smearing on his middle finger.

"Let me get that." I take his hand and slip his finger into my mouth, tasting the sweetness against my tongue.

His eyes darken and he bends down to grip the back of my thighs and scooping me into his arms, my legs naturally wrapping around him.

"Careful, baby. The cake won't be the only thing I eat tonight."

Oh my.

I grip his jaw and peck his lips. "I have some gifts for you."

I need to nip this conversation in the bud, or I'll never get to show him what I got.

He pouts but sets me down on my feet, ducking down until we're eye level. "I already got three from you this month." He chuckles. "You're spoiling me."

"I love doing it, hold on." I lift a finger before I scurry into our bedroom, yelping when he smacks my behind on the way out.

Laughing, I slide open our nightstand drawer, swiping

the envelope, and slip it into my back pocket before grabbing the other gift from the closet.

"Close your eyes!" I call out before walking back in, grinning, and holding part one of my gift between us. "Open."

He opens his eyes, and his whole face lights up. "Amelia…"

While he was out of town for an away game a few months ago, I booked a pottery class and made him something special. A heart-shaped bowl with our initials carved into the center, along with the exact date we became a couple. The design matches the carving we made as friends all those years ago.

But now this one has a new meaning.

"You're perfect." He turns the plate over in his hands, feeling the ceramic. "This means a lot to me. Thank you."

I grin, take the bowl from his hands, and set it down carefully.

"And here's the next one." I spin my back to him and point toward the envelope in my pocket, unable to contain my excitement. "I think you'll like it."

His hands slide into my pocket, fishing it out and opening it.

Anything You Want Punch Card

With three punch holes along the bottom.

As I turn around to catch his expression, his eyes darken with lust.

"You can use it anytime." I chuckle. "Whatever you want, I'll do."

"Can I redeem it now?"

"I mean, you can, but don't you wanna save it for—"

"I want to use it now," he interrupts quickly.

"Let me grab a hole puncher—" before I can finish my sentence, he shakes his head, snatching me off my feet, tossing me over his shoulder like a sack of potatoes.

Blood rushing to my face as I squeal.

He hurries toward our bedroom, tosses me onto the bed, and my lips curve with anticipation as I prop myself up on my elbows. He kneels, fingers hooking into my jeans, tugging them down impatiently.

"Lay back for me," he groans, not once looking up, his eyes locked on my damp underwear.

I obey, lying flat, as anticipation swirls low in my stomach as I yank my shirt and bra off.

He slings my legs over his shoulders, his lips trailing along my inner thighs sending jolts of pleasure through me.

Then, hovering over my center he drags his tongue over my clit through the thin fabric in one long swipe.

"Oh ffuu—"

"Sensitive." He grins, then glides his tongue up again.

"Please..."

He traces the edge of my panties delicately with his fingertips as he watches the way my hips shift in silent desperation.

I swallow hard, feeling the ache between my thighs grow. "You're teasing."

"It's more like savoring." He finally yanks my underwear down.

A low, guttural groan rumbles from his chest as he stands, quickly undressing.

Then he sinks to his knees again.

I mumble a curse as he hooks my thighs, dragging me to the edge of the bed. Before I can process a single thing, his tongue slides up my center. A sharp gasp tumbles out of me.

He moves with purpose, his tongue stroking the spot that has my vision going black as I grab a handful of his hair.

That makes him happy as he flicks his tongue faster, pushing me closer to the edge, my orgasm threatening to come any second now.

His fingers tighten around my thighs, keeping me in place as I writhe. "Stay still, baby. I'm trying to eat my dessert."

"I can't."

"Yes you can." His tongue plunges inside me, and my entire body convulses as a strangled cry rips from my throat and I push up onto my elbows. My fingers tugging harder on his thick brown hair.

Then he reaches down, wrapping a hand around his length, stroking himself slowly.

My breathing rapidly picks up as I watch him pleasure himself while devouring me. It's officially the hottest thing I've ever seen.

His hand moves faster while his tongue matches the speed. My eyes squeeze shut as pleasure builds within me and just as I'm about to come he draws back.

"Caleb—"

He licks his lips, glistening with my arousal. "You taste so fucking good."

Heat rushes to my cheeks as I groan, still twitching from the denied release. "So, why'd you stop?"

A dark laugh rumbles from Caleb as he settles beside me in bed, smirking like he's about to watch a damn football game. "Use me."

"What?"

He grabs my waist. "You heard me."

A shiver runs down my spine as I swing a leg over him. The moment I settle, his hard length presses hard against my core.

A desperate whimper spills from him. "Oh fuck."

"I need you." I whine, pressing my palms against his chest as I lift my hips.

The moment I do, he grips the base of his cock, teasing my entrance.

"Tell me what you want to do to me."

"I want to ride you."

He grins, flicking his tip over my clit. "Then put it in."

Swallowing hard, I reach between us, gripping his hard cock and guiding it inside me. My eyes flutter shut as I slowly sink down.

"God," I rasp, my nails digging into his chest, leaving crescent-moon marks as he fills me completely.

"Please use me," he breathes, trailing kisses between my breasts. "Hold onto the headboard."

I listen, gripping the wooden board as I roll my hips, and find my rhythm.

"That's it, you're doing so well." He praises, digging his blunt nails into my hips. "Take what you need."

The praise and control he gives me is all I need to keep going. I roll my hips faster, rocking against him as he lets me take control. My curls fall around his face as our eyes lock, heat simmering between us.

He moans, leaning forward to take my breast into his mouth, and I grip the headboard tighter until my knuckles turn white.

Our skin slaps against each other as I pick up my pace, bouncing and rocking back and forth. "More." I cry.

I need him to take control now…

His hands clamp onto my ass, yanking me down as he pounds into me with force, hitting the perfect spot and unable to hold back.

"Holy fucking shit—"

"I know baby, I know," he coaxes, as he spreads my ass wider. The deeper he goes, the white-hot bursts of pleasure crash over me, hitting me without warning as I clench around him.

"Oh, god!" I grip the headboard tighter as it bangs against the wall with each thrust. I hope we don't get any noise complaints later but I'm too far gone to care. I'll apologize if I have to.

"Best birthday ever," he murmurs, cupping my face and kissing me. Our moans tangle and spill into each other's mouths as we come together.

Let's just say, we had a lot of stamina and used the rest of those punches one after another.

EPILOGUE
AMELIA

SIX MONTHS LATER

"I haven't been here in what feels like forever." I step onto Manhattan Beach, the soft white sand slipping between my toes, cool and comforting. The light breeze brushes my skin, and memories as a teenager rush in with every crashing wave.

"Let's find a good spot." Maya says, looping her arm through mine.

Tia's ahead of us, rubbing her baby bump, which has grown so much over the past month. Between pregnancy classes with Amir and getting their baby girl Leah's nursery ready, she's been more than occupied.

But tonight, we all finally had the chance to get together and have dinner. We wanted to catch the sunset, and what better place to witness it than at the beach? The saltwater in the air and the sounds of waves gently rolling?

The perfect evening.

Once we walk further onto the beach my heart flutters seeing a glimpse of a marriage sign.

"Oh my god," I whisper-yell to Tia, tugging my light pink sweater tighter around me. "Get back over here. Someone's about to get proposed to, let's wait a few minutes."

"You're right, someone is."

A sultry voice drifts behind me through the cool air. I whirl around, breath catching, to see Caleb standing there looking all handsome in a white button-down shirt and black dress pants.

Maya and Tia squeal as they speed walk away from us and my brows furrow, confused mixed with excitement.

He steps forward, taking my face in his hands and kisses me. "Hi, pretty girl."

My eyes flutter. "What are you doing here? I thought you had a meeting?"

"Change of plans." He says, taking my hand and leading me further down the beach.

The sand is scattered with rose petals arranged in a heart shape at the center, surrounded by LED candles. Nearby, marquee letters glow boldly with the words: Marry Me?

"Oh my," I inhale sharply, covering my mouth with my hand as I take it all in, my vision blurring as tears fill to the brim. "Caleb."

He takes my now shaky hand, leading me toward the center of the heart and I glance up at the setting sky. Golden with purple hues.

Lowering himself onto one knee, I gasp again. He reaches into his pocket, pulling out a small black velvet box.

Oh my god. Oh my god. Oh my god. Is this really happening?

"Loving you has been the greatest privilege of my life,

and I can't imagine spending it with anyone else." His voice softens, tender and sincere.

My cheeks grow wet as tears spill out, and then he flips the box open, revealing an elongated cushion cut ring that leaves me speechless.

It's the exact ring I pinned to a forgotten Pinterest board years ago.

"I want to love you in every way I know how and make you the happiest woman in the world."

He already has for as long as I've known him.

"You have my heart, and I don't ever want it back." His voice cracks, barely above a whisper. "You are my home. My best friend. My everything."

A soft sigh slips past my lips as my chest tightens. This is happening. This is real.

"Amelia Cruz-Taylor." He holds up the ring, his hand trembling. "Will you please marry me?"

My shaking hand shoots out as my heart pounds against my ribs. "Yes! A million times yes!"

His eyes shine as he slides the ring into its place...the one that had always been reserved for him.

The second it's on, I yank him up and grasp his face, tears streaming down my cheeks. "I love you so much."

Loving him has been the easiest thing I've ever done.

He leans down and kisses me in a way that steals my breath away.

Our crazy group of friends rushes out from the beach deck, shouting congratulations as they approach. Marcus and Amir pull Caleb aside, slapping him on the back, and a smile blooms across my face. Then my girls rush over to me, eyes fixed on the ring, gasping in surprise.

"It's gorgeous," Tia shrieks.

"Oh my God." Maya leans down so close to my hand,

squinting at the diamond. "I can see my reflection through this thing."

Once we all finish chatting, our friends slowly drift away, giving us a moment of privacy.

"You know, I've always chased my dreams, running toward the next goal." Caleb gently grasps my wrist, pulling me closer. "But now I can stop, because I've finally reached my destination."

Tears threaten to fall again as he cups my face, sweeping his thumb across my cheek.

"Because that destination has always been you."

THANK YOU!!

If you had fun and enjoyed *It's A Win For Me*, please consider leaving a review! Your support means everything.

Thank you again for taking the time to read Caleb and Amelia's love story unfold.

COMING SOON

MAKING THE CATCH SERIES
STAY TUNED…

ACKNOWLEDGMENTS

It's A Win For Me has my entire heart, this book started off as a thriller believe it or not! Well, not exactly, but let me explain. Back in December, I was coming up with a concept for a movie and it happened to be horror/thriller. My mind was moving a thousand miles per hour trying to figure out how I could pitch this to a media company.

Then, my dad told me, why not just write it yourself first? It was like a lightbulb went off. I opened up my computer and started typing away, then randomly it turned into a romance novel…don't ask me how. Another light bulb went off and I was like wait a second, I love rom-coms and fake dating movies/books… why not create my own? And the rest is history. I've fallen in love with this book and I hope you did too.

To my family- thank you for putting up with my endless rambling about this book when it was just an idea on a blank page. Your encouragement has kept me going, even though I begged you not to read it (lol).

To my beta readers- Gabi, Jinny, Jersey, Amina, Jenikka, Arya, Zee, and Moriah- thank you so much for your feedback and reactions! This was my first time sending a copy of my book and I was so nervous but you all made it easy for me to relax. It made my entire day to hear how you were kicking your feet and giggling to Caleb Hayes and relating to Amelia Cruz Taylor. And thank you for giving me suggestions that helped shape this story.

To my editor- Thank you so much Roxana Coumans for handling my story with care, you have transformed my book into the best it can be and I'll forever be grateful for your dedication and hard work.

To my readers- thank you for absolutely everything. Thank you for supporting me throughout this publishing journey and reading Caleb Hayes and Amelia Cruz Taylor's love story. Also if you're from the Philippines or Filipino yourself, I hope this story showed you the representation we all need to see more of and had a fun time reading the little bits of Tagalog and traditional foods mentioned. Again, truly from the bottom of my heart I can't thank you all enough for taking the time to read my book baby.

Love,
Clarissa Mae

ABOUT THE AUTHOR

Clarissa Mae is an indie romance author who graduated with an associate's degree in Medical Office Administration and a bachelor's degree in Sociology, magna cum laude, from the University of North Carolina at Pembroke (UNCP).

She loves steamy contemporary romances with all the banter and tension. When she's not reading or writing, she enjoys learning dances at 2 a.m., trying out the latest makeup products, and filming content. She's most likely binge-watching her favorite comfort movies and TV shows while stuffing her mouth with White Cheddar Cheez-Its.

Instagram: instagram.com/authorclarissamae
Threads: https://www.threads.com/@authorclarissamae
TikTok: tiktok.com/@authorclarissamae
Goodreads: goodreads.com/authorclarissamae
More of me:
Lifestyle IG: @itsrissa
Lifestyle TikTok: @allthingsrissa
YouTube: ItsRissa

Printed in Dunstable, United Kingdom